The List of Unspeakable Fears

Also by J. Kasper Kramer

———————

The Story That Cannot Be Told

The
List
of
Unspeakable
Fears

J. KASPER KRAMER

Atheneum Books for Young Readers
NEW YORK LONDON TORONTO SYDNEY NEW DELHI

ATHENEUM BOOKS FOR YOUNG READERS

An imprint of Simon & Schuster Children's Publishing Division

1230 Avenue of the Americas, New York, New York 10020

Text © 2021 Jessica Kasper Kramer

Jacket illustration © 2021 by Deena So'Oteh

Jacket design © 2021 by Simon & Schuster, Inc.

For information about special discounts for bulk purchases, please contact Simon & Schuster Special Sales at 1-866-506-1949 or business@simonandschuster.com.

The Simon & Schuster Speakers Bureau can bring authors to your live event. For more information or to book an event, contact the Simon & Schuster Speakers Bureau at 1-866-248-3049 or visit our website at www.simonspeakers.com.

The text for this book was set in Bely.

Manufactured in the United States of America

0821 FFG

First Edition

2 4 6 8 10 9 7 5 3 1

Library of Congress Cataloging-in-Publication Data

Names: Kramer, J. Kasper, author.

Title: The List of Unspeakable Fears / J. Kasper Kramer.

Description: First edition. | New York : Atheneum Books for Young Readers, [2021] | Audience: Ages 8 to 12 | Summary: In 1910 New York City, four years after her Irish immigrant father dies of tuberculosis, ten-year-old Essie's fear and anxiety continue to grow uncontrollably, so much that when her mother, a brave nurse, remarries and the family moves to North Brother Island, where Essie's new stepfather runs a quarantine hospital for the incurably sick, Essie imagines all manner of horrors, including the ghost of a little girl—which might not be imaginary after all.

Identifiers: LCCN 2020055007 | ISBN 9781534480742 (hardcover) | ISBN 9781534480766 (ebook)

Subjects: CYAC: Fear—Fiction. | Emotional problems—Fiction. | Grief—Fiction. | Supernatural—Fiction. | Stepfathers—Fiction. | Communicable diseases—Fiction. | North Brother Island (N.Y.)—Fiction. | New York (N.Y.)—History—1898-1951—Fiction.

Classification: LCC PZ7.1.K696 Li 2021 | DDC [Fic]—dc23

LC record available at https://lccn.loc.gov/2020055007

To my mom,

who taught me to be brave,

even when I'm most afraid

Chapter One

A red door.

A dark hallway.

A terrible feeling of dread.

My dream always starts just like this. The only noise is a rhythmic dripping behind one of the walls. I'm so sick with fear, I can't move. I squeeze my eyes shut, but when I open them, the red door is still there. Looming.

A tingle prickles up my spine, like the toes of a hundred black spiders.

Someone whispers my name.

And right then, on most nights, I wake up.

Usually I'm crying, my sleeping gown soaked in sweat. Usually I plead for my mam to light the gas lamp by our bed, and she holds me till the shaking has stopped.

But sometimes I can't wake up at all.

Sometimes, still asleep, I thrash about or crawl to the floor. Sometimes I run screaming straight across the room, my eyes wide open but not seeing.

Mam calls it "getting stuck."

On those nights, when she catches my cheeks between her hands, she can tell that I'm not really with her. She says she calls to me over and over, trying to lead me back to the world of the living with the sound of her voice, but it's like I'm deep underwater. I hear nothing at all.

In the distance, on the other side of the East River, a lighthouse beam pierces the late afternoon fog. Five seconds of burning light. Five seconds of chilling dark. For a moment, I'm certain it's happened again. I'm certain I'm stuck in the nightmare.

I realize that the shadow forming across the murky, churning water is North Brother Island, and a shiver passes through me. I turn to go back inside the ferry, but Mam takes my wrist.

"You promised," she says under her breath. Since I can hear her, I know I'm awake. "Come now, Essie. Be a brave girl."

That's easy enough for her, I suppose. Mam is the bravest person in all of New York City. Everyone says it—the cranky landlord in our crumbling tenement; my best friend, Beatrice; the nuns who teach us at St. Jerome's Catholic School. I've seen Mam pick up dead rats without flinching. I've seen her stomp a fire out with her boot. When she was half my age, just five years old, she crossed the whole ocean with her mother to join her father in America. I can't even take a ferry up Hell Gate without turning white as a petticoat.

January wind, freezing and damp, spits into my face. There are slushy puddles of water on the deck and it's so cold that I'm shaking even in my big coat, but Mam takes a step toward the rail, tugging me after. I get an irritated look from her when I dig in my heels, but I refuse to risk my life for a view. Besides, anyone with sense knows that the shadow in the distance is no sort of view to be glad for.

"Brought a lot of luggage, you did," someone says, and Mam and I both turn.

A crewman in a long, wet rain slicker smiles, tipping his cap. The water is getting rough, so he's checking cargo secured to the deck, pulling on ropes and doubling knots. One of the big wooden crates beside him reads MEDICAL SUPPLIES. Another reads LABORATORY EQUIPMENT. Tied up on top of the pile is our dented old steamer trunk and Mam's pretty metal hatbox— a gift from her new husband.

My new father.

I cringe.

"A lot of luggage just for a visit, I mean," the crewman continues, several questions hanging at the end of his comment.

He's not the first curious person we've met today, but I don't like the look of him. There's something suspicious—his hair, perhaps, or his shoes—so I shrink behind my mother and narrow my eyes.

"We aren't visiting," Mam says, raising her voice to be heard over the waves. "We're moving to the island."

The crewman tilts his head. "You can't be patients."

"Heavens, no!" says my mother.

I don't want to look out over the water again. I don't want to see the lighthouse, warning us away from the growing shadow it guards. But the ferry rocks violently and I stumble from my mother, crying out as a huge wave splashes up over the bow. Terrified I'll be swept overboard, I lurch to the side railing and cling on tightly.

Behind me, Mam is giggling like a schoolgirl, pressing her fancy new hat to her head. She's hardly even lost her balance, as poised and confident-looking as ever.

"What weather!" she says to the crewman, and then, as if I didn't just nearly fall to my death, "Not too close, Essie dear."

I shut my eyes, trying to keep from looking down at the icy rushing water below. All I want in the world is to go back inside—and then, after that, to turn the boat around and go home—but I'm frightened I'll fall if I let go of the railing. And our home in Mott Haven is no longer our home. The rest of our possessions, few as they are, have already been packed up and sent ahead to the island. Our tenement back in the city is empty.

Our apartment, where I've lived my whole life.

Our apartment, where I lived with my mam and my da—my *real* da.

When the beam from the lighthouse strikes me again, I force my eyes open, squinting through the brightness, then the gloom that follows.

North Brother Island is desolate. The scattered trees look like the arms of skeletons. The shoreline is rocky and seems to be waiting for someone to step wrong and twist her ankle.

"You're a nurse, then?" the crewman asks my mother. "To replace the ones gone missing?"

I let go of the railing and turn around, my eyes wide, but then the ferry crashes into another high wave and I'm sent tumbling toward Mam, shouting. She catches me as dirty brown water sprays up over the side of the boat.

"I'm drenched!" I cry out.

"You are not," says Mam.

"I'll catch cold!"

"Goodness, Essie. Don't be dramatic."

My mother turns toward the crewman and excuses us politely before leading me back inside the ferry. By the time we make it, I'm a shivering, blubbering mess.

"Stop it now," says my mother. "You're causing a scene."

I can't help myself, though. It's terrible, picturing all the ways you might die.

Mam pries my fingers from her waist and begins patting her clothing down with a handkerchief. Her wet skirt is black-and-white-striped. Like the hat and hatbox, it's new. Another gift.

"We might have picked a better day to travel." She tries to smile at me.

"We might have not traveled at all," I say.

A sharp look is enough to get me quiet again, so I cross my arms, teeth still chattering, and pace away. Our ferry sways. North Brother Island creeps closer. The storm clouds darken above. When someone begins coughing, I glance over my shoulder. There aren't many other passengers on the small boat, though I saw two police officers board with us. They must be up top with the captain. It seems the ferry is mostly just delivering a last run of supplies before bad weather makes crossing the river impossible. But then, in the far corner of the room, wrapped in a shabby blanket, I see a skinny man, his face flushed with fever.

Anxiety knots in my gut. I take a step back.

"Come dry off," calls Mam, wiggling the handkerchief as she sits down on a bench. Her eyes dart to the man, and I quickly do as I'm told.

For a while, neither of us speaks. We've said everything already, after all. Yelled everything. Shouted everything. Called each other terrible names. I've already cried till I was purple, gasping and begging like my life was in danger.

Because, truly, it is.

The ferry crests wave after wave, rolling my stomach.

"We're going to sink," I whisper.

"No, we aren't."

"Ships sink in this part of the river all the time. Hell Gate is a graveyard."

Mam sighs. "You know, my first time on a ship, I was so excited. I couldn't stop thinking about what my new home would be like. And we had quite a few worse nights than this. Have I told you about the time we started taking on water and the cabin filled up to my bloomers?"

Of course she has. I've heard about every moment of my mother's journey from Ireland. Even when she tells me the most frightening parts—the ship catching fire or the food spoiling or sharks circling in anticipation—she speaks as if it were all some grand adventure I missed out on. I suppose, in her mind, anything was better than what they were leaving behind. Mam and Granny were starving. Getting on the boat to America was a last chance at survival.

The beam from the lighthouse pierces the fog, fracturing through the ferry windows. Light. Dark. Light again.

"He's a good man, Essie. You'll see."

I go rigid. I don't want to hear my mother try again to convince me that this is the right choice—the only choice. I don't want to hear about Dr. Blackcreek and his hospital.

"We're going to get sick," I say, my voice low as I glance at the other passenger.

"No, we aren't," Mam replies, and she puts her arm around me, kissing the top of my head.

I understand why my granda came to America. I understand why my granny followed him. But even though, through her pretty new dress, I can feel how thin Mam has gotten—even though, this past Christmas, we could barely afford coal to keep from freezing, much less any presents—I don't understand why my mother's remarried. I don't understand why she agreed to move us to this strange man's estate.

Because North Brother Island isn't like other islands.

Our new home is where the incurable sick of New York City are sent to die.

Chapter Two

The precise moment I knew all hope was lost came yesterday at half past three.

I arrived home from school late and found nearly our entire apartment packed away. The biggest shock wasn't the emptiness of the place, since we own very little. It wasn't even the hulking steamer trunk, half-full with its heavy lid open, sitting right in the middle of the kitchen. No, the biggest shock was seeing Mam standing there in the midst of strewn clothing and hastily wrapped dishes, trying on a new hat. It was fashionably tall with a gigantic, wide brim and topped with piles of ribbon and lace. My mother was humming to herself, admiring her reflection in a tarnished hand mirror. For how much mind she paid me, I might as well have been see-through. She only turned and noticed me when my arms went limp and my schoolbooks thunked all over the floorboards.

"Oh, Essie!" Mam said cheerfully, taking off her hat. "Thank goodness you're finally home."

Her hair was pinned up, as usual, in a large, lush puff on her head. She was always threatening to chop it off and complaining about how it got in the way, but so far, I'd talked her out of such scandal. Clearly, my recent efforts to talk her out of ruining our lives hadn't been as successful, because the next thing she said was, "You need to go pack your things. Tomorrow we're leaving for North Brother Island."

The death sentence was so matter-of-fact, so perfectly simple and undebatable, that she might have been correcting my arithmetic homework. She'd used the exact same tactic two weeks ago. While cooking colcannon, she'd casually announced that she'd remarried.

"We met marching together at a women's suffrage rally," she'd said with a smile, mashing together potatoes and cabbage. "His real name is Alwin Schwarzenbach, but he goes by Alwin Blackcreek because people get flustered when they try to pronounce 'Schwarzenbach.' Essie love, you're going to get on *so* well. I can't wait for you to meet him."

It was clear my mother had lost all common sense.

Not only had she married a stranger—a *German* stranger, at that—but she'd married a man with the most unfortunate of occupations. Dr. Blackcreek was the director of one of the most feared places in New York City—Riverside Hospital on North Brother Island. People who were thought to be sick with infectious diseases, usually poor people or immigrants like us, were regularly rounded up by the Board of Health and shipped to one of the quarantine hospitals on the islands in the East River, often against their will. Everyone said that if you had the bad luck to wind up on North Brother, you'd never leave.

During that first conversation about my new stepfather, as Mam had described how grand his estate would be compared to our tenement, I could do little but gape. Yesterday afternoon, coming home to find our whole life stuffed into suitcases, I had much the same reaction.

"Bad weather's on the way, so we've no choice but to leave quickly," Mam had said. "Alwin sent a letter this morning from the hospital and there will be room for us tomorrow on a late ferry. It might be weeks till we can travel otherwise."

I didn't argue that "weeks till we can travel" would be just fine with me. I didn't say a word, in fact. I just turned and left the apartment. In the narrow hallway, where the yellowed wallpaper was peeling, I took off at a run. At the rickety stairs I slowed, worried I might trip and fall, but once I made it to the bottom and through the back door, I sped up again. The fenced-in dirt yard behind our tenement was bitter cold. Half-frozen clothes hung on lines overhead. The row of slanted wooden outhouses blurred as I rushed past them. With more than seventy people in our little building, usually all three were occupied, but thankfully, today no one was around.

At the back end of the yard, I collapsed behind a stack of wooden barrels and hugged my knees, sobbing.

"You sound sniffly as a babe with the pox," someone called from nearby.

I didn't have to look up to tell it was Beatrice.

"If you haven't anything nice to say, leave me alone," I muttered, wiping my eyes with my patched mittens.

My best friend walked up in front of me and crossed her arms. The hem of her dress was caked with mud. Her hair was dirty and her stockings were ripped at the knees. In short, she looked much as she always did. Beatrice was forever going places she shouldn't and coming out tattered.

"What's the matter then? Found another mouse living in your pillow?" she asked.

I shook my head.

"Got teased by the older boys on the street corner? I'll have my brothers ring their ears."

I shook my head again.

"You heard a loud noise that scared you? Or your pencils rolled into the dark place under your bed?"

"It's nothing like that!" I cried, frustrated. "It's more terrible than anything you can guess."

Beatrice frowned. "Well then, what?"

"I'm moving."

Her eyes widened. "When?"

"Tomorrow. *To North Brother Island.*"

At this, Beatrice dropped down beside me, taking my hands. "Saints forbid," she said. "That really *is* terrible."

My friend knew all about my mother's recent marriage, about Dr. Blackcreek and his hospital. In fact, she probably knew even more than I did—upsetting things she hadn't the heart to tell me—because Beatrice was a snooper. She listened in on people's private conversations. She read their letters or followed them if they were acting odd. This was all in preparation, of course, for her future career as a detective, so it should come as no surprise that her favorite dime novels were sleuth ones, like *Nick Carter Weekly*, or that she liked to ask new neighbors weird questions and search down dark alleys for clues. Often she forgot about studying, or even going to school, because she was so busy tracking grifters and creeps.

Beatrice's mam and da didn't much notice her sleuthing, not even when she came home from St. Jerome's with bad marks and welts on her palms because the nuns had smacked them with a ruler. This was mostly due to the fact that Beatrice's three older brothers took up all their parents' attention. The Murphy boys were a real terror—the worst on our block. They started street fights and swiped sweets from shopkeepers. They spent their money from selling papers on gambling, cigarettes, and nickelodeons. In the evenings, they were frequently dragged home by the police, and even all the way up on the fifth floor, I could hear the yelps when the boys got the belt from their da.

In any case, Beatrice was known to have the inside scoop on everything, so I appreciated that thus far she'd kept any rumors about my mam's new husband to herself. Knowing I was moving to an island for people with cholera and yellow fever and typhoid was quite enough for me to worry about.

I pressed my face into my hands. "I'll never see you again. I'll get sick and die."

"Essie, Essie, Essie," Beatrice chided, nudging me with her shoulder. "Don't be silly. If you can take a ferry there, you can take a ferry here to visit. *And you're not going to die.*"

"I don't want to live with some strange man!"

"It could be worse," she said seriously. "I mean, it sounds like he's loaded, so I bet your new house will be posh. You might even have electricity!"

I gasped, horrified by the idea, and began sobbing all over.

My friend sighed. "Sometimes I worry you're hopeless."

And then Beatrice got a look in her eyes that I knew all too well. A wide, eager look that meant she knew something—and that I wouldn't want to hear it.

"No. Stop right there," I said quickly, sniffling and scooting away.

"But, Essie—"

"Whatever it is, don't tell me! I'm frightened enough!"

"I just . . . if you see her . . . Oh, I'm *so jealous!*"

"See her?" I sputtered. "See *who?*"

"Typhoid Mary!" Beatrice exclaimed. "North Brother Island is where they shut her away!"

At this, I felt myself go cold.

Typhoid Mary.

Two years ago, she'd been all over the papers. It was discovered that her cooking had infected multiple households with typhoid fever, so she'd been forcibly quarantined. Then, this past summer, the *New York American* had printed a terrifying picture that showed Mary spicing a dish on her stove with a sprinkle of skulls, which started the tabloids back up again. Beatrice thought Mary's story fascinating. She'd followed it obsessively, snatching discarded papers from reeking trash bins to keep up.

"Do you remember her famous dessert? Ice cream and sliced peaches!" Beatrice exclaimed. "Can you imagine? Ice cream and sliced peaches? I'd risk getting ill to eat that."

"I don't want to hear any more," I pleaded, wringing my mittens. "I don't want to think about living near someone so dangerous."

"They say Mary took a carving knife and went after the sanitation engineer who tracked her down! Or maybe it was a fork? Either way, she was screaming and cursing. Oh, Essie, do say I can visit! I should very much like to meet her."

"Beatrice, please!"

She rolled her eyes and put an arm around my shoulders. "Let's go inside. You're shivering. Isn't frostbite on that list of yours?"

It was, of course—catalogued under the *F*s on the List of Unspeakable Fears. But my impending move to a quarantine island, and my mysterious new stepfather to boot, utterly outranked it.

"I don't want to go in. I don't want to pack," I said.

"Well, unless you plan to show up at your new home with no change of underwear, you haven't much choice."

"I don't want to leave you," I said, and this time, the sad noise I made was very small.

For a brief moment, Beatrice's expression fell, and I thought she might cry too. We'd gone to the same school and been best friends since we were little. We'd lived always in the same building.

Finally Beatrice straightened up, turned away, and replied gruffly, "Well, buck up. Because there's no room for you in our apartment. I suppose if you'd like to try for a life of crime on the streets, my brothers could help you get started. But just know, once I'm a famous detective, I'll come after you all the same. Fair is fair."

I wrapped my arms around her neck and pressed my face into her coat. "What will I do without you?"

"I honestly don't know," she said, patting the top of my head. I could feel her smiling. "But we won't have to find out. You aren't moving to the moon. If you need me, just write. I'll always write back."

Eventually, the cold got the best of us, so we walked together past the old, stinking outhouses, past the metal-ringed wooden buckets of coal, past the piles of filthy clothing, waiting to be washed. Beatrice said farewell at the door, off for more sleuthing, I expected, and up the rickety stairs I went, all alone. On the fifth-floor landing, I slipped quietly into my apartment. The kitchen was clean, and under an old knitted warmer was a loaf of soda bread, hot out of the oven. Mam's hat was tucked away in its box and one of our hand-me-down suitcases was sitting on a chair, ready for me to pack. My mother herself must have been out, because she wasn't in sight.

In the kitchen, there were three doors. One led to the hall. One, to the right, led into the tiny sitting room where Mam and I spent almost all our time. The third one, to the left, led to a large bedroom. It was where our boarders lived, the most recent ones newly arrived from Ireland. The family had four young children and they all slept together in the same room. A quick listen told me no one was home.

I turned right and stepped into the small sitting room, where Mam and I had pallets made up on the floor. There wasn't space enough for a real bed. I crossed to the far wall and stared out our only window. It faced the street. Outside was a fire escape. I hadn't been on it in more than three years. But if Mam and I were to leave in the morning—if this was my last chance—I couldn't stop now. Seeing this view was far too important.

I gritted my teeth, opened the window, and climbed out.

From our block, if you lived up high enough, you could see the East River and its many islands: North and South Brother Islands, Randall's Island and Wards Island, Blackwell's Island in the distance. You could see Hell Gate too, a dangerous, narrow strait of water near Queens. A chill breeze bit at my cheeks.

Da had loved this view.

He was comfortable, up above the rest of the city. For most of his life, he'd worked on dangerous construction sites—bridges and tall buildings and places like that.

"Because us Irish are expendable," he would say, grinning. "Lucky I've got good balance."

Da was never afraid of heights. And when I was with him, I wasn't either—at least not a lot. We'd swing our legs over the edge of the fire escape, side by side. He'd talk baseball and roll cigarettes, and the smoke would drift out above the streets far below. For hours, we'd watch steam-powered ships travel up the river, water foaming and rough all around them.

"Look at those tugs," Da might say, admiring even the ones heaped with garbage and barrels of night soil, on their way to dump the city's waste into the Atlantic.

He might point at a pretty boat. "You know, I came over on a charmer just like that."

It hurt to think of these things, but I knelt down on the fire escape anyway, a safe distance from the edge, and clasped my mittens tight together. The sight line to the river wasn't as direct as it used to be. A new building across the street was partially in my way. But I could still close my eyes and remember.

It wasn't really the *view* I wanted to see, after all.

I tried to picture Da's smile. I tried to hear his laugh. I wanted to feel my father's presence beside me one more time. Before I was too far away.

And then, like a prick to the thumb, something appeared, clear as ice.

A memory I did not want.

It was morning. It was summer. I was nearly five years old.

I'd come onto the fire escape to bring Da his coffee, as I always did, taking great care not to spill. Mam sometimes hovered nearby, prepared to lend a hand if I needed it, but that morning, she was not there. And when I climbed out into the sunlight, I found my father's eyes wide open in horror. He grabbed for me, pulling my sleeve as he pointed, and hot coffee sloshed over my hand. The burn would be bad enough to leave a scar, but I didn't cry out, and Da didn't even realize what he'd done. Because we were both staring down at the river.

At a passenger ship. A big one.

Huge, black clouds of smoke tumbled from its hull.

I'd seen fires before. In the Bronx, cramped, cluttered buildings like ours went up in flames all the time. Charcoal irons tipped over or were left unattended. Embers from fireplaces hopped out onto carpets. Smoking pipes dropped into sleeping men's laps. In New York City, with the old buildings so close together, once a fire got started, it was hard to put out. Later, in school, I'd read about our city's three Great Fires—how they'd spread faster than the men could fight them, how one was so massive it could be seen from Philadelphia.

But the blaze Da and I saw was bigger than anything I'd ever seen. It was more frightening than anything I'd ever read about.

Far off as we were, with the wind pushing hard in a different direction, we couldn't smell the ship's decks as they burned, fueled by a lamp room filled with straw and oily rags. We weren't forced to breathe in the dust from the rotten life preservers, thick enough to make you choke. But we could see little bright spots of light, sometimes two at a time, sometimes more.

Some jumped. Some were thrown. Some toppled over the railings.

Falling.

Spinning.

They all vanished into the dark, churning water.

That morning in 1904, I'd gripped my father's calloused hand with my hurt one and held on for my life. The *General Slocum* turned in desperation toward North Brother Island, a thousand of the women and children it carried soon to be dead.

But yesterday afternoon, there was no one's hand to hold.

I'd thumbed the faint scar through my mittens and gone back inside.

Climbing out onto the fire escape, what I'd wanted was to find happy memories, something to take with me to my new home. Instead, I'd found a burning ship.

Chapter Three

It's almost dark now. It's started to rain. Our ferry slows and comes to a stop at the dock on North Brother. The waves, getting stronger, rock our boat up and down, making it difficult for the crewmen outside to secure the ramp and unload. At the last moment, I grasp my mother's arm and cling to her, pleading.

"Please, please, let's stay inside! Just until the storm passes," I beg.

She shakes me off, sighing, and opens an umbrella. Then she picks up our two small suitcases and goes on without me, making it across the swaying ramp all alone. When I finally gather enough courage to follow her, three shrill blasts from the steamer's whistle nearly make me jump out of my dress. After that, I'm such a trembling mess that the crewman with the suspicious shoes has to carry me over the ramp. On the other side, I walk with him down a long wooden dock, water splashing up over the sides. The freezing rain starts coming harder. My mother meets us on the shore, and I hurry to her.

"Is that the main hospital building?" she asks the crewman, nearly having to yell over the wind. She points to a long brick structure at our left. It's two stories tall, with five massive chimneys and dozens of dark windows.

Even though the trip wasn't long, my legs feel strange and wobbly now that I'm back on solid land. Since I'm busy worrying about this, I don't notice at first that the crewman is still on the dock—that he won't step onto the island.

"Aye. The pesthouse," the man says, nodding, and I look up, my heart skipping a beat. When Mam frowns, he adds quickly, "The smallpox pavilion, I mean."

The steamer whistle sounds again—three shrill blasts—and then two nurses in white smocks and high rubber overshoes emerge from the building, hurrying toward the boat. The crewman eyes them anxiously, then tips his wet cap to bid us farewell. He joins his mates unloading the rest of the cargo. Ice-cold wind heaves against me, and I huddle closer to Mam under her umbrella. I can feel the bottom of my skirt soaking through.

"Alwin said he'd be here to meet us," explains my mother, struggling to keep hold of her hat. "I'm sure a carriage is due any moment."

She's right, of course. She usually is. Just then, in the distance, a shape comes into view through the gusts of rain. The closer it gets, though, the stranger it looks. The colors are wrong. The size is odd. I can't make out the horses.

It's not a carriage at all. It's an *automobile*.

Red-and-black top and doors. Golden trim. White tires. There are two plush black leather benches. The back one is completely enclosed from the weather, with little windows and everything. The automobile stops right in front of us, and I stand there blinking. My mother stiffens in surprise. A driver steps out and hurries around to us, opening a sturdy umbrella with a hooked silver handle.

"So sorry to keep you waiting, Mrs. Blackcreek," he says, his curled mustache dripping. It's the first time I've heard my mother called by her new name, and I can't help but make a nasty face. The driver just smiles. "And you must be Essie!"

After taking our luggage and putting it in a covered space at the rear of the auto, he opens a little door to the back seat and gestures for us to climb in.

"Dr. Blackcreek sends his apologies," the man says, helping my mother up. "He meant to greet you himself but was called away to the hospital to attend to some visitors. I've just returned from dropping him off. Quite the storm coming, isn't it?"

He reaches for my hand so I can step in, and I notice that his eyes dart toward the swaying dock, where the police officers who boarded with us are now standing. Before I can think too much about this, though, I'm settled in the back seat and over-whelmed by the noise.

I very much intend to be frightened. The automobile is loud: growling and clicking and whirring as it idles. I've heard terrible stories of these contraptions crashing into things—turning turtle and killing passengers. How much can one young lady take? Traveling by boat and then auto, for the first time, all in a single day?

I very much intend to be frightened, but soon I'm too mes-merized to tremble and fret. I run my numb fingers along the slick, bouncy cushions and look into the front. There's a steer-ing wheel attached to a long pole, with three foot pedals below it and a hand brake to the left. To the right is a round glass dial with numbers. When the driver closes our door and climbs in, I sit back and Mam pinches my arm.

"Isn't this exciting!" she says.

I almost nod before remembering myself and burrowing down in my coat.

The ride to our new house doesn't take long, and the driver talks through the glass between us the whole way. His name is Frank and he's the groundskeeper at the estate, as well as the chauffeur, apparently, and whatever else Dr. Blackcreek needs him to be. He says he's been on the island six years, just as long as the director—followed him over to North Brother, in fact. Before Dr. Blackcreek took the job at Riverside, Frank worked for him in Manhattan.

"Always been a good man," Frank says, calling back to us over the noise of the car. "Fair man. Treats me well."

I let the groundskeeper's words roll through me, pressing my nose to the window as I listen to the automobile engine grumble and clickety-clack. I watch a blur of red brick pass by. The rain is still coming down, but the fog is clearing, and through the dreary landscape I make out a gigantic smokestack, spitting black clouds into the air.

When the auto pulls into a circular drive, Mam whispers, "Oh, Essie, look."

And the way her voice vibrates—almost as if she's going to cry—makes me lean forward, peering outside.

"One of the island's oldest buildings," says Frank, squeezing the hand brake and changing pedals after the automobile comes to a stop. "Don't fret, though. It's been fully renovated. Up to date with the latest modern conveniences. Gas heating. Electric lighting in several rooms. Plumbing, too. There's a fully functional toilet on the second floor! We've no telephone yet, but we will soon enough. For now, there are a couple at the hospital, if you're needing one." Frank glances back at us through the glass, smiling. "You've married a man with a mind for progress, Mrs. Blackcreek."

At any other moment, I would have swooned in terror over the thought of a house so full of danger—electric lighting, indeed!—but as it is, I only gape.

Dense white mist swirls around the great old mansion. The sleeping beast is three stories tall, made up of sharp angles and steep peaks. There are several dark dormer windows with sagging hoods, but the only light comes from two flickering lamps guarding the front door.

I lean over my mother's lap and tilt my head, looking up. Through the remaining fog, I can just make out the sloping tiled roof, and after I've been watching for a moment, I see the reflection of an attic window.

"Oh!" I gasp, ducking into my seat.

I hate attics. If you look up into them too long, it's inevitable that something horrifying will look back. I hate cellars for the same reason. Staring down a dark stairwell is an open invitation to be frightened. Closets aren't much better. Or the musty spaces under sinks. Really, anything with shadows and cobwebs is too much for me.

Mam glances my way, but Frank is already opening her door,

umbrella in hand. He helps her out and she insists on carrying her own suitcase as they walk together up the path. I watch them for a moment, then curl up in the seat and close my eyes, fear pooling in my gut. Even though I'm frozen and exhausted— even though I'm terrified of catching a chill and dying on this god-awful island—I can't stand the thought of going into that house.

Who would live in such a bleak place all alone?

What sort of man has my mother married?

When Frank comes back to retrieve me, extending a hand and another smile, he cocks his head at the house. "A sight, isn't it?"

I twist my fingers together, looking down, and don't answer.

"Is something wrong, miss?" he asks, smile fading into concern.

I shake my head quickly, ready myself, and climb out of the auto. But just as I step to the ground, a gust of wind passes through the yard, and the stone walkway to the house clears of fog right up to the door—creating a path just for me.

I suck in a breath as I see the house in full for the first time.

Dr. Blackcreek's estate is the most miserable, frightening place I can possibly imagine, and it's calling for me to come inside.

Chapter Four

Once we're through the front door, Frank closes it behind us. As always, my mother is one step ahead, already speaking to a tidy-looking woman in a black dress and white apron about how the house is run.

"I knew the estate would be large, but this . . . this is enormous!" says Mam, gesturing to the wide staircase and vaulted ceiling. She's clearly flustered. "A single maid-of-all-work in a house of this size is unthinkable. You must run yourself thin keeping up with the place!"

The maid blushes. She's younger than Mam by several years, with a plain, round face and pointy nose. Her dark hair is pinned on top of her head.

"It isn't so much trouble," she says, and I guess from her accent that she came to America from Germany, like my new stepfather. "We never have company. And Dr. Blackcreek leaves rarely a footprint in the hall. I hardly know anyone is here."

I glance down at my own footprints, tracking mud through the foyer, and bite my bottom lip.

"It's too much for one person," says my mother, looking serious.

She would know. I would too. Shortly after Da died, Mam lost her job as a visiting nurse, and since then, she mostly made money by cleaning fancy people's fancy toilets or taking care of their old, sick relatives. Often, I went with her to help, at least when I wasn't in school, and together we scrubbed the floors of houses just like this.

Frank opens the big front door suddenly, and freezing rain gusts into the foyer—a carriage has arrived with the rest of our luggage. Moving away from the cold, I wander alone a bit deeper.

The foyer is huge, with heavy carpets and curtains and twisting brass gas fixtures along the walls. The bright flames cast monstrous shadows up to the ceilings. There are expensive-looking, oddly shaped decorative vases and bowls along the tables and shelves. I tip a nearby urn toward me, peeking inside, and find it full to the brim with strange little colored pieces of glass. I set it down, perplexed, then turn to the grand staircase, which is wide enough for three people abreast. It has carved dark banisters, gleaming with wood polish. To the right of the stairs is a parlor. Fireplace crackling. Double pocket doors wide open.

The whole place is conspicuously inviting, like a vampire's den in one of those dreadful novels Beatrice reads.

The hall past the parlor seems to lead back to a dining room, and I can smell something smoky and peppered cooking, so there must be a kitchen. Left of the stairs is another hall, which bends out of sight. The door closest to me is shut, but I take a step forward anyhow.

The knob is golden and polished. The thick wooden frame is etched with flowers and vines. I reach out, my face reflected in the knob, but then stop. A chill goes up my spine.

Because it's not my face looking back.

The eyes are the wrong shape, too round. The nose in the reflection is too small. This morning I left my auburn hair loose. But in the doorknob, I see a dark braid with a ribbon tied at the end. I touch my head, fingers trembling.

"Essie," says Mam. "Come meet Fräulein Gretchen."

I look up, startled, then back down at the shiny doorknob. I blink twice. Certain as day, there I am. My eyes. My nose. My hair. Mam and the maid resume talking.

"Since you've mentioned it, Mrs. Blackcreek—" starts Fräulein Gretchen.

"Do call me Aileen." My mother smiles.

"Yes, of course." The maid smiles back uncertainly. "Well, since you've mentioned it, we do need to post in the papers for new staff. You'll want a lady's maid. And Essie must have a governess, yes?"

My eyebrows go high in my reflection, and I finally turn around. I don't even know anyone who knows anyone with a governess. On our block in Mott Haven, if parents didn't have time to take care of their children, children took care of themselves.

"Oh gracious," says Mam, laughing a little. "I knew things were bound to be different here, but I doubt I'll start needing help getting dressed."

I cross the room and stand next to my mother. "And I don't need a governess."

Fräulein Gretchen looks at me, surprised. "But someone must help you with your studies. We have no school on the island."

I'm so shocked that I just stand there staring till Mam nudges me.

"Don't be rude," she says. "Introduce yourself."

I blink. "Hello, I'm Essie. Nice to meet you, Fräul—Fräu . . ." I hesitate, looking at my mother for help, and it's my turn to blush.

"*Fräulein,*" says the maid slowly, smiling. She pronounces it "Froy-line." "It is like 'Miss' in English."

I nod but don't try to say it again, afraid I'll keep getting it wrong. After another moment, I ask nervously, "If you clean everything here, does that mean we don't have to?"

Mam gasps in horror. The maid stifles a laugh. I grimace, because though I know it sounded impolite, that's really not how I meant it. Honestly, after seeing the size of this place, I'm worried Dr. Blackcreek has simply brought us here for free labor.

"Mother Mary, hold her tongue!" my mam says under her breath.

"Well, I expect you will need to keep your own room tidy," says Fräulein Gretchen, still chuckling a little.

My mouth drops open. "My *own* room?"

The maid looks to Mam, as if asking permission, then reaches out, smiling. "On the second floor. Would you like to see?"

I hesitate but then pick up my little suitcase and nod, taking her hand. The maid's skin is soft and warm, not much like the hands of people back home. Her voice is soft and warm too. When she asks what foods I like, and if I'm tired from the big move, it seems she truly cares. By the time we reach the second floor, I'm almost feeling a bit better, even after the creepy door-knob reflection. Fräulein Gretchen chatters as we walk.

"This is the master bedroom," she says, pointing, "where your mother and stepfather will sleep. This is the library, where you will have tutoring."

After that is a sitting room and two guest rooms, and I think there can't possibly be any more. But then we turn a corner and there are three. First is the bathroom, with a big porcelain claw-foot tub and a flushable toilet, just like Frank boasted about. The bowl is off-white and has engravings of fanned leaves. The wooden tank is high up on the wall, with a pull chain hanging down. Fräulein Gretchen shows me how to use it.

"Isn't there an outhouse I can go to instead?" I ask anxiously.

"No," the maid replies, sounding curious. "Whyever would you want that?"

I shake my head and look down at my toes, surprised she doesn't know about the dangers of sewer gases escaping into the house. Since she works for a doctor, one expects he would have told her—unless he himself doesn't know. I take a slow breath, again fretting about the quality of man my mother has married.

When we continue down the hall again, I notice that even up here the old house is decorated with the same odd little pieces of colored glass. They overflow from jars and vases. They're piled in large, pretty bowls. I want to ask about them, but the next door leads to my room.

"Go ahead, then," says Fräulein Gretchen.

I look up at her cautiously, then reach forward and turn the knob. It won't budge.

"I think it's locked," I say.

Fräulein Gretchen puckers her lips, pulling a large iron ring, overfull with jingling keys, out of her apron pocket.

"Frank must have shut it up behind me," she says. "We aren't used to having guests." Then she looks down apologetically. "You aren't a guest, though, are you? I am so happy to have you here, Essie. This old place could use some new life."

For the first time all day, a smile edges up at the corner of my mouth. I try to think of something nice to say. But then my eyes wander down the hall.

And suddenly, I can't form any words.

I try. A sound creeps up my throat and squeaks out, but it's only a whimper.

How did it get here? *Did it crawl right out of my dreams?*

Fräulein Gretchen tilts her head, a familiar expression on her face—the one I often get from adults, especially those who don't know me. Confusion. Concern.

"Essie, are you well?"

The flames in the gas lamps along the walls jump. I stick out a shaking hand, pointing to the last door, down at the end of the hall.

The red door.

"Wh-where . . . ?" I barely whisper.

I mean to ask, *Where did it come from?*, but when Fräulein Gretchen follows my gaze, her expression loses its tension.

"Oh, that just leads to the attic," she says, smiling. "Lovely, isn't it?"

Staring at the great door at the end of the hall, *lovely* isn't a word that comes anywhere near to mind. *Grotesque*, perhaps.

Bloodcurdling. The wood is stained dark, dark red, nearly black. The frame is carved with deep gashes and swirling patterns. A less imaginative person might mistake the curves and swells for roses or brambles, but I can see horrible things—anguished faces, mouths open in terror, warning me away.

Fräulein Gretchen sticks the key to my bedroom into the lock, and I realize that there are scratch marks all along the lower wall leading to the red door. There are scratches at the base, too, like something has been trying to get in. I shiver violently, but the maid is still talking like nothing's amiss.

"It is only storage upstairs. Items left over from Dr. Blackcreek's previous home. It's been a long time, but he never finished unpacking." She turns the key. "Outdated laboratory equipment. Clothing. Moldy books. The attic is kept locked for good reason. There are spiders up there. And lots of dust. Not a safe place for a young girl."

A knot tightens in my gut. Suddenly I'm trying hard not to think the thing that I'm thinking.

But I know already it's true. Something's there. Something's behind the red door. Something's waiting for me.

Fräulein Gretchen opens up my bedroom. "Here we are," she says.

She steps through the doorway, and I start to follow, distracted, but stop short when I realize the room is pitch black. A frigid breeze rushes by, fluttering both our dresses. I grab the maid's forearm to halt her. She looks back at me, so deep in shadow that I can't see her expression.

"The window," she says reassuringly. "Loose latches. That is all."

But the window isn't why I've stopped.

I've stopped because there's a sound. Movement along the floor. Skittering. Slinking. I can hear claws tapping wood.

"We aren't alone," I whisper, hardly able to breathe.

Before I can run back out into safety, something rubs against my ankle—something awful and hairy—and I scream at the top of my lungs. I drop my suitcase as I stumble away, and its contents burst all over the floor. I collapse in the hallway, curling up, and am still screaming when I realize Fräulein Gretchen is doubled over with laughter, clutching her chest as she tries to regain her composure.

In the doorway between us is a mangy mass of black fur— the ugliest cat I've ever seen in my life. I cover my face with my hands and scream again.

"What's wrong?" Mam calls, rushing up the stairs. When she reaches me, she peels my fingers from my face, and I squint, because the bedroom is now illuminated with an oddly bright light.

Fräulein Gretchen, still trying to catch her breath, points at the creature. "It's only Old Scratch," she says when I've quieted. "He gave poor Essie a fright."

My mother helps me stand. "I thought you'd been hurt!" she says reproachfully.

I can't take my eyes off the scrawny, horrible animal, though, and when he opens his mouth and makes a ghastly noise—a broken rattle of a meow that's more bird than cat—I cower back into Mam's arms. Fräulein Gretchen shoos Old Scratch off, and he hisses at her before sashaying over to the attic door, stretching tall as a child, and dragging his yellowed claws down the frame.

"Stop that! Stop that now!" the maid cries, shooing him again.

The monster drops to all fours and scurries past us toward the stairwell.

"Not a cat lover?" observes Fräulein Gretchen, clearly fighting a smile. She goes back into my room and closes the bedroom window, still talking. "Don't mind him a moment. He looks nasty, but he is harmless. He doesn't even have all his teeth."

Mam untangles herself from me, walks into the bedroom, and kneels down to collect the items spilled from my open suitcase. She gestures for my help, but I'm still staring at the turn in the hall where the cat disappeared.

"Does it live in the house?" I ask warily.

"When he chooses," says Fräulein Gretchen, bending by Mam.

"Essie, please come help," says my mother in a tired voice.

After a moment, I do, squinting again in the strangely bright bedroom. We've almost finished picking up the mess when the maid's fingers stop on something unexpected amidst the spilled garments, something light and silver and small enough to fit in her palm—something I didn't pack.

"What a pretty trinket," says Fräulein Gretchen, and though I haven't seen it in months, I immediately recognize the little bell. It's plain but polished, with a straight, thin handle the length of a pinky. *The sick bell.*

My heart jumps into my throat. "Don't!" I shout.

But it's too late. I can't stop her.

She rings it.

Chapter Five

I throw my hands over my ears and brace for the awful sound, but of course there's only silence. Fräulein Gretchen glances at me, then turns the sick bell up to look in its mouth, confused. There's no clapper inside. Without a word, Mam reaches over and takes the silver heirloom from the maid's hand, perhaps more frantically than she intends. Fräulein Gretchen's eyes widen. She looks between us.

"I'm sorry—I . . . ," she falters. "Did I do something wrong?"

I'm still rigid with terror and covering my ears. My mother's face has gone pale, but she forces a smile, trying to lighten the air.

"No, no, no," she says. "Nothing like that. If you might excuse us a moment, though? I need a word with my daughter."

Her voice is perfectly calm, but her eyes are furious when they turn on me—a special art she's mastered over the years. I look down and see she's squeezing the sick bell between her palms so tightly that her knuckles have whitened.

Fräulein Gretchen glances between us a second time, then says softly, "Of course, Mrs. Blackcreek." She rises. "Shall I let you know when dinner is ready?"

My mother nods, not taking her eyes off mine. I know the look well, so my heart is already racing.

"Please do. Thank you," Mam says. "We won't be long."

When the door closes and we're alone, she immediately starts in on me.

"How could you, Essie? How could you!"

"I didn't pack it, I swear!" I stand up, shaking my head. It's ridiculous of her to accuse me. She knows I hate the bell. She knows I dread even touching it. Why would I bring it here?

"For months I've been asking where it went! *For months,*" says Mam, her voice shaking. Her fingers clench tighter around the piece of silver, and she looks very much like she's about to start crying. "All this time you've been saying you didn't know. Lying right to my face! How could you?"

"It wasn't a lie! I didn't know where it was!"

"Yet here it is with your things."

She picks up my suitcase and chucks it down on my bed, then heads for the door, bell still clutched in her fist. Right before she leaves, she turns around and stabs a finger toward me, eyes glistening.

"I pray your new father doesn't realize what a selfish girl you are. If I took in a girl like you, I'd put her right out!"

It's clear she wants to slam my bedroom door, but this isn't our house. Not really. So Mam takes a deep breath and closes the door quietly behind her.

She's obviously had more practice at pretending to be civil than me, because I shout, "Have him put me out, then! I want to go home anyhow!"

Then I take off my shoe and throw it across the room.

Since I have terrible aim, it strikes the little table near the door, rocking an unlit lamp. I cry out, dashing forward, and fortunately avert disaster, steadying the spiral-cut glass before it crashes to the floor and douses the room in oil that could light with the smallest of sparks.

Slumping against the wall, I breathe a sigh of relief.

I fully expect to perish on North Brother Island, but I'd much prefer it wasn't my own fault. And I certainly don't want to die in a fire. Witnessing the burning of the *General Slocum* has forever ensured *Fire* a spot on my List of Unspeakable Fears.

Thinking of the list, I suddenly realize why the sick bell mysteriously appeared in my luggage. I stand up, meaning to cross the room, but a whistling sound stops me in my tracks. I turn in a slow circle, really taking my first look around, and my eyes land again on the oil lamp. It strikes me as strange—that the room is so bright, yet the lamp is unlit—and my gaze continues upward, landing on two horrors, one after the other.

First is a small tin mouthpiece sticking out of the wall by the door, about a foot above my head. It's shaped like a cone and has a tiny lever. The whistling sound—which has stopped abruptly—was coming from somewhere deep inside its metal throat.

I take a step backward, heart racing, and then look up directly above me, squinting once more as I spot the large gilded light hanging from the ceiling. It has three scrolling branch arms, each shaded with frosted glass. I can *see* the electricity. It's buzzing about inside the bulbs, so bright I have to look away.

I gasp, nearly calling for Mam, but at the last moment I remember we're fighting and instead snatch my suitcase off the bed and run to the far side of the room. Could the electricity reach me from here, if it escaped the glass bulbs? I desperately want to turn the light off to be safe, but I don't know how. Two white buttons on a panel by the bed look promising, but I'm certain I'll be shocked if I press the wrong one.

I can feel myself starting to panic, so I hunch down in the corner and start fishing around in my luggage, feeling for the tear in the blue cloth lining. When I find it, I reach inside and pull out my pencil and the papers I hid there. Just the act of unfolding them, smoothing the rumples and creases, makes me start to feel better. I run a trembling finger over the pages, touching the word *Cats* and then *Doors*. Farther down, I find *Electric Lights* and glance up at the fixture again. I press my thumb over the words, picturing them, and say them a few times in my head. Eventually, I'm calm enough to think clearly.

Three years ago, shortly after my nightmares began, Mam thought it would be a good idea for me to write down all the things I was afraid of. In the beginning, the List of Unspeakable Fears was nothing more than a few notorious items: *Tuberculosis*, followed by *Fire*, followed by *Thunderstorms*, then *Unlaced Shoes*. That spring, I'd seen a boy from school trip on his laces and break his nose walking home. There was a lot of blood.

The list went on from there, though, growing over the next couple of days.

Haggis.

Rats.

Ships of All Kinds.

Hard Candies and *Talkative Strangers* and *Moths.*

A few weeks later I'd written ten pages, front and back, and I was quite proud of the accomplishment. I showed it to my teacher, Sister Maud, who called Mam into school, and they had a long conversation with me about putting aside "morbid obsessions." I'd tried to explain that I wasn't interested in death. I was interested in *avoiding* it. But no one seemed to understand the difference. My teacher kept the original list "for her records," and Mam insisted she'd made a mistake by encouraging my behavior—I needed to stop writing things down.

Of course I started over in secret, organizing my fears in alphabetical order, and adding as I saw fit.

Alligators, Ants, Anything with a Sharp Point.

Bats and *Big, Hairy Noses.*

Candles That Flicker.

Cats, Creaky Closets.

The Dark.

DOORS. DOORS. DOORS.

Electric Lights and *Empty Boxes.*

Fires, Fog, Folding Fans, Furnaces.

Ghosts.

The list has grown a great deal since those early days. I still try to keep the items generally alphabetical, but since there's always something new to be afraid of, I've hardly room to be picky. Fears are written in the margins and the soft, worried corners. They're written upside down. Some are so smudged they're unreadable. Some have been retraced with a pencil so many times that the letters have cut through their page.

I skim till I find the *S*s, thinking of the whistling metal mouthpiece sticking out of the wall by the door. In a tiny space between *Smokestacks* and *Spiders* I write *Speaking Tubes* with the nub of pencil. I let out a slow breath.

After a moment, I remember the sick bell and scan the rest of the page, just to be safe. Thankfully, that fear hasn't magically appeared on my list like the bell appeared in my suitcase. It might not make sense to others—writing down the things you're most scared of and leaving off the worst one—but I'm so afraid of the sick bell that the thought of scrawling those letters is simply too much.

Because the sick bell is haunted.

Just the sound of it tinkling summons paralyzing feelings of dread—even Mam, brave as she is, pulled the clapper right out so it couldn't be rung.

Thinking of this, everything tightens inside me again, and I clutch the List of Unspeakable Fears in my fist. I didn't pack the bell. Truly. When it was missing in our apartment, I didn't know where it was any more than my mam did. I wasn't lying.

But I also wasn't being totally honest.

What my mother doesn't know, though obviously suspects, is that I was the one who lost the bell in the first place. I could no longer stand looking at it. Even without a clapper, the fear that it would somehow start ringing was more than I could take. So I hid the bell in an empty hand-me-down suitcase, naively certain we wouldn't be moving anytime soon. However, Mam got so upset—believing the heirloom was lost—that I opened the suitcase back up to retrieve it. Much to my horror, the sick bell was gone.

Still curled up in the corner, I hear Mam down the hall talking to someone, and I know I must get ready for supper, but it takes a moment to gather my courage, rise, and walk back across the room. I do my best not to stand directly beneath the electric lights as I stuff my papers under the mattress and put my clothing away. Before closing up the suitcase, I feel again for the small tear in the lining. I hadn't noticed it till yesterday, while looking for somewhere to hide the list while we traveled, but without a doubt, that's where the sick bell had been. I hadn't found it when I'd searched the suitcase before because it had slipped into a place between places.

For more than six months, the sick bell has been missing. And now it's returned.

Like the red door, it's followed me to this horrible island.

Chapter Six

The table in the dining room is so long and so large that it must have been built inside. I've seen tables this grand before while cleaning for rich people, but I've certainly never *eaten* at one. The thought that it now belongs to me doesn't fit in my head—just like the table wouldn't have fit through the doors in this room. I suspect you have to be born surrounded by lavish things to feel like they're truly yours. No matter who my mother marries, no table this big will ever be ours.

Though there's more than one candelabra in the room, most of the light comes from the giant chandelier hanging from the center of the ceiling. It's decorated with sparkling cut glass and has several brass arms—half pointing up and half pointing down. To my relief, the arms pointing up are burning with gas flames. The arms pointing down, clearly electric, are dark.

Fräulein Gretchen notices me staring at the light when I come through the doors and says, "I can turn it on, if you like. It is only that the bulbs are quite dim. The ones in your room use a new, experimental material. Dr. Blackcreek made sure to install them before you arrived."

I shake my head quickly, even more frightened now that I

know the electric lights in my room are *experimental*. The head of the table is reserved for my still-absent stepfather, so I take the seat across from Mam and try my best not to stare at his empty chair, fretting about what he'll be like when we meet. Soon enough, though, I'm overwhelmed by other concerns, such as the remarkable number of utensils set at my place. Why would anyone need two forks? I nervously whisper at Mam, "How do I know which one to use?"

She blushes, clearly not knowing herself, and suddenly Fräulein Gretchen is explaining each utensil in the most gracious way, as if she does this for every guest at her table. She even demonstrates how to cut meat like a proper lady.

"Won't you eat with us too, Fräulein Gretchen?" asks my mother when the maid has finished showing me how to hold the fork in my left hand, tines down, and the knife in my right.

Fräulein Gretchen looks up, surprised.

"I took my meal already, ma'am. In the kitchen," she says. Then she adds with a sincere smile, "But thank you."

My mother insists that we wait for my stepfather before eating. Besides this, she says little to me, so we sit in silence for what seems an eternity. Fräulein Gretchen stands patiently by the door, which makes me terribly uncomfortable. Each tick of the oak longcase clock against the wall seems to echo louder and louder. Finally there's a knock at the big double doors, and I look across the room in anticipation. When Frank lets himself in, though, he's alone, hat in his hands and rain dripping onto the floor from the bottom of his coat.

"So sorry, Mrs. Blackcreek, Miss Essie," he says. "It seems the doctor won't be making it home in time to dine with you. He sent me to make sure you went on and ate."

Mam's pretty face falls in disappointment before she can politely reply. Soon after, Fräulein Gretchen steps into the kitchen and returns with platters of smoked fish and crisp vegetables and hot, crusty bread. I try not to look too eager, but it's an enticing feast.

"I'm sure Dr. Blackcreek is sorry to miss you," the maid says. "If the hospital needs him to stay, he stays. He works very hard. He retires in his office sometimes, rather than return home."

"I see," says my mother unhappily.

I almost smile. It's terrible of me, I know. But I'm looking everywhere for disappointments to prove that her sudden marriage and our even more sudden move were an awful mistake. Perhaps, if it turns out to be awful enough, we'll find ourselves back home soon.

After we eat, Mam tells me to go to bed. She'll stay awake a bit longer, she says, touching the fresh curls in her hair. She wants to read in the parlor by the fire.

I nod, watching her, and start to pick up our dirty dishes. It takes some restraint not to lick the remaining morsels of German crumb cake off my plate. Even though she laughed when I was frightened by the cat, Fräulein Gretchen's cooking is so delicious, it's impossible not to start liking her. This is even more true when I walk toward the kitchen door and she swoops in to take everything from my hands.

"Thank you, sweet girl," she says. "You had a long journey today. Please go rest."

I glance at my mother, certain she'll insist I at least do the drying. In Mott Haven, I often cooked and cleaned up our whole meal. Mam is lost in thought, though, staring at Dr. Blackcreek's empty chair, so I turn back to Fräulein Gretchen.

"All right, but . . . can you please show me how to turn off the light in my room?"

A red door.

A dark hallway.

A terrible feeling of dread.

My breath grows faster. The dripping behind the walls becomes louder. A light appears around the door's frame that has never been there before. It's burning hot. And though I haven't moved a step forward, everything's suddenly closer. I squeeze my eyes shut. I don't want to see or hear any of this.

Someone whispers my name right next to my ear.

I sit up in bed, crying and sweating. I call for Mam, but there's no answer. When I pat the mattress beside me, searching for her, I'm surprised by the touch of soft sheets and feather pillows. I'm disoriented, thinking my mother must be visiting some poor, sick neighbor. Even though she no longer works for the settlement house, she can't help but go take care of people when they're unwell.

Suddenly the world fills with muted light, and I blink in surprise at an unfamiliar room.

Just as suddenly, the light disappears.

It's not till this happens again, a few seconds later, that I realize the glow is coming from behind curtains—and I remember that these are *my* curtains, *my* windows, *my* room. I remember the dreary mansion on North Brother Island. I remember the lighthouse, its gigantic lantern turning in circles to warn ships away from the shore.

I reach down quickly, feeling along the edge of my mattress for the spot where I hid the List of Unspeakable Fears. Perhaps, if I write *Lighthouse*, I'll get it out of my head and stop shaking. But how will I be able to see the words on the page? Through the curtains, the spinning light isn't bright enough.

After supper, Fräulein Gretchen came upstairs and showed me the speaking tube and electric switch on the wall. The tube's tin mouthpiece, she explained, had a little piece with a lever so that you could blow through it—to make it whistle and alert the servants below—or speak through it and listen for replies. She thought maybe a draft was the cause of the tube whistling earlier, but added that the contraption wasn't working. Frank believed a pipe was loose somewhere in the walls. As for the electric lights, Fräulein Gretchen insisted there was no chance of shock, no matter which button I pressed on the switch, but I'm still not convinced.

However, I have no matches for the oil lamp, which means my only option, if I want to see clearly, is to open the curtains across the room.

Just as I start to rise, though, a sound makes me freeze.

Voices. *Angry voices.*

Coming from under my bed.

I'm almost too scared to breathe. The beam from the

lighthouse on the other end of the island continues to cast my room in a rotation of muted light and suffocating dark. For a moment, I can make out the large wardrobe and empty bookcase along the far wall. Then everything vanishes. The room turns so black I can't even see the foot of my bed. I go still, terrified, waiting to hear the voices again. I want to run to the door and down the hall to Mam, but I'm certain once my feet touch the floor, something will reach out and grab me.

I picture Old Scratch, his dirty claws sharpened to points.

I picture things much, *much* worse—things with tentacles and too many teeth, things that walk upside down on fingertips or slither so flat on the floor you can't see them till they're gnawing your ankles.

When the voices return, I squeak, drawing my knees to my chest. But then the spinning light fills my room, and my head calms for an instant, and I realize that though the sounds are coming from *below*, they're also coming from *outside*.

The voices aren't under my bed—they're beneath my window.

Men are arguing. A carriage door slams.

I exhale, but I'm still nervous. Who would be outside at this hour? I want to roll myself up in my quilt and stuff my head under the pillows. Unfortunately, Beatrice's voice is already ringing in my thoughts, encouraging me to go have a look.

"I'm so frightened, Bea," I said when she came to wish me farewell at the ferry docks, rough water crashing nearby. I hugged her neck as tight as I could, like I might drown if I let go. "I know my new stepfather will be monstrous!"

"If that's true, I'll come save you," my best friend promised, hugging back. "But remember the boiler room, Essie. Not everything is a monster, even if it seems like it at first."

The boiler room was the scariest place at St. Jerome's, located deep in the bowels of our school at the bottom of a dank stairwell. The room was off-limits to students, of course, and I was happy to keep my distance. But once, when Beatrice and I were stuck late after class, desperately trying to finish a difficult sewing project, I noticed the door to the stairwell ajar. From its depths came a horrible sound—like the raspy hacking of a witch.

"There's only one solution," Beatrice declared confidently. I was trembling all the way to my toes. "We have to go see what it is. If there's truly a witch or some other vile thing, we can make a run for the police call box. And if there's not, well, problem solved! Either way, it's better to go see than to sit here worrying."

I protested and begged and tried to block Beatrice's way. I sat on the floor and held on to her skirts, pulling her back, but she just wound up dragging me through the halls. In the end, Beatrice went down into the boiler room and I followed in tears. When we discovered old Mr. O'Shea, the janitor, smoking an overstuffed pipe and coughing, my friend was smug as the devil.

"See," she told me. "Nothing to fear. You just needed to be brave enough to go take a closer look."

I don't want to climb out of bed. I don't want to see who's outside my window. But when the light from the lighthouse spins back around, I force myself to jump up and run quick as I can across the floorboards. Nothing dashes after me, thankfully, and I yank back the curtains before the beam has fully passed. It's incredibly bright for a moment, but then the light spins away and my eyes adjust to the dimness.

The first thing I see clearly is a big mason jar full of colored glass on the windowsill. After that, I spot a carriage below, parked in front of the house. Standing outside it are the dark shapes of three men. When the beam comes back around, a few seconds later, it lights the men up like they're on stage at the theater, and for a moment, the scene below almost doesn't seem real. One of the three people is unusually tall, with gaunt cheeks and a ghostly complexion. He has on a long, black wool overcoat, round spectacles, and a bowler hat. He has a full beard, which is an uncommon sight. He's holding a cane, and in his free hand there's a rolled-up newspaper. While snarling at the others, he shakes this viciously.

The others are the police officers from the ferry.

I gasp as the darkness returns. Without a doubt, the tall man is my stepfather. From my mother's descriptions alone, I can guess it. What he's doing talking to the police so late at night, though, I have no clue. The freezing rain turned to snow while I slept. White is still flurrying down from the sky. This makes the voices below drift up muffled, but even in the dim light, I can see that Dr. Blackcreek is irritated—and losing patience.

I catch a few words here and there, coming out of the shadows.

"... accusations ... slander ... outrageous ..."

And then I make out half a sentence sharp as a hiss, and the blood goes chill in my veins.

"... those damned disappeared women ..."

I remember Frank's concerned glance at the officers when he saw them on the dock. Then I remember the crewman and his questions to Mam. He said something about nurses who had gone missing. My mind starts racing. How could someone go missing on an island this small? And why is my stepfather so angry? Certainly the police don't suspect he's involved. My mother wouldn't have married a man caught up in a scandal.

Just as the light returns, I see the officers climb back into the carriage. They must be staying the night somewhere on the island, since no ferry is running this late. Dr. Blackcreek, left alone in the snow, looks at the newspaper crushed in his fist.

Once more, darkness blankets the world, and I hear horses' hooves and wheels echoing on the brick path. I lean close to the glass. I squint down at the front stoop of the house, waiting for the lighthouse beam to spin back around. Finally, it does.

Dr. Blackcreek is staring straight up at my window.

I cry out, letting the curtain drop as I stumble away. It takes less than a breath before I'm back under my covers, pillow over my head and eyes tightly closed. I try to block out what I saw. I try to erase it from memory. But I realize that though I love her— though I think her incredibly clever—Beatrice isn't always right.

I should never have looked out the window.

We shouldn't have followed that noise down into the boiler room either.

When we emerged from the stairwell, Sister Maud spotted us, and we both got the yardstick, which left bruises for a week. And, worse yet, what did it really matter that we'd found Mr. O'Shea making weird noises? That didn't mean there wasn't *also* a witch. She might have been watching us from the shadows. She might have been waiting to catch us alone.

Not everything is a monster.

But *some* things are.

Some things you can look at just once and regret your whole life that you saw them. Some things are so terrible you know no matter how hard you try, you'll never get them out of your head.

Seeing my stepfather staring up at me through that window is one of those things. Because in that small moment, I knew I'd never seen anyone so furious. I'd never seen anyone look so sinister in my entire life.

Dr. Blackcreek had appeared positively murderous.

Chapter Seven

My whole life, I've had responsibilities early in the morning, and after Da died, those responsibilities grew. Even before dressing, packing my lunch in an old tobacco tin, and walking to school, there were chores. Mam and I would hang laundry, bring coal up from the yard, and bake our bread for the day. Sometimes we'd have odd jobs, so we could earn a little extra money, and we'd squeeze the work into the early, dark hours before dawn or the late, dark hours before bed. My least favorite of these was when we made paper flowers. They're very popular in New York City in autumn, and the work could all be done at our kitchen table, but Mam and I would have to paste together almost 1,500 to make our full eighty cents, and it left my fingers so sore I'd have trouble writing at school.

I knew my mother hated that I had to work. She considered my education of the utmost importance. And technically, it's against the law for children to have jobs. But most everyone we know would have been out on the streets if not for their whole family's help earning money.

Because of the way we've always been forced to live, I'm used to getting up very early. So when I sleep till nearly ten my first morning on North Brother Island—and no one comes to wake me—it's quite a shock. I get dressed in a rush and open my door with my hair still untidy, certain that *someone* must be waiting for me to do *something*. I nearly trip over the breakfast tray laid out in the hall.

There's a covered bowl of porridge, still hot, some cut fruit, and a tall glass of milk.

I hesitate for quite a while, standing there and debating whether the food is for me. Since there seems to be no other possibility, I bring it back into the room and eat at the writing desk. It's delicious, except for the milk, which has a very strange taste.

When I'm finished, I carry the tray downstairs. The house seems different in daytime—larger, but also less intimidating. The thick curtains are open in most rooms, and bright light reflects off snow outside. In the grand foyer at the bottom of the staircase, I find no one, so I walk down the hallway to the dining room. There's no one there, either, so I go through a door at the back that leads to the kitchen and wash all my breakfast dishes in a large white sink.

When I'm through, I look around. Signs of Fräulein Gretchen are everywhere—a cup of tea still steaming, a damp dishrag balled up on the counter. I turn in a slow circle, blinking at the towering wooden cabinets and hand-painted serving bowls. There are jars of dried herbs lining shelves on the wall. There's a heavy-looking cast-iron stove and a wooden Knickerbocker refrigerator beside a tall window. I go over and open it, marveling at the fresh cream and meat and fish. I peek into the top left cabinet and find the biggest block of ice I've ever seen in a house. Since we didn't own a refrigerator, in the summer we only bought what we could eat in a day. In the winter, we kept our food out on the fire escape, but it often froze, and our bottles of milk sometimes exploded like cannon fire.

"Man yer stations!" Da would shout when this happened, diving under furniture dramatically. "We've raiders attacking the starboard bow!"

If I was still scared stiff by the loud noise, he might shout, "Essie, lass, gather your courage! We must defend our vessel! Except for your mam's stew. The meat cooked too long and is dry. Let the scurvy dogs have it."

After that, Mam would storm in, yelling, and Da would snatch the broom from the wall, swinging it in front of him like a sword.

"Here be Fanny Campbell—the world's most ferocious female pirate! Back, Fanny, back, I say!"

By then, I would no longer be scared. I'd be too busy snorting with laughter and thinking that even in his patched, oversized clothes, my father looked gallant—like a hero from one of his favorite stories.

Da was a romantic, a lover of adventures and heart-pounding tales. Unfortunately, the only book we owned was an Irish songbook, passed down from my granda and granny, and none of us could read music. But sometimes Da's boss lent him novels. My father was a slow reader—much slower than me—and had to ask for help with big words, but it never discouraged him. When the Bronx's first library opened in 1905, just two blocks from my school, he was one of their most devoted patrons.

Thoughts of Da remind me that there's something I want

to see, so I stand up on my toes to try and look out the nearby window. This, in turn, reminds me of last night—of the angry, muffled voices rising up through the snow and Dr. Blackcreek's frightening glare. I step away quickly, suppressing a shiver. The window is too high, anyhow, and more importantly, it's not facing south. That's the direction I need, where I might get a look at some of the other small islands in the East River.

I scoot out the far door into a dimly lit hall. There are no windows here—no people, either—just storage rooms and linen closets and more of that decorative glass sharing corner tables with lamps and piled up in vases on shelves. I accidentally wander into what turns out to be Fräulein Gretchen's bedroom. I can tell by a small framed photograph of her and some handsome young man. I reach to pick it up, but then stop, feeling guilty. Beatrice would call this "an investigation," but I call it "being nosy," so I leave.

Farther along the hall is a door that opens to the backyard. I hurry to the window beside it, but there's no clear view of the shore. What I see instead is a winter-bare garden covered in snow—icy stone benches and pathways, a frozen fountain, a trellis of black, brittle vines. I also see Old Scratch perched by some shrubbery. I watch him for a moment. Ugly as he is, the cat appears somehow majestic, as if he were a king surveying his lands. Tufts of dark fur frame his bony face. He lifts a paw and starts cleaning it, looking rather self-important.

And then I see the ragged little dead bird at his side.

"You cruel, evil beast!" I sputter.

Old Scratch barely deigns to glance up at me. He narrows

his foggy eyes and goes back to cleaning his paw. I feel faint and stumble away. The maze of carpet and drapery closes in. I start breathing faster. The image of the tattered bird flashes past my eyes. Just as I'm about to start crying, I emerge unexpectedly into the foyer.

The grand stairwell is to my left, as is the warm parlor, its open doors beckoning me to a quaint yellow sofa and a tray of cookies in front of a dwindling fire. I resist, but the cozy scene is enough to shock me back to my senses.

"Essie, love?" Fräulein Gretchen appears with a basket of firewood. "Oh, there you are!" she says, smiling. "Did you sleep well?"

"Y-yes," I stammer, still recovering. "Have you seen my mother?" At the last moment, I remember my manners. "And thank you for the breakfast."

"You are welcome. I hope the porridge was not cold," says Fräulein Gretchen. "I'm afraid Mrs. Blackcreek left early this morning, though. She is touring the island with Frank and meeting some of Riverside's staff."

I make a wary face. I want to tell Mam what I saw out my window last night. I also want to apologize for the bell. I need her to trust me again. Seeing Dr. Blackcreek fight with the police has given me a terrible feeling. If something criminal is happening on the island, I need Mam to believe me when I talk to her.

"Did my mother seem angry with me?" I ask.

Fräulein Gretchen looks surprised. "Not in the slightest. She said, 'Let Essie sleep all the day if she wishes, and when she wakes, tell her to do as she pleases.'"

I try to match the maid's cheery smile, but I can hear those words in Mam's voice, and I am positive beyond all doubt that she's still furious. My stomach twists in a knot.

"Pretty, isn't it?" Fräulein Gretchen says, nodding to something beside me.

I look down to find that I'm standing right next to a bowl of that strange glass. It's sitting on a side table near the stairs. Light glints off the pieces, creating a rainbow of colors. Some of the glass is smoky inside. Other pieces are clear enough to see straight through. I pinch one between my fingers and lift it up. It's about the size of my thumb, smooth to the touch and quite beautiful. When I peer through it, the whole world tints orange.

"Drift glass," says Fräulein Gretchen. "It washes up on the shore."

I set the piece of glass carefully back down in its bowl.

"There's a lot around here. There's even a jar in my bedroom."

"You can call it Dr. Blackcreek's . . . hobby," says Fräulein Gretchen, as if she couldn't find the right word. She walks the rest of the way into the parlor, on the opposite side of the foyer, and I follow her, watching as she rolls up her sleeves and kneels down to add wood to the fire. It makes me anxious seeing someone do these things for me. I fidget.

"The doctor walks the beaches during low tide and brings the drift glass back in his pockets." Fräulein Gretchen pauses again and turns to me knowingly. "You can find many unusual things on North Brother Island if you look."

My skin tingles. It's like an echo of Beatrice's advice.

Be brave. Take a closer look.

In less than a day, though, I've looked close enough at North Brother already. I don't want to find "unusual things." I'm afraid as it is. All that matters is telling Mam what I saw. She surely won't make us stay here if my stepfather is up to something villainous. I decide to go write Beatrice immediately. It's best to keep her updated on these sorts of goings on.

The antique grandmother clock by the front door chimes loudly, and both Fräulein Gretchen and I turn our heads.

"Good timing!" she says. "Low tide is very soon. If you hurry, you can see the drift glass for yourself."

I hold my hands up. "Oh, n-no, thank you! There's snow outside and likely ice, too." I wring my fingers together, taking a step back. I twitch when I spot my shadow out of the corner of my eye. "I could easily slip into the river or catch frostbite or—"

I stop talking when I see Fräulein Gretchen blinking at me. "Angsthäschen," she says.

"What?"

"My new name for you." She gives me a wry look, then goes back to her work. "Do not worry. It is a cute name."

I feel defensive instinctively. "What if I meet a patient and get ill? What then?"

"The patients are quarantined in their rooms," Fräulein Gretchen says simply, placing the last piece of firewood. "Sometimes the nurses take them outside for fresh air, but not in the winter. The buildings are too cold already. They would not risk making the sick even colder."

I bite my lip, searching for another excuse, but then realize that going for a walk is *exactly* what I want to do after all. Even if it's dangerous, from the shore I'll be able to see South Brother Island. "Which way should I go if I want to look south?" I ask suddenly.

Fräulein Gretchen turns to me, clearly confused by my change of heart. "Use the back door and follow to the right. If you walk a little way, you will have a nice view."

"Thank you," I say, and she nods, curious. I excuse myself to go get my coat before she can ask any questions.

A letter to Beatrice can wait. Worrying about Dr. Blackcreek and his mysterious visit with the police can wait too. I get bundled up, put on my boots, and hurry to the door. I've almost made it outside when I hear someone call my name. Fräulein Gretchen is coming down the hall, and in her hands is a soft brown leather satchel. She offers it to me, along with her smile.

"In case you find something," she says.

Chapter Eight

Down at the water, the wind whips at my gray dress. It twists the cloth around my boots, which lace up past my ankles. The air is freezing, but there's no snow here—the waves have washed it all away. I pick a careful path to the edge of the shore, watching for ice.

I've only ever been to the beach once. On my sixth birthday, Mam and Da took me to Coney Island. It was the middle of July. It was hot. Surf Avenue was packed full of people so tight we barely had room to move. First we went to the ocean, where Mam begged me to swim. I refused, so my parents rented striped swim costumes for themselves. The company's advertisements boasted that their clothing was "sterilized," which sounded painful, but when Mam and Da came back from changing, they both seemed unharmed.

At the water, Mam and Da followed a rope past the first, strong waves. I watched from the shore, fretting that they'd be swept under and vanish. When they started playing like children, though, splashing around and giggling, I finally began to relax. Mam swam back to me, and I agreed to let her tie up my skirts so I could wade in to my knees.

That afternoon we ate a picnic lunch, then headed to Luna Park. Admission was ten cents a person, and I worried we couldn't afford it, but Da handed over the coins without blinking and tipped his hat at the vendor, just like he was rich. He led Mam and me through the entrance with a grand gesture. The whole place was spellbinding, with a circus and carousel and a spectacular train ride called Dragon's Gorge. Mam wanted me to go with her on Shoot the Chutes—a boat trip that would take you up a tall, steep track and send you splashing down into water. I refused, for all the obvious reasons, so she went alone while Da bought me sweets. When Mam got off the ride, giddy from screaming, I gaped at the sight of her—drenched clothing, hair a tangled, fallen mess. I turned to my father, expecting shock, but he just started laughing.

I remember him taking both her hands. I remember his smile. *That smile.*

He loved her so, *so* much.

On the shore of North Brother, the memory has gone sour.

Some small part of me had hoped that being on a beach again would feel good. But thinking of the happiest day of my life just makes me sad. And this is a miserable excuse for a beach anyhow. Low tide hasn't revealed pretty treasures. It's only revealed what I already knew—that when people in New York City decide something is too broken to fix, this is where it winds up. There's more garbage on this shoreline than sand.

Beside my right foot is a piece of rusted scrap metal, half-buried under rocks. I dig it loose with the toe of my shoe, then kick it as hard as I can, sending the rubbish flying out over the water. For a long time, I stare at the dark waves, daring them to send the trash back.

And then I get an odd feeling, like I'm being watched. I turn, glancing over my shoulder, and nearly leap out of my shoes.

Old Scratch is a few yards away, sitting on a boulder. He flicks his ratty tail.

"You followed me!" I cry in horror.

The mangy cat narrows his yellow eyes and meows—or at least I think it's supposed to be a meow. It sounds more like a creaky, dented trunk lid opening up.

"You can't even talk like a proper cat," I say, frowning. I lift my chin to match his gaze. "Stay put, murderer. I don't want you near. Do you hear me?"

Old Scratch flicks his tail faster.

I move on, making a point not to look back, but after walking for quite a while, I can tell I'm still not alone. One glance and I scrunch up my face. Old Scratch is following from a distance. I move quicker, eyes on my feet.

If Beatrice were here, she'd start getting suspicious.

That cat's trailing you, she'd say. *He knows something.*

"Don't be ridiculous," I mutter out loud.

Trying to take my mind off Old Scratch, I start scanning the shore, looking for drift glass. At first I don't see any, just more garbage, but then I slow. Then I look a bit closer. A bright bit of yellow catches my eye on the left. A few steps later, there's a green glimmer among the rocks on my right. Fräulein Gretchen was telling the truth—there's drift glass everywhere. I finger her satchel but don't stoop to pick anything up. The bend around the north side of the island is getting closer. I'm sure I'll see South Brother soon. But the buildings that make up Riverside

Hospital are getting closer as well, and one in particular draws my attention. It's very near to the shore, made of concrete, and has a big window on the ground level. Through that window, I see movement.

I guess I still don't really understand where I am—what sort of an awful place this is—because I don't feel scared right away. I leave the water behind and walk across a flat, snowy yard. I stop next to a tree by the window. It's bare, and not nearly big enough to hide me, but when someone runs past on the other side of the glass, I duck behind its trunk anyway. I hear voices, and that's what reminds me to be afraid—because they're the voices of other children.

Sick children.

Peeking from behind the tree, I watch through the window in a sad kind of awe. Boys and girls, some my age, some a bit older or younger, lie in nightgowns on metal beds along the walls. One is reading a book. One is playing with a rubber doll. Some are sleeping. Most are just staring vacantly. A nurse in protective clothing picks up the boy who ran by the window. She scolds him, and he starts coughing.

That's when I see the girl in the pretty dress, on the far side of the room. She sticks out because she's not in bedclothes. Instead, she's all done up in lace, like she's going to church. I tilt my head. Something is wrong. The way that her dress hangs is funny, like it's heavy. And her face . . . It's familiar. The brown braid and white ribbon. The dark, staring eyes. I'm certain I've seen her before.

There's a sudden noise, the sound of something running

very fast, and when I turn, I see a creature barreling toward me through the snow.

It's hairy and hideous, growing larger as it approaches.

I cry out, spinning away, but make it only a few yards from the tree before I slip and fall. To my surprise, the beast bounds right over me, and Old Scratch starts screeching. The cat has followed me all the way from the shore. For a moment I actually feel bad for him, watching his fur stand on end as he swats and hisses. But then the mangy thing abandons me, darting off, and the hairy creature—clearly some kind of terrible mutt— recognizes Scratch isn't worth the chase.

Not when I'm right there on the ground, helpless and injured.

I scream as the dog runs toward me, snarling and slobbering. His front paws pin me down. I writhe in terror, turning my face away from his rancid breath.

"Heel, you brainless thing! Heel!" a woman shouts.

The dog gives me a disgusting lick, all the way from my chin to my forehead, then rolls over onto his back beside me, as though he believes I'll repay his assault with a belly rub. I scoot away, mortified, my hair and clothing a shambles. The beast isn't as big as I first thought. In fact, he's not much bigger than the cat. His fur is white with brown and black patches. His ears flop over at the tops and his muzzle is particularly scruffy, as if he has a large, unkempt mustache. I shiver convulsively, suspecting he's some kind of fox terrier. When he realizes I'm not going to pet him, he gets up, starts sniffing for Old Scratch's trail, and trots away.

The woman who called the dog off hurries over and helps

me up. "Curse that no-good wretch," she mutters, wiping snow off me rather forcefully. "Are you all right? Are you hurt?"

I'm too much in shock to speak for a moment, and when I gather the strength, all I can say is, "M-maybe?"

The woman's expression turns annoyed. "Well, are you all right or aren't you?"

"My knee is hurt," I say, surprised by her tone. "And my coat is dirty. And it was a terrible fright."

She glances down at my knee, where I'm sure there's a grotesque wound. I'm too nervous to look at first, but when she doesn't say anything, I risk a peek. There's nothing more than a scuff on my stocking. My knee might bruise, but it isn't cut. I let out my breath and gingerly poke the injury.

"Is he your pet?" I ask, looking sideways at the beast. He's found something to bark at in a small tidal pool and is hopping around like a buffoon.

"I suppose," says the woman, eyeing the dog.

I consider her more curiously. She's the picture of health, with rosy cheeks and strong shoulders, dressed in a long coat and boots. Most likely one of the staff, though it's strange she's not in a uniform. Her dark hair is styled on the top of her head. She's tall, with a handsome quality, but there's something intimidating about the way she holds herself. Too confident, perhaps.

I cross my arms and say pointedly, "Well, is he or isn't he?"

The woman turns back to me, raising an eyebrow. "Aren't you a cheeky one?" I've nothing to say to that, so after a moment of silence, she smiles coyly and asks, "Essie, isn't it?"

My eyes widen. "How do you know my name?"

"I know everything that happens on this island."

I realize right then that I should turn and leave. The chill down the back of my neck tells me as much. But I'm still upset by what I saw last night, and it's important I learn what's happening on this island—and how my new stepfather might be involved. So I gather my courage and ask, "If you know everything, do you know about the missing nurses?"

The woman's eyes light up. "Cheeky *and* nosy, it seems!" She grins. "What business do you have with those poor women?"

"Well, I saw Dr. Blackcreek . . . I mean . . . Yesterday there were police here. And a crewman on our ferry mentioned the nurses." I stop trying to explain myself and stand up a bit straighter. Beatrice would ask direct questions. "How many people are missing?"

"Three," she says. Her grin grows. *"So far."*

A lump rises up in my throat. "Wh-what happened to them?"

"I've my suspicions." The woman looks me over for a moment, then adds in a low voice, "Plague Island is a horrible place. You realize that, don't you? You realize the danger you and your sweet mother are in?"

I can barely swallow now. I certainly can't form any words. And there's no time to try, anyhow. Someone is calling my name from across the yard. I look up to find Fräulein Gretchen hurrying toward us.

"Stay safe, Essie," says the strange woman. "I wouldn't want to see anything happen to you."

By the time I turn back to her, she's already started down the beach after her dog.

Chapter Nine

Back at the house, Fräulein Gretchen makes me immediately wash my hands—not just once, but *twice*, declaring that I didn't do it thoroughly enough the first time. The whole thing is peculiar, but I do as she asks, then go up to my room to write Beatrice.

Dearest Beatrice, my letter starts out.

> *I feel like it has been one hundred years since I left*
> *Mott Haven because I miss you that much. I'm*
> *going to write you as often as I can so you will know*
> *everything bad that has happened to me.*

After describing the awful ferry ride and the creepy house and the strange occurrence last night, I tell my friend about the drift glass and the woman I met on the beach.

> *I'm pretty sure she was Irish because of her accent.*
> *So even though she was rude and scary, I feel better,*
> *knowing there are other Irish people here. Fräulein*
> *Gretchen is very nice, but she's German.*

I blush a little after reading this part. I suppose I didn't even realize I felt this way till now. But it's only natural to be more comfortable around people who are like you, isn't it?

> *You know how in school they're always telling us that we are Americans—not Irish or German or Italian—and that we must speak only English and forget our parents' foreign ways? Well, I'm starting to feel like Dr. Blackcreek doesn't know about all that. The books on his shelves are in German and Fräulein Gretchen cooks German food. It's very delicious, but I'm not sure it's American of me to eat it. I think I'd rather stick to corned beef and cabbage.*

I continue writing, and time passes quickly. After the sun sets, there's a knock at the door and Fräulein Gretchen peeks into my room. Instinctively, I hide the letter under my hand, which makes me feel guilty about the whole thing.

"Time to get dressed for supper," says the maid. "Your mother's woken up from her rest, if you want to see her."

I'm surprised, because I didn't even know Mam was back from the tour, much less that she took a nap.

"Thank you," I say politely. And since I'm not sure what getting "dressed for supper" means—I'm dressed already—I wash my face and brush my hair and quickly read over what I've written. At the end of the letter, I sign my name big and loopy, in a way that would have made Sister Maud go *tsk-tsk-tsk*, and then I fold the pages together carefully and stuff them into an envelope. With a bit of damp cloth, I wet the gum and seal it, since licking paper is both disgusting and incredibly dangerous. Once a man named Sigmund died after cutting his tongue on the edge of an envelope. Beatrice told me all about it.

I haven't seen Mam since last night, so I'm hoping I can talk to her before we go downstairs, but the moment I step into her room, I know it's not the right time. Though she looks elegant in a fashionably low-cut red dress, my mother is still clearly tired, staring blankly at her pale face in the vanity mirror. In fact, she looks so tired that it frightens me. The move has taken more out of her than I guessed.

Mam glances to where I'm hovering in the doorway and sighs. "Your dress is dirty. And you wore it yesterday, too, didn't you? We need to buy you more clothes."

I look down, not understanding. At home, though I'd change my underthings most days, I often wore this same dress all week. I had only two, after all—and the other was for church.

Mam gets up and we walk together downstairs. When we go through the dining room doors, we find Dr. Blackcreek waiting for us.

"Alwin!" exclaims my mother, her eyes lighting up as he rises from his seat. "I was worried you wouldn't able to join us."

My stomach rolls, losing all notion of hunger. I foolishly expected that Mam and I would again eat dinner alone—that I could avoid meeting my stepfather for another night, or two, or forever. I'm unprepared for the way my legs tremble when I come to a quick stop.

Mam hurries to her new husband's side and plants a kiss on his cheek, but I just stand and stare, thinking only of the women on the island who are missing—and what this man my mother is kissing may have to do with them. Does he know where they are? Does he know why they left? What if he's somehow involved?

My blood goes cold when Dr. Blackcreek smiles—too briefly, too tight—and pulls out my mam's chair. He's more intimidating in person than two stories below. He's a full head taller than Mam—and she's taller than the average woman. His eyebrows are thick, his eyes set in deep behind round glasses. His long beard is streaked with gray. I notice the black cane propped beside him at the table. Its silver head is shaped to look like a raven.

After my mother is settled, Dr. Blackcreek walks around the table and pulls out my chair, gesturing. It takes a great deal of strength to cross the room. I'm not sure what I think will happen when I reach my stepfather, but I'm thankful he doesn't try to hug me, like my real da would have done. He simply holds the back of the chair till I sit, then pushes me in and takes his place at the head of the table. He nods toward me, clearly uncomfortable.

"It's nice to finally meet you, Essie."

I swallow but don't reply, managing only to nod back. Across from me, Mam makes a face. Before she can insist I say something nice, though, Fräulein Gretchen comes into the room with three large stoneware mugs on a tray. The first two she places in front of Mam and Dr. Blackcreek. The last she gives to me. It has just a little liquid inside, but the smell tells me it's wheat beer.

My stepfather stands up again, glances briefly at his cane, then raises his heavy mug.

"A toast," he says. "To this new family." He looks Mam in the eyes. "Frau Blackcreek, I am so glad to have you as my wife and to have you here in my home." Mam smiles brightly. Then he turns to me. "Fräulein O'Neill, I hope you will be happy here. And I hope we come to learn a great deal about each other."

I'm terribly anxious now. I don't like the names he's using for Mam and me. I don't like his formal way of speaking. On top of that, his eyes are cold and gray and too intense. He clinks his mug together with Mam's and then faces me. As our cups touch, I can't stand it anymore and look away. He makes an odd noise in his throat.

When I glance up, I find my stepfather staring at me with the strangest expression—shock, for certain, but something else, too—and I can't help but remember again his anger last night. I'm so frightened, I fear I'll be ill. Dr. Blackcreek's gaze darts down to the table, where he taps his mug once and then drinks deep. I don't even pretend to take a sip.

We eat most of the meal in awkward silence, but as we're finishing, Mam starts up light conversation. She thinks the island is "remarkable" and the house is "just so lovely" and everyone she's met has been "entirely friendly." Mam's certain we'll be "happy as clams here." The rest of my food loses its flavor.

My new stepfather doesn't say much, only nodding or adding a word now and then. His mannerisms are unusual. He sits so straight in his chair, it appears that he's ready to bolt. He never sets his utensils down except to take a drink and keeps his hands always above the table. When he pauses to pat his mouth with a napkin, he lays his silverware neatly side by side in the center of his plate. It all seems rather unnecessary. More than once, holding my fork and knife the way Fräulein Gretchen showed me has resulted in dropping perfectly good bites of sausage into my lap.

I look up, watching the maid flutter around making sure everyone has enough of everything. Her behavior in front of the doctor is formal and distant, which sets me on edge even more. I realize she's been acting odd all afternoon.

"We saw the staff house today," says Mam. There's color in her cheeks again. "The coal house too. The boiler plant. The cistern. That little church is just lovely. And the old lighthouse—how charming! Frank says there are plans for tennis and handball courts near the nurses' home?"

Dr. Blackcreek nods. "Pleasurable activity, particularly taken in fresh air, is important for the recovering patient. And our patients here do frequently recover, contrary to whatever the papers report."

"Pleasurable activities are also important for doctors, you know—especially those with such demanding positions," says Mam. "I hope you intend to enjoy a little tennis yourself?"

I'm surprised by my mother's forwardness. Usually I like the way she speaks her mind to people, especially men. It's part of how I know she's brave. But I've heard her called awful things because of the way she talks—things like "damned suffragette" or "nasty bit of stuff." And I don't want Dr. Blackcreek to call her those things. I don't want him to get angry.

I look over, waiting for his reaction, but he just raises his brow. "Do you play, Frau Blackcreek?"

"I do," Mam replies with a smirk. "I was rather good as a schoolgirl."

"Then I will play with you," my stepfather says.

A memory of Da playing tennis with Mam at the park near our house comes to mind, and I get so dizzy so fast that I drop my tiny dessert spoon. My mother glances at me before turning her attention back to her husband.

"I'd like to tour Riverside when it's convenient," she says. "Frank was hesitant to take me inside any of the hospital buildings."

My stepfather frowns. "Unfortunately, that will have to wait. We have lost three nurses in as many months and are terribly understaffed. Overcrowded, as well. Three hundred twenty beds in the new tuberculosis pavilions and it is still not enough. It makes me vastly uncomfortable—the size of this empty house—when so many of the sick are in need."

I'm already listening intently because of the comment about missing nurses, so my breath catches at the word *tuberculosis*. I feel myself go white as a hospital sheet.

"What about volunteers?" asks Mam. "Have you no one to lighten the load?"

Dr. Blackcreek smiles his tight smile again. "I can see what you are suggesting, but truly, I would rather you not trouble yourself. To put it kindly, conditions at Riverside are not up to my standards. I should be embarrassed for you to see them." He sighs. "Do you know tuberculosis accounts for more than ten percent of the deaths in this country? Here in New York City alone, that was over eight thousand people last year. Eight thousand people!" He gets animated. "And I can assure you, tuberculosis does not distinguish the derelict and indigent man from the prosperous, no matter what the fools say. The disease is only more widespread in poor communities—like those of the immigrants—because of the sorry quality of living conditions and inadequate access to fresh food."

Tuberculosis.

The word repeats in my head till I feel the breath evaporating from my lungs. I know Mam's gaze has fallen on me, but it doesn't do any good. My stepfather still doesn't notice.

"There are physicians in France working on a form of immunization, though it will take some years still before it is ready for human trials," he says. "But there are many precautions that could be taken immediately. If only the worthless health commissioner would listen! Have you noticed that the milk here on North Brother tastes different?" He gestures to my glass, which, like the beer, remains untouched. "It is pasteurized. All of it. I won't allow anything else. Tuberculosis can be transmitted through raw milk."

Tuberculosis. Tuberculosis. TUBERCULOSIS.

"Essie," says Mam, but I don't really hear her, just as if I'm stuck in a dream. I try to picture the word on the page of my list. I try to get it out of my head. Nothing works.

For the first time since he started talking, Dr. Blackcreek seems to notice I'm in the room. "Is she all right?" he asks.

"Do you need to excuse yourself, Essie?" asks Mam.

I nod, and somehow I get to my feet. I'm shaking.

"Is she not well?" asks Dr. Blackcreek, though I don't think he's really concerned.

"She just doesn't like to talk about sickness," says Mam. "I should have warned you."

"That is unusual from the daughter of a nurse," says my stepfather, and though I'm almost to the dining room doors, I can feel his gray eyes on my back. He clears his throat. "Essie?"

Something about my name sounds like trouble.

"Fräulein Gretchen informed me that you met Mary Mallon today," he says.

My heart sticks in my throat. I turn around slowly. "M-Mary Mallon?"

"I believe the papers are calling her Typhoid Mary? I find it a crass name." He lifts an eyebrow. "So it is true? You spoke with her?"

My mouth goes dry. My eyes widen in horror. "Old—Old Scratch . . ." I can hardly make a complete sentence. "Her dog . . . I didn't mean . . . I didn't know she was . . ."

"If it is the dog you are fond of, I will get you your own," he says, then takes a drink before adding, "Just see that you stay clear of Mary."

Even my mother looks concerned now. "Is she that dangerous?"

"She didn't look sick!" I sputter, bracing myself on the wall. "She didn't look sick at all or I would have gone away at once!"

My stepfather lowers his mug, blinking up at my reaction. "She wouldn't look sick. She does not have any symptoms. The city confined her to the island because she is a carrier of typhoid fever—an irresponsible one. Her cooking resulted in the infection of several households. People died. Surely you have read all about this?"

I feel as if I might faint. "Am I *infected*?"

Dr. Blackcreek frowns. "Of course not," he says, and then attempts something like a grin. "Unless you let her make you dessert."

Mam seems to relax, but I gape, horrified.

"I've always felt bad for the poor woman," says my mother. "I read that she came all the way from Ireland alone when she was only fourteen. She worked hard to get her position as a cook, so she must feel very discouraged. And I suspect it's terribly lonely for her on North Brother. Is there not a safe way for Essie to visit? If she wore protective clothing? Or washed her hands with—what did you say you used? Chlorine?"

I intend to tell my mother I don't *want to* visit with Mary Mallon, but I'm too busy trying to breathe.

My stepfather's grin fades. "To be honest, it is not Mary spreading the disease that I fear most. As long as she avoids jobs where she might infect others—such as her previous employment as a cook—there is little danger. The trouble is that she doesn't take her illness seriously. She doesn't believe she is to blame for the families she worked for getting sick. No matter how I explain her condition—that she can carry typhoid fever but not have any symptoms—she refuses to accept it. She sees her quarantine as imprisonment. And the stories about her in the papers made everything worse. She has been writing her lawyer, whom I suspect is paid for by the papers themselves. She's having private lab tests done. Demanding to be released." He shakes his head. "What I fear will spread is Mary's mistrust of science. And her *fear*. She thinks everyone on the island is against her. She thinks I—" He hesitates, then purses his lips. "She is angry. To put a point on it, she is angry with me."

At this I look up, and I remember Mary's expression when I asked about the missing nurses.

I remember her warning.

"I won't talk to Mary again," I say quickly. "I promise."

My stepfather turns to look at me by the door, his eyes widening, as if he'd forgotten I existed at all. He nods, and I take it as permission to finally leave the dining room.

On my way up the stairs, the taste of the lie is still tart on my tongue.

Chapter Ten

As I climb into bed, there's a knock at my door. I've just finished resealing Beatrice's letter and added it to the outgoing mail. I had to reopen it to include a short note about the woman on the beach being Mary Mallon and meeting my peculiar stepfather. Mam comes into my room, holding something. She slips it into her pocket before I can see what it is.

"Can we talk?" she asks, and I nod.

I remembered to bring up a box of matches tonight. They're nonpoisonous safety matches, much to my approval, and I used them to light the oil lamp by the door. The little flame casts a long shadow over my mother's face as she crosses the chilly room and sits down on the edge of my mattress. From the way she's looking at me—from the gentle touch of her hand on my forehead, pushing back my hair—I know she's not angry anymore.

This is all very predictable. We fight. We storm apart. Then we lose our lightning and thunder and drift back together. Only now we're stuck on this horrible island, and I can't help but sense a new storm already approaching, threatening to force us farther and farther away from each other.

"I realize the past couple of days have been quite a lot for you," Mam says. "They've been a lot for me, too. But we need to put on our best faces. Give North Brother some time. Give *Alwin* some time. Once you get to know him, I'm certain you'll be friends."

I bite my tongue to keep from asking how she's so sure, when she doesn't really know him either. She told me all about the women's suffrage meeting they'd met at, and it was only a few months ago. He'd walked up and signed the petition her union had written, and that got them talking. They agreed to have dinner the next night at a café. Those women's suffrage meetings always were trouble. Mam started attending them after Da died, and sometimes she'd come home wearing sashes and ribbons and carrying big paper signs with the words VOTES FOR WOMEN printed in black. Two years ago, she even participated in a march. The police had said the march wasn't allowed, but the women walked around New York City anyway. Mam got stale bread and wet sponges thrown at her head, which she told me about very proudly.

"Just look at this room, Essie," my mother continues, motioning to the high ceiling and fine furniture, the thick, soft, warm blankets. "Can't you already see how much more comfortable life will be for us here?"

I certainly can, but I suspect it will also be shorter.

My mother sighs. "I'm sorry for calling you selfish last night. And for all the rest of it too. We've both suffered a great deal of hardship. Da dying. Me . . . getting sad."

I cringe, turning my face to the pillow, trying to keep my thoughts blank, but just the sound of Da's name makes my heart ache. Memories flood into my head without warning. I hear the sick bell ringing. I see Mam lying in bed, thin as a skeleton. I wish, desperately, that I was alone—that I could take out my list and start tracing words to calm down—but my mother reaches for my hand on top of the covers. She keeps talking.

"You've never dealt with change happily, no matter if it was bad or good. And in the last three years we've had a lot of change." She takes a breath. "But can't you see that it's more good than bad now, Essie? Can't you see that I love him?"

I look up at my mother, right into her eyes, and her face is so earnest—so hopeful—that I forget to stay silent. "Can't you see we're in danger?"

Mam smiles slowly. "You'll have an ulcer before you're eleven."

"People don't live on quarantine islands unless they're sick. It's not safe here."

"Some of the staff on North Brother have been here a decade or more—without incident, I might add," says my mother. "If you had come with me on the tour today, you'd have learned that."

I frown, about to remind her she *didn't invite me* on the tour, but she's talking again before I can get a word in.

"There's no reason to worry. Alwin takes every precaution. He studied at a prestigious school in Germany—and you do realize the Germans have far surpassed us in their understanding of medicine?"

I roll my eyes.

"Alwin was at the top of his field before he even immigrated to America. So I'm certain Riverside is the picture of cleanliness and advanced practices—even understaffed, as he says. Especially compared to the places I've tended patients before, in tenements where people sleep on the roof in the summer and six to a bed in the winter. When Alwin was talking tonight about the hospital being *overcrowded* . . ." Mam stops and shakes her head.

"There are other things, though," I say, and I glance at the closed window. "There are things besides illness that might make a place dangerous."

My mother tilts her head, obviously trying to hold in a smirk. "Such as?"

"Last night I saw Dr. Blackcreek with the police."

To my relief, some of the mirth leaves Mam's expression. "Where? *Here?*"

I nod. "Outside my window. It was very late. They were arguing about the missing nurses. Dr. Blackcreek . . . looked angry. He was yelling."

My voice is subdued. Cautious. What I want is for her to be shocked. What I want is for my mother to declare that she's off to get answers, and that if they aren't to her satisfaction, we'll pack up and be gone.

For once—*just once*—I want her to be scared like me.

But instead, to my anger, Mam is only amused.

"So *that's* what this is all about." The smirk she tried to swallow appears in full display. "You think Alwin has something to do with the disappearances!" Mam laughs. She actually *laughs* at me. "Sweet Mother Mary, if my daughter's head were any fuller of clouds, she'd float up to join you in the sky!"

I narrow my eyes. "So what happened, then? Where are the missing women?"

Now Mam purses her lips. "We've been here not even two days, Essie. Do you want me to poke my nose in every drawer? Is that what you spent your day doing? Snooping around like Beatrice?"

"Beatrice doesn't snoop!" I say defensively. Though, of course, she does.

"No more of this," says Mam. "I won't hear it."

"You don't care what happens to us." I scowl. "You don't even care what's happened to those poor women."

"Of course I care," Mam says, scowling too, and I can tell she's trying her best to keep calm. "And you want to know who else cares? Your new father. I didn't know the police had come by the house, but he told me this morning that the reason he was late getting home last night was due to their visit. He invited them himself. Doesn't sound much like something someone would do if they were up to no good, hmm?"

Clearly, my mother hasn't read the same dime novels as Beatrice. The Murphy boys dig them out of the street trash, and once they've finished them, they pass them to their sister. Whether I want to hear about the vile stories or not, eventually Beatrice tells me every last gory detail. So I *know*. Asking the police to investigate a disappearance sounds *exactly* like something someone would do if they were up to no good. My friend would call it an "excellent cover."

It takes only one look at Mam's face to see that I shouldn't explain my suspicions any further, though. She won't accept the truth: that moving us here was a bad choice. She's too stubborn.

That makes me think of someone else, someone who's not so different.

I have to go see Mary Mallon.

I don't want to jump to conclusions. Beatrice would insist that a good detective first gather clues. But now that I've met my stepfather—now that I've seen his cold eyes up close—I feel certain he's the kind of person who might do something villainous. It's not hard to suspect that he's part of the reason the nurses are missing. Did he frighten them away? Did he . . . hurt them? I picture his creepy cane with the raven head. I remember how terrified I felt sitting beside him.

And between Mary's cryptic warning and Dr. Blackcreek's insistence that I avoid her, it's clear the woman knows something—something he doesn't want me to find out. If I'm brave enough to speak with her again, maybe this time from a safe distance, I might get Mary to tell me what has happened. I might be able to prove to Mam the trouble we're in.

"You should get some sleep," my mother says. "And go out and see more of the island tomorrow. Your schoolbooks will be arriving later in the week, and you won't have as much time for exploring."

"My schoolbooks? There isn't a school here."

"No," says Mam. "Fräulein Gretchen will be in charge of your lessons for now. We've put out an advertisement for a governess, but . . . well, Alwin isn't optimistic that we'll find someone quickly. Thankfully, Gretchen has some experience tutoring, and she's agreed to help for a while."

I'm aghast at the idea. "But she's German!"

My mother frowns. "What on earth does that have to do with anything?"

"What if she doesn't know the right words?"

"Don't be silly. Her English is exceptional," Mam says, annoyed. Then she smiles wickedly. "And lucky for you, arithmetic is the same in every language."

I make a miserable face. "I'd rather go back to St. Jerome's and let the nuns smack me with their yardsticks," I say.

"You're being rude."

"But why can't you teach me?" I ask.

"I . . . I just can't," says Mam. "I won't have time."

The way she says this gives me pause, and I recall something she mentioned at dinner. Was it something about volunteering at Riverside? I don't have time to panic and start asking questions, because my mother is digging around in her pocket.

I remember that she was holding something when she came into the room.

Something small.

"There's one more thing we need to discuss," says my mother. "I think you know what it is."

I don't. Maybe, mostly, because I don't want to know. It's not until she opens her hand and reveals the silver heirloom that my heart drops into my stomach. It takes every last ounce of willpower not to leap off the bed and out the window. I press myself into the pillows, staring down at the sick bell in anguish and fighting the urge to cover my eyes.

"I know you didn't mean to hurt me," says Mam, "hiding it all this time."

I try to protest, but she quiets me.

"It's all right. You don't have to explain." And then she offers the bell, as if I should take it from her—*as if I would touch it*—and I scoot as far back as my bed will allow. "I didn't realize what it meant to you," Mam says. "I didn't realize . . ."

She sniffles, shaking her head, and pinches the little handle. Even though the bell has no clapper, she holds it straight up and down out of habit, keeping the open mouth flat to her palm till she can place it safely on my bedside table.

"You keep it," says my mother. "Da was as much yours as mine." She laughs a bit. "Maybe more, even."

"I—I don't want it," I finally manage.

"It's all right, Essie," says Mam. "I was the one being selfish."

As much as I wish that I could, I can't take my eyes off the little silver bell. I can barely even whisper, "Please, *please* take it back."

"No." My mother pats my hand. "It's yours now. I'm trying to put all that behind me."

It's like a punch to my gut, realizing "all that" means *Da.*

Mam gets up from my bed and blows out my lamp. "I understand you aren't ready to let go—and that's all right. Keep the bell, love, as long as you need it."

And then she kisses my forehead. And then she leaves me.

Alone.

In the dark.

With the thing I fear most in the world.

Chapter Eleven

Someone is out in the hall. I know it before I'm really awake—
before I even hear the sounds.

Footsteps.

Someone is standing just outside my door.

I sit up slowly, fighting to see in the dark, and realize I fell
asleep with the List of Unspeakable Fears clutched tight in my
fist. The lighthouse beam passes through my windows, filling
up the whole room, and I look immediately to the bookcase on
the opposite wall.

The sick bell glints in the light—a small silver trinket in
the middle of an empty shelf. I placed it as far away from me as
possible. It isn't far enough.

Floorboards creak in the hall.

The room goes dark again. I stop breathing. My imagination takes off. I picture someone pressing their ear to my door,
shifting their weight as they listen. I don't want whoever is out
there to know I'm awake, so I sit still as stone. The seconds
stretch like hours, but finally the footsteps move on. They're
light. Almost too quiet to hear. The person must be small, bare-
foot, tiptoeing along the cold wooden floor. Down the hall, to
the left of my room, the sound stops. It takes me a moment to

remember the layout of the house—to remember where the hall leads.

The light returns and my heart clenches.

The attic. *The red door.*

I hear it swinging open, slowly. Its hinges protest with a growl, as if a bright-eyed, fanged animal has just spotted me. The handle taps against the far wall. In my mind, I can see that gaping doorway. It's so black that stepping through would feel suffocating, like dropping down into deep seawater.

Whatever has opened the red door has opened it just for me. I know this as certainly as I know the fears on my list.

I know it, because the speaking tube has started to whistle.

At first it's so soft, I can pretend it's not real. But then it gets louder. Soon the whistle is so piercing and shrill it's disorienting, and I burrow under my blankets, pressing my hands to my ears. I refuse to answer the call. I pray someone will come to my rescue. My mother, Fräulein Gretchen, even Dr. Blackcreek would do. Surely someone has heard the noise. Surely no one on this cursed island can truly sleep anyway, not with the dizzying, rhythmic light from the lighthouse.

But perhaps the house is too large to hear the whistling in my room. Perhaps the haunting, spinning light only reaches my windows. Because no one comes.

I want to be like Beatrice, or like my mother and father. I want to get up out of bed and yell into the speaking tube for it to be quiet. I want to stomp down the hall and slam the red door. But I can't. I'm too scared.

Once, I told my da the same thing. We were sitting together

on the fire escape, looking out at the skyscrapers he'd helped build as they lit up from the streets to the stars.

"You're so brave," I said, thinking how frightened I would be standing at the top of the world. I could only bear the fire escape because he was beside me, holding my hand. "I wish I was like you."

His reply confused me.

"But you are like me," he said simply. "Little love, don't you know? Every single time I climb up, I'm terrified that I'll fall."

For a long while, hands still pressed to my ears, I remain in bed, taking the smallest, quietest breaths. I repeat my father's words over and over silently, and it's almost as calming as tracing the fears on my list. If I could only understand what he meant, I might find the strength to look closer—to put my ear to the speaking tube or walk through the door. But it still doesn't make sense. I don't see how you can be brave when you're so afraid.

When I finally lower my hands from my head, I realize that the whistling has stopped. I don't give it the chance to start up again—I just jump out of bed and dash down the hall, without looking even once at the red door. I mean to wake Mam up and tell her what's happened, but as I'm rounding the corner, a new sound makes me come to a halt.

Downstairs, in the foyer, the front door opens and shuts.

It's just one turn more to the grand staircase, so I tiptoe past the master bedroom and peer over the second-floor railing into the entranceway. One of the curtains on the big downstairs front windows is partially drawn. Through it, I see my stepfather, his grim face lit from below by a lantern in his hand. I watch him tip his hat low and set off at a brisk pace toward the shore.

Was it him outside my door, checking to make sure I was asleep? It must be nearly midnight, and it's freezing cold. *Where on earth is he going?* I have to follow him. I realize it at once. And it doesn't matter that I'm afraid. If I want Mam to believe me about the danger we're in, I need to see what he's up to—certainly nothing good, late at night, in the dark.

The winter coat and boots I wore today are still by the front door, so I put them on and slip outside, bracing against the icy wind. Clouds hide the moon, making it nearly impossible to see when the lighthouse beam circles away. I have to wait till it returns before picking a path toward the river. It's slow going, pausing each time the shadows come back, but it's better than slipping and breaking my leg. Finally I hear water lapping close by, and I wrap my arms around myself, coming to a stop. When the light returns, I make my way down to the beach. The long, empty stretch of shoreline doesn't offer any hints about which way my stepfather traveled, so taking a guess, I turn left.

It would be easy to trip over rocks here. The ground is uneven. There's a lot of ice. So I keep my eyes pointed down as I continue. It's because of this that when the lighthouse beam comes around again, I see the shore start to glitter.

Red. Yellow. Green. Blue.

I blink, watching strange, bright bits of color sparkle and glint for a breath in the dark, as if the Fair Folk had danced in this place, sowing the sand with their starlight. Finally I understand. *Drift glass.* It's low tide.

The air changes, suddenly colder. A breeze pushes in from the East River. And when the lighthouse beam spins toward me again—when I once more point my eyes down—I see something that I wish I had not. I see something so frightening my whole body goes numb.

Footprints.

Footprints leading out of the water.

For a moment, a patch of sand lights up in front of me. The footprints are distinct, so deep, in fact, that I could believe they were made just seconds before.

Bare feet. Small feet. Like a child's.

Before the light disappears, my eyes quickly follow the tracks from the surf, where the waves are lapping at the impressions, already erasing them. The footprints continue up the shore till they reach the rocks and vanish entirely.

They're headed straight for the shadowy, hulking shape of the house.

The light again disappears. And in the darkness that follows, time stops. I can't hear the water. I can't feel the cold air. All I can do is imagine those footprints—imagine that the person who made them is watching me right this moment. Unexpectedly, I think of the girl in the children's sick ward from that morning. Something was wrong with her—really, *really* wrong. It had something to do with her dress, with the way it was hanging all funny off her shoulders, like it was heavy.

Like it was wet.

My heart is already in my throat when the lighthouse beam returns, and I spot a dark figure down the beach, running toward me. I scream, stumbling backward. I fall into the surf. Frigid water soaks through my long coat. I manage to pull myself up, but my boots feel like muddy bricks strapped to my feet, and I trip nearly every third step, racing along the rocky shore. In the yard by the house, I collapse to my knees, scrambling on all fours and shouting for help. The windows light up just as hands close around me.

Strong hands. Big hands.

I writhe violently, but the hands pick me right up off the ground. It takes a moment to realize I've been set down on my feet. It takes longer than that to hear someone calling my name over and over and over.

"Essie! Essie, calm down!"

Dr. Blackcreek's face is shocked, perhaps even frightened. I recoil at the sight of him, trying to wrench away. Then I look over my shoulder and see both Mam and Fräulein Gretchen running out the front door. My cheeks are streaked with tears. My breath is coming in gasps. When my stepfather picks me up again, I go limp in surprise, and he carries me toward the house.

The lighthouse beam circles back around, casting its burning eye over the world. Even in all the commotion, I can see the spot on the shore where I fell. I'm awake. I'm not stuck in a dream. This is real. But the only footprints in the sand are mine and my stepfather's.

Chapter Twelve

Mam is upset. She keeps readjusting the blanket over me and fussing about my bruised knee. She doesn't listen when I try to tell her that the injury is from my encounter with Mary's dog.

"I thought you were getting over this!" she says.

"I wasn't stuck," I insist for the millionth time. "I was *awake*."

"Stuck?" asks Dr. Blackcreek, raising an eyebrow.

My mother turns to him. "Essie sleepwalks."

Till now, my stepfather has appeared rather shaken by the whole ordeal. He's barely spoken a word, his eyes wide and face pale. But in a single sentence, he transforms back into a doctor. "How long has this been going on?" he asks.

"Since her da died," says Mam, and I cringe.

After carrying me inside, Dr. Blackcreek set me on the yellow sofa in the parlor. Fräulein Gretchen rushed to get a fire lit, then went to the kitchen. Now the wood is crackling and the chill has left the room. Fräulein Gretchen returns with a tray of warm drinks. None of this makes me feel any better. I'm too anxious. I can't take my eyes off my stepfather.

"She has nightmares," my mother explains, accepting a cup of steaming tea.

"About what, exactly?" asks Dr. Blackcreek. When the maid offers him a drink, he turns it down.

"A door," says Mam. She looks at me. "Isn't that right? Usually there's a door?"

I don't answer, hunching deeper into the blanket.

"She doesn't like to talk about it," says Mam. "But some nights she starts thrashing around and can't wake up. I've sat with her for hours, calling her name. She's always confused when she finally comes out of it. Sometimes she's even violent."

My mother seems embarrassed, and I realize she's apologizing for me—for my kicking and hitting and screaming tonight by the shore. Dr. Blackcreek glances my way and I look quickly into my lap. I'm grateful for the distraction when Fräulein Gretchen offers me a mug of warm, sweetened milk.

"That's quite common, actually, with somnambulists— sleepwalkers," my stepfather says. "Has she seen a doctor for the condition?"

"Yes, but not with any result," Mam says, pinching the bridge of her nose. "I'm so sorry for all of this. Really. Waking you both in the night and upsetting everyone."

"Do not fret for an instant," Fräulein Gretchen assures her.

At the same time, I mutter, "You didn't wake him."

My mother turns to me. "What?"

I gesture to my stepfather. "He was already awake." My voice trails off as I catch his narrowing eyes. A shiver scurries up my spine.

Mam didn't know about his midnight walk.

He'd intended it to stay secret.

"A *dream*, Essie," my mother says, sounding exhausted, but her husband clears his throat.

"Not entirely, perhaps. I did go out for some air."

Mam lowers the cup in her hands. "You went out? In the middle of the night?"

"I suffer from my own sleep troubles," says Dr. Blackcreek, pursing his lips. "I should have told you before. Sometimes a walk clears my head."

"I see," says my mother, looking uncertain. She wraps her own blanket tighter around her shoulders.

Dr. Blackcreek deftly changes the topic, squinting behind his glasses at me like I'm a record of symptoms on a chart.

"It would be useful if you told me more about your dreams, Essie. There are many studies today that suggest dreams are like a window into the human psyche. If we discover what it is that you fear—what causes you to have nightmares—then I might be able to help you," he says.

This is highly suspect—him wanting to know about the things that I fear. Beatrice would certainly say he was searching for weaknesses. Once more, I stay silent.

Dr. Blackcreek turns back to Mam, stroking his long beard. "We should consider some changes. A new diet, perhaps, along with strict steps to ensure she gets quality sleep. Sleep disruption can result in a variety of health concerns—both mental and physical."

I frown, wanting to protest, but then Fräulein Gretchen sets her tray down and reaches out for my hand. "We had better get you dry and back to bed. Come along, Fräulein O'Neill."

I blink at her, but then nod. She helps me off the sofa and out of the parlor. All the way up the grand stairs, we can hear Mam and Dr. Blackcreek continue talking about me.

"I don't need a change in diet. I wasn't asleep," I repeat, mostly to myself.

Fräulein Gretchen looks down with a wary expression. "You were screaming very loudly," she says. "You were wild with fear."

"Not because I was dreaming."

We reach the second floor, and I flinch when she turns on the electric lights. I try to walk only in the middle of the hall, hugging myself and keeping well away from the buzzing, bright fixtures.

"Whatever was so frightening, then?" Fräulein Gretchen asks.

For a moment, I'm not sure that I'll answer. I'm not sure that I trust her. I suppose the fact that she doesn't press me to say anything is what changes my mind.

"When I was in bed tonight," I start quietly, "I heard someone standing outside my room. After they left, the speaking tube started whistling again."

"Oh my goodness," says Fräulein Gretchen. "That would be upsetting. But, sweet Angsthäschen, you must learn that old houses make lots of noises." She sounds sympathetic, even when she uses the funny nickname.

"There's more, though," I insist, shivering as we step into my bedroom. "Something else scared me too."

Uncomfortable, I stop talking, but Fräulein Gretchen smiles reassuringly. "Go on."

"I saw . . . footprints on the shore. In the sand. That's why I was already screaming. They were . . . they were coming out of the water."

Her smile fades.

"They were small footprints. No bigger than mine. And they were headed toward the house. It made me think of a girl I saw today, through a window at the hospital." I pause before saying very softly, "Her dress was all wet."

Suddenly Fräulein Gretchen turns away. "You should not go near the hospital," she says. Her voice is stern, but it's also trembling. "You should not leave the house after dark."

I mutter an apology, then a promise. I get undressed. But even after I'm tucked up in my bed, I can't stop shaking. Because I know why Fräulein Gretchen is afraid.

She's seen the girl too.

The red door.

The hallway lengthens, stretching far out before me, but somehow, the door only grows taller. Closer. I feel queasy. Dizzy. Like I've been spinning and spinning on a ride at Luna Park. Behind the red door, there's a fire. I can hear the crackling now. I can see the flames through the thin, bright line around the frame. The hallway fills with smoke and I cough. My eyes blur. But I can't even raise my hand to shield myself from the heat.

Essie.

I can't take it.

Essie.

I don't want to see what's behind the red door. I don't want to look. I'm not brave enough. I don't want to remember who's calling my name.

The smoke thickens, making it even harder to breathe. It thickens till it's not smoke at all. It's chalky dust. It's ash and particles of burnt, rotten cork. Charred decay piles up at my feet, reaching my ankles, then my knees, then my stomach. It swirls around, getting caught in my hair. I try to shake it off. I start coughing.

Essie!

I wish I didn't know that voice. I wish. I wish. I wish. *I wish.* But I do.

Chapter Thirteen

When I wake, my sheets are tangled and I'm dripping with sweat. For a long time, I stay sitting in bed, blinking at the room. Morning light pokes through my windows. The commotion of the night before feels like a dream. I get up slowly, quite groggy. After pulling on my dress and long wool socks, I notice the sick bell on the center shelf of the big, heavy bookcase across the room. A nasty feeling twists in my stomach, so I hurry downstairs.

In the dining room, Dr. Blackcreek is eating his last bites of breakfast. I give him a wide berth as I round the table to my chair. Mam is across from me, but the moment I sit down, she rises, in an obvious hurry. I want to explain what happened last night—what *really h*appened—but before I can even open my mouth, I notice her white smock and high rubber overshoes, and all my words fall away.

I raise an arm, pointing. "What . . . why . . . ?"

My mother swallows her last sip of coffee and starts to gather her belongings. "It's just for a while. Just till things settle."

"No! No no no!" I shake my head, frantic. "You promised!"

"There are too few nurses and too many patients. Would you rather the poor, sick people go without someone to help them?"

"I don't care about other people! I care about you!"

"Essie!" gasps Mam.

"She is right to be nervous," says Dr. Blackcreek with a sigh.

I snap my head toward him, ready for a fight—I don't care if he's dangerous—but then I realize he's agreeing with me. It's so confusing that I go silent.

"The conditions are terrible at Riverside," my stepfather says. "It is not a safe environment."

"The *conditions* are exactly why I'm doing this," insists Mam. "I won't sit around useless while people are in need. No one in pain should be left to suffer alone. A single volunteer might not solve the problem, but it's the least I can do."

My stepfather frowns. "I'm concerned you will be overwhelmed. You are still tired from the move. And if you are already weak when exposed to—"

"I'm perfectly fine," says my mother. She picks up the rest of her things with a look in her eye I know far too well. It's the same look she gets when she goes out the door to shout in the streets about women's rights, even knowing she might get arrested.

I can't let her leave, though. I absolutely can't. I can't let her catch some awful disease that takes her away from me.

I turn to Dr. Blackcreek and sputter, "She lost her last job as a nurse, you know. The settlement house called her 'unreliable.'"

My stepfather stares at me blankly, too shocked to react, but my mother—whose back is turned toward me—goes stiff. I expect an explosion. I brace for it. I *want* it. An explosion will keep her safe a while longer.

But Mam just walks out the dining room doors.

My stepfather sets his fork and knife at either edge of his plate and picks up his napkin from his lap. He folds it before laying it on the table.

"I assume you know that was uncalled for," he says.

I'm not sure whether he's looking at me with those cold eyes, because I'm not looking at him. I try my best not to let my hands tremble under the table.

"I—" My voice catches in my throat, and the feeling that I'll start crying comes abruptly. I do my best to swallow it down. "I'd say anything to keep her safe. I'd do anything."

It's a moment before Dr. Blackcreek responds, and when he does, his voice is so sincere and soft—so different from the practical, direct tone he's been using—that I have to look over to make sure it's still him.

"I would too," he says, and we lock eyes. "But you must also know that your mother is not the sort of woman who can be stopped from doing what she thinks is right."

I'm taken aback by this, because it's true. Mam is brave and stubborn and sometimes as foolhardy as Da. But that's why I have to protect her. I let my anger boil up till I feel strong enough to whisper, "You shouldn't have let her volunteer in the first place."

Dr. Blackcreek raises an eyebrow. "You think I could have stopped her? Flattering."

As frightened of him as I am, I feel as if I could scream. My hands tighten into fists out of sight. He doesn't really care about her. It's a show, I'm certain. He would have stopped her otherwise.

"Please do not worry," Dr. Blackcreek says, offering me a tight smile. "I promise to watch out for your mother."

"Can you promise she won't get sick?" I spit back without missing a beat.

My stepfather's gaze narrows, but I don't look away.

"No," he says.

"That's what I thought," I reply. Then I stand up and walk right out of the house.

Chapter Fourteen

Barely one minute outside and I backtrack for warmer clothes. It's freezing. Flurries sputter around wildly, swirling into my eyes. The waves at the shoreline are slushy with ice, the rocks slick under my boots. I trudge through the bare garden, beneath its trellis of dead vines. Fräulein Gretchen opens the door before I even reach for the handle.

Storming out into the snow after a fight is quite satisfying. Returning to find the maid waiting for you, holding a scarf and your mittens and coat, along with a lovely, fresh pastry wrapped in brown paper—well, it just doesn't have the same *oomph*.

By the time I'm on the shore, bundled up and munching on the treat instead of determined and furious, I feel limp and soggy, like a knit hat left out in the rain.

"Come back if the weather turns bad," Fräulein Gretchen said with a smile.

I burrow down into the scarf as my cheeks redden.

At first I'm not sure where I'm headed. My mind is full of furious thoughts about Dr. Blackcreek and fear for my mother. But when I reach the northern tip of the island, near the spot where I met Mary Mallon, I pause, remembering what it is I need to do. First I'll go see South Brother Island. Then I'll find Mary and question her.

The idea makes my stomach tighten in knots. Mam's treated patients with typhoid fever before. I know how awful it is and I'm terrified that I'll catch it. In truth, I'd be happy if I never saw Mary Mallon again. Dr. Blackcreek made it seem like I would be fine if I didn't eat anything that she cooked, but unfortunately, I don't trust him.

I don't trust him.

So maybe he's wrong about Mary. Maybe she shouldn't even be on the island at all.

More importantly, if I don't speak to her, I won't figure out what she knows.

It's truly, bitterly cold. And I don't want to get caught outside if the weather does get worse, so I start to move faster, pushing fears about illness to the back of my mind and replacing them with fears about terrible things that can happen when it snows. *Frostbite* and *Hypothermia*, for instance. I try to remember other snow-related items on my list.

Ravenous Polar Bears.

This makes me giggle. I giggle even harder when I think of Beatrice. Once, last winter, she was on a serious case—something to do with a pair of stolen baby booties—and she wanted to investigate the suspect while he was walking to work. It was snowing hard, though, and Mrs. Murphy forced Beatrice to put on this gigantic oversized coat that one of her brothers had outgrown. It nearly reached her knees. Beatrice came barreling through the yard of our tenement, pointlessly trying to shake off the snow as it fell.

"Man alive!" she shouted at the sky. "This won't look suspicious at all—a polar bear hot on the trail!" She sniffed the coat's collar angrily and recoiled before adding, "Forget that—the thief will smell me first!"

I'm still laughing about polar bears and stinky brothers, so I decide to make some changes to my list when I get home. It's been a long time since I erased anything, and it makes me feel good, knowing that at least I'm not afraid of polar bears anymore. After everything I've seen on North Brother Island already, it does seem a bit ridiculous to worry about something I'll likely never encounter. There are probably a few other similar items that I could cross off. *Pythons*, for instance. And *Erupting Volcanoes*.

I scan the island. There are buildings blocking my view, bare trees and wiry brush, but I'm certain that if none of it were there, I could see every bit of North Brother at once. Walking the shoreline will likely lead me to both destinations I have planned in short order. I'll beat out any potential bad weather.

Confident now, I round the northern bend, passing the huge concrete building where I saw the children's ward. There are three others just like it, lined up perpendicular to the shore. In the distance is a tall brick smokestack puffing out white clouds as the boiler plant works to heat the hospital. I think of the warm parlor in the house—of how I shouted that I didn't care about the sick patients—and feel suddenly guilty.

A tingle spider-walks up my neck.

Someone is watching me.

I resist the urge to snap my head around, but it takes all

my courage. I think of the girl in the pretty dress, soaking wet.

The wind picks up, and I wrap my arms tighter around myself, then wrinkle my nose in disgust. There's a terrible smell. To the southeast, Rikers Island is plainly visible, and most of it is covered in great mounds of garbage. The island is quite a great deal larger than North Brother, and barges towering with refuse have been using it as a dump site for years. All along the shore is heavy construction equipment—steam shovels and pile drivers and the like. A few men, probably inmates from the workhouse, are toiling away in the cold, expanding Rikers Island with trash, just like they did here at North Brother.

I plug my nose and kick a piece of rubber tire out of my way. No wonder there's garbage everywhere. I consider leaving the beach and walking through the island proper, but there's a concrete border wall around much of the shoreline, and here it's too tall for me to climb. There's no choice but to go on.

The snow starts coming down hard. The smell gets worse.

The feeling that someone's watching returns.

This time, I can't ignore the gooseflesh prickling up my arms and stop in place, spinning around.

There's a small figure in the distance, facing me, standing perfectly still.

In an instant, my pulse is pounding, and I recall the terror I felt when I spotted footsteps in the sand. I squint through the snow. Do I see a dress? A brown braid? Bare feet? Did she leave the children's ward to follow me? Did she follow me last night?

Is she even alive?

I take one step backward, then another, and then I turn on

my heel and I'm running as fast as I can, whimpering with every breath. There's a break in the concrete barrier wall up ahead, and I race toward it. But then something else—out over the water—catches my eye, and I come to a sliding, stumbling halt.

South Brother Island.

All my fear slips away. My heart tightens in my chest.

"Da."

I don't mean to say it out loud. I don't mean to remember. But suddenly I'm picturing my father next to me on our fire escape, rolling his cigarettes, a book tucked under his arm, pointing out shapes on the horizon—the different boroughs of New York City, the buildings going up taller each year, the islands in the East River.

Da was always fascinated with North and South Brother. He told me that when the land was first claimed, in the early 1600s, the two islands were named "the Companions." South Brother, the smaller one, was owned by a beer magnate and politician named Colonel Ruppert. Like my father, Ruppert was a baseball fanatic. He'd tried, unsuccessfully, to purchase the New York Giants for years. When Da learned that Ruppert had a summer home on South Brother, he became obsessed with the idea of getting a look for himself.

"Likely full of memorabilia, don't you think?" my father would say, a gleam in his eyes. "Photographs and mitts and signed balls. A treasure trove, I suspect, ripe for the pillaging."

I'd start to squirm. "Da . . ."

"If the current was with me, it might not be such a big thing, swimming out to North Brother," he'd go on.

"Da, *please*."

"Have to watch out for the nurses at Riverside, mind you. You know how those types can be." He'd wink at me, glance back in the apartment at Mam, then return to stuffing his cigarette paper or thumbing through his book or staring out at the water. "I'd stay out of sight, though, keep low along the shore. Soon enough, I'd be dripping dry on South Brother! Get myself a good look-see through dear Ruppert's windows. How's a rich man like him to remember what's stashed away in one place or another? He wouldn't likely notice a small thing or two gone."

"Da!" I'd exclaim, mortified.

This charade would continue for some while—my father never reassuring me, no matter how I pleaded, that he wouldn't actually attempt such a ridiculous stunt. He'd always leave me fretting.

"Maybe next week, if it's warm enough," he would muse.

It makes me sick now, thinking of how I made it to North Brother without him.

It makes me sicker, staring at the only visible structure on South Brother Island—a strange, charred heap of wood—and realizing slowly what it is that I'm seeing.

Jumbled-up stacks of broken, black beams. The splintered remains of a door. Collapsed roofing. Snow-covered piles of ash.

Ruppert's house has burned to the ground.

Chapter Fifteen

The sight of Colonel Ruppert's ruined summer home makes me feel like part of my father—a part I didn't even realize I loved—is gone forever.

Of course I loved Da when he sang to me. I loved Da when he brushed my hair in front of the stove. I loved Da when he didn't understand the big words in his books. I loved how, when I helped him sound them out, he made me feel like the smartest person in the world. I loved Da when he drank a little too much and got so silly Mam had to tell him to be quiet. I loved Da when he bought raw oysters from a pushcart late after work and woke me up—*just me, only me*—to share them while watching the stars.

I loved Da for all these things and so, *so* many more.

But I loved him for his faults, too.

For his recklessness. For his constant teasing. For his absurd, foolish dreams.

And now, it's like some piece of that—some piece of *him*—has burned away to nothing at all.

I don't care anymore about the other place I wanted to visit on my walk. I don't care about investigating Dr. Blackcreek's suspicious behavior. I don't care about whatever creepy figure is following me or why I'm hearing strange noises at night. Tears well up in my eyes, and I roughly rub them away with the back of my mittens. All I want to do is return to the house and go up to my room and into my bed.

The snow starts coming down harder. Big, chunky flakes pile up on the ground. At the southern tip of North Brother is the tall white lighthouse. I can see the lighthouse keeper's woodpile and his little rowboat. There's the outline of a small, dead garden. I can tell that going straight instead of backtracking around the island will get me home faster. So I start shuffling through the snow in my boots. I'm moving very slowly, though. And it's not just because of the weather. It's that I can't seem to stop crying. The world distorts and blurs. I blink tears away again and again. It's so strange, because I don't feel anything, not really. It's been a long time since I've felt anything but afraid.

Wind sprays up icy water from the East River. The snowfall thickens. Soon I can't see very far ahead. And then, once more, the feeling that I'm being watched returns. Stronger this time.

I stop and turn around, flushed, huffing and puffing. I'm not crying anymore. And I realize, even as the familiar anxieties start knotting in my gut, there's something else inside me now too—a feeling that I can't quite describe. I squint, peering through the snow. If the watcher from before is behind me, I don't see them.

When I start off again, I crunch down on an icy patch and my foot sinks into water. I step back quickly, so disoriented that it takes a moment to understand I'd been about to walk right into the river. That's how heavily the snow is coming down—I can barely see what's right ahead.

Panic rushes to the front of my thoughts, pushing out everything else.

What if I can't make it back? It's a small island, yes, but I'm already nearly blind. Does anyone even know I'm still gone? If they come to find me, will they make it before it's too late? My cheeks are so cold that they're burning. The wet streaks from my tears feel like ice. My thighs are numb to the touch and so is the tip of my nose. What if I've already gotten frostbite?

I think of the homeless man who used to beg on our block and sleep in the narrow alleys between tenements. One winter, he lost three toes and a finger. Last winter, he lost all the rest.

I think of Mam, waiting for me. I think about how, if I don't make it home, she'll be all alone here, stuck with a stranger—a stranger who I'm worried is hiding something.

I think about what happened last time, after Da died, when Mam got sad.

I grit my teeth, huddle into my coat and scarf, and stuff my hands under my armpits. I keep moving. And suddenly, out of the white nothing, a small cottage appears. Light shines from its windows as brightly as the lighthouse beam shines into my bedroom, and I follow just like a lost boat to port, nearly weeping in relief when I make it to the door and start knocking.

There's no reply from within. Or at least, if there is, I can't hear it. I can't hear anything, in fact, except the sound of falling snow whizzing past my ears. I'm shaking with cold. I look left, and when the wind blows wildly, I see the outline of another building close by. The point of a bell tower. Rounded stained-glass windows. It's the island's little church.

I knock again, louder, thinking this cottage might be where the priest lives. Did Mam say North Brother had its own priest? Or does someone ferry back and forth across the river for services?

"Hello?" I call out. I cup my hands around my eyes and peek through a window.

The cottage is small but nicely furnished. There's a fireplace with a big cast-iron gas heater blazing inside, like some of the rooms have back at my new house. There's a bed stacked with quilts. A sturdy wooden desk and chair. A sink with plumbing. The cottage appears to be lit with electricity, too. All of this is normal enough—at least here on North Brother Island. What's *not* normal is the stuff pinned up to the walls.

Papers. *Papers and papers and papers and papers.*

Newspaper clippings. Torn scraps of notes. Yellow ones. White ones. Ones stained with smudges and spills. Letters typed. Letters handwritten. Letters with dark, fancy borders. Swooping cursive scrawls. Pages ripped out of books. Lab reports. Drawings and diagrams. A calendar covered in *X*s, counting down to a date circled roughly in red.

"Fancy meeting you here," says a voice, and I spin around, gasping. Mary Mallon is standing behind me with her arms crossed, bundled up in a big tan coat and fuzzy black hat and holding her dog on a leash. "You do know you're being followed?"

I blink in horror. "You—it's you? *You've* been following me?" This doesn't make sense. She's much too broad and tall. And she clearly hasn't been outside for long. There's hardly any snow on her.

The woman gives me a bland look. "Do I seem the sort of person with time to follow a little girl around? Of course not *me*."

She points over my shoulder and I turn, expecting something horrific. A few paces away, though, all I find is Old Scratch, half-hidden in the snow, his ratty tail flicking back and forth. When he spots me, his tail starts flicking faster.

"I knew it!" I say, and then shout over the wind, "What on earth do you want?"

Mary glances between us, then down at her dog, who's started to pull on his leash. She sighs, opening the cottage door. "Come on, then. Both of you. It's freezing."

For a moment, Old Scratch and I go equally still. I realize how close to Mary I'm standing. I realize that inside her home, I'll be surrounded by the air that she breathes. For a moment, I contemplate turning and walking back out into the snowstorm. But if Beatrice were here, she would walk through the door. And that, most of all, is what encourages me. I'm not brave like my friend, but I want to be—at least brave enough to get some answers and protect Mam. I tell myself Mary isn't really sick. I tell myself I'll be safe. I step inside the cottage.

Behind me, Old Scratch's eyes twitch from me to the dog to the door. The poor, nasty cat's fur is so tattered and patchy, he must be even colder than I am. When Mary wraps her dog's leash around her wrist tighter, Old Scratch zips past us all and vanishes under a bed. The dog pulls wildly at his restraints, whimpering, and Mary follows everyone inside and removes her big coat.

When she lets the dog loose, I flinch, expecting another assault, but the hairy beast couldn't seem to care less about me. He runs straight to Old Scratch's safe place, and the cat hisses and wiggles farther under the bed. Even pressed to the floor, sniffing frantically with his mustached snout, the dog can't reach.

It's clear this isn't the first time Old Scratch has visited the home of North Brother's most notorious patient. I take a look around and my heart pounds a bit faster.

"So what is it?" asks Mary, turning up the gas heater. The elements start to glow deep red and the room warms, fog spreading from the edges of the windows.

"What—what is what?" I know I sound barely alive. And I must look ghastly. If I saw my reflection, I'd be afraid of myself.

"Was it chance you got caught in a snowstorm outside my house?" the woman asks, blunt as always, and I timidly shake my head no.

Before seeing South Brother Island, I had a plan. Finding Mary Mallon was part of it. She knows things about my stepfather. She has answers I need. Now, though, with the sight of the charred building—with the memories and the snowstorm—all the words I prepared to convince her to help me have sunk down to the bottom of my mind, out of reach.

"So what is it? What do you want?" Mary repeats.

I picture Da on his fire escape, staring out at the East River, dreaming of places that will burn to the ground.

"I want to go home!" I say suddenly, and Mary Mallon stares at me, surprised. "I hate it here. I hate the hospital. I hate my stepfather. I think he's up to no good. I saw him arguing with the police. He walks the shores at night, when he thinks no one's awake. He talks funny and eats funny and he married Mam far too quickly."

The dog stops rooting and sniffing. Under the bed, in the darkness, Old Scratch's yellow eyes glint. The corner of Mary's mouth edges up.

"Hmph," she says. Still watching me, she sits down at her desk, where there are two stacks of crisp papers. "Have you told your mother all this?"

"Yes, but she thinks I'm overreacting. I have a history of being easily frightened." I shake my head furiously. "That's not it this time, though! Something awful has happened on North Brother Island! I can feel it everywhere. There are strange things going on in the house. I keep seeing this girl. . . ."

Mary tilts her head, raising a curious eyebrow.

"Dr. Blackcreek is hiding something," I say. "I just don't know what."

For a long while, the whole cottage is quiet. Mary taps a finger on her desk. She eyes me like a recipe with a list of mismatched ingredients, trying to figure out how I add up.

"Do you know who I am?" she asks finally.

I hesitate, then nod once.

"Do you know why I'm here?"

I nod again.

Mary smirks. "I'd like to hear you say it."

The look in her eyes makes the lump in my throat—already quite large—entirely impossible to swallow.

"You—you made people sick," I squeak out.

Every bone in my body tells me to leave at once, blizzard or no. Even swimming the icy East River wouldn't be as cold as her stare. And if she is contagious after all, freezing to death might be slightly less terrible than dying of typhoid fever.

"I made people sick?" Mary's mouth twitches. "Are you certain?"

I can tell she's not asking a question, not really. Answering honestly won't do me good, but I sputter out anyway, "I—I read in the papers—"

"The *papers!*" exclaims Mary. She gestures around the room, walls plastered so thick with clippings they could be mistaken for wallpaper. "What did you read? Go on. *Tell me.*"

I'm paralyzed but for my eyes, which bounce around like crickets trapped in a jar.

WOMAN COOK A WALKING TYPHOID FEVER FACTORY, proclaims one headline.

WANTS TO LEAVE THE ISLAND: 'TYPHOID MARY' DECLARES THE HEALTH BOARD IS HOLDING HER ILLEGALLY, another black-and-white clipping cries.

"I—" The room spins. I back away till I'm pressed to the door.

PRISONER ON NEW YORK'S QUARANTINE HOSPITAL ISLAND, reads the *New York American*, and I recognize the accompanying drawing from this past summer. It's a copy of the paper Beatrice dug out of the trash.

A tall woman with a double chin and dark-shaded skin cracks eggs into a fiery skillet. But they aren't eggs. They're miniature skulls.

"I read—" I grind my teeth and look up. "You served ice

cream and sliced peaches to a family in Oyster Bay. They got sick. And there were others, before them. You're here because keeping you locked up keeps people safe."

Mary's face loses all its expression. Her mouth briefly opens.

"I'm sorry to hear you think that," she finally says, recovering. "I was almost starting to like you." She looks down at the two stacks of papers on the desk. "These are the results of bacteriological examinations—laboratory tests for typhoid fever," she says. "I won't upset you with unfortunate details about how samples are collected. You've heard of my encounter with the esteemed Mr. Soper, though, yes? That sanitation engineer they say I attacked? Let me assure you, if a strange fellow approached you, demanding the things Soper demanded of me—with no proof, mind you!" She shakes her head. "I suspect, in such a case, even a skittish thing like yourself might manage a touch of bravery."

I'm not sure where my voice comes from, but it's reassuring to find it still works. "Are you really trying to get off the island?"

"More than trying," says Mary. "Ever since I arrived at Riverside, they've been treating me like a peep show. Prodding me. Poking me. Your stepfather. His army of nurses. Orderlies. Staff. They all ogle about, whispering when I walk by."

Mary's dog seems to sense her agitation. He crosses the room and plants himself at her feet. She reaches down absentmindedly and pets him.

"These tests were done on North Brother," Mary says, pointing at the stack of papers to her left. "As you might expect, they're positive. They declare me a carrier of the bacillus. But

I've no symptoms. None at all!" Her brow lifts, and she points to the other stack of papers. "These, though—*these* tests—they're from a private laboratory. Ordered by my lawyer." Mary leans forward conspiratorially. "Can you guess how they read?"

I nod out of habit, then stop and shake my head no.

"Negative," says Mary. "Every. Last. One."

I frown. "So you're not sick?"

"Of course not."

"But then why do they keep you locked up?"

"Don't be dense, girl," she snaps, and my eyes widen. "You're Irish too."

I puff myself up. "I'm American. So are you."

Mary laughs in my face. "You might tell that to the rest of the country!"

At first I'm not sure I understand. America has so many Irish people. New York City even has an Irish mayor! Lots of immigrants, from other places, get treated much worse than us. But then I remember that Mary came over on a big boat, like Mam and Da both did, and I remember their stories about how hard things sometimes were. People thought they were dirty because of where they were from. People thought they were lazy or immoral because they were poor. They got called "hooligans" and "bogtrotters." I've been called those things too, most often when I'm with Beatrice and her brothers, and the thought makes me queasy.

"I can tell they've scrubbed the Irish right out of you at school," Mary says. "But I'll always be seen as a foreigner. And to top it off, I'm a woman—one who knows my mind and has the sense to speak it. Of course the papers paint me as a fiend."

I glance back at the clippings, mottled with crude drawings and accusatory language: *menace to the public health; Robust Irish Cook; taking up valuable space; large and buxom; a walking pestilence; Typhoid Factory; more to be dreaded than a professional poisoner or homicidal maniac.*

"Believe me or don't." Mary's dog paws at her and she bends to pick him up, scratching his beard. The terrier wags his tail, slapping it rhythmically against the wood desk. "I'll be gone from Plague Island soon, anyway." She looks out the window, too casual, then turns to me. "Might have room for one more when I leave." She shrugs. "Then again, I might not."

Old Scratch slinks out from under the bed and curls up in front of the fireplace. We exchange a shared look. This woman isn't to be trusted. But neither is Dr. Blackcreek. And right now, Mary's the only lead that I have to find out what sort of danger I'm in. If Beatrice were here, she'd press on. She'd wring every last detail out of the witness before letting up.

I put on a tough face. "You said you knew what happened to the missing nurses. That's why I came here. I need to know if my stepfather's involved in their disappearance."

"Your stepfather's involved in *everything* on North Brother Island."

I want to shrink into my coat, but I don't. "But—but how, exactly? Did he . . . did he do something to the nurses?"

Mary considers me. "You want to hear what I know?" I nod quickly. "What I know is that I'm not sick. But this island could burst from all the people who are. Smallpox. Leprosy. Tuberculosis."

I cringe and she sees it.

"You clearly can't handle this," she says, then shifts like she's going to stand up.

I shake my head, frantic, and almost reach out and touch her. At the last moment, I tuck my hands under my arms. "No! Please continue."

Mary eyes me as she settles back into her chair. "Blackcreek is a tyrant about cleanliness and schedules and rules. He wants everything under his control. Considers himself an epidemic fighter, like the man who put me here—that villain George Soper." She gestures to herself. "And you know how your stepfather gets results for the Health Board? *Experimentation.*"

My eyes grow big as serving plates when I realize what she means. "But . . . but the nurses, if they were healthy, why would he—"

"*I'm* healthy!" Mary cries. "He experiments on me! They want to cut out my gallbladder, you realize. They keep trying to get me to agree. I've had so many regimens of drugs, I can't keep track. Urotropin was the worst. Nearly killed me." She points to her left eye. "Did you know, for six months I was so stricken from grief, my eyes began to twitch? This one even became paralyzed! No doctors came to treat *that*, though. Only by the grace of Almighty God was I cured."

I blink, overwhelmed, then glance again at Old Scratch. He's staring at Mary intently, the fur on his big tail all fuzzed out. After a deep breath, our host seems to calm down.

"Besides, why assume these missing nurses were healthy? The staff here catches disease too. They aren't immune. And to have his own nurses sick with the very things he's charged with containing . . . Well, it would reflect rather poorly on the dear doctor, yes? Just one more reason a poor woman might be made a victim."

My heart is racing. I'm thinking frantically of Mam but somehow manage to whisper, "So you think he . . . *murdered* them?"

Mary shrugs. "I suppose it depends on your definition of murder. In any case, if someone was to die during one of Dr. Blackcreek's experiments, well, I expect he'd be inclined to dispose of the evidence. That would explain why the women are *missing*, after all."

I feel an uncanny twist of horror and hope. "And it would mean that there's proof! Proof I could show Mam. But where?"

Mary taps her chin with a finger. "On the island, for certain. Too risky to ship the bodies elsewhere."

"Is there a graveyard?" I ask.

"Yes, a tiny one. But it's mostly temporary—and rather obvious, besides, don't you agree?"

I nod, swallow, and gather the courage to ask, "What if he sank them in the ocean?"

She thinks for a moment about this. "Wouldn't the tide carry the bones back to land?"

I shrug, uncertain, and almost say something about her being the accused murderer, not me—but then I regain my sense of self-preservation.

"Have you heard of the *Slocum* disaster?" asks Mary. "You were a wee thing then—and it was before my time here—but people say the victims' remains sometimes still wash up on North Brother's shore."

Images of fire and ash again fill my head, and I try to push past the gruesome memory. "Yes. I know about the *Slocum*. So if not the ocean, where, then? What would my stepfather do with the bodies?"

We both go quiet. Thinking. Old Scratch stretches his front paws, claws out and glinting. Suddenly Mary sits up straight. And in the same instant, I recall the huge boxes of equipment stacked up with my luggage on the ferry.

"The laboratory!" we both say at the same time.

"Why stop experimenting at death?" Mary asks, a vile gleam in her eyes.

I take a slow breath, composing myself. "So you think my stepfather is doing experiments in the laboratory—"

"I *know* that. *Everyone* knows that."

"—on d-d-dead nurses?"

"Might be," says Mary. "Easy enough to cover up. There's a variety of plausible excuses for missing nurses, after all. New job. Got married. Took a long holiday! A few interviews with the police later, and Blackcreek's cleared of suspicion."

Trying to breathe steadily, I look away.

"If he's . . . if he's been doing experiments, in the laboratory, on the . . . b-bodies . . ." It takes a great reserve of willpower to keep standing. "Then that's where the proof is." I harden my resolve. I look up. "That's where I have to go."

Chapter Sixteen

During a lull in the snowstorm, I take my chances and leave Mary's cottage. Old Scratch darts outside to follow me. The flurries begin coming down hard again after we reach the docks, but luckily, that's where our walk ends. A honk from an automobile horn makes me jump, and I turn to find Frank in the car, waving. Someone came out to look for me, after all.

I'm about to leave the shoreline and run up to the groundskeeper, but then I pause and consider the cat. He's watching from nearby, sitting as small and tight as possible, obviously freezing. His crinkly whiskers and black fur are covered in snow. Almost without thinking, I walk over and pick him up. We're both very surprised. I gasp at the weight of him—here I thought he was all bones. Old Scratch writhes wildly, then goes stiff. He's clearly upset, but contrary to his name, he doesn't scratch. Once I'm settled in the back seat of the automobile, holding the cat awkwardly to my chest, Frank does a double take.

"Hello, Miss Essie," he says, and then nods at the bundle of black fur in my arms. "Old Scratch."

"Thank you for rescuing us," I say, teeth chattering.

"You're welcome," says Frank. "Fräulein Gretchen and I got a touch concerned when we noticed you still weren't home."

He starts to drive toward the house, and I learn quickly that Old Scratch is even more frightened of automobiles than I am. I hug him tighter as he squirms and don't let him go till we're through the front doors. As soon as the cat's paws hit the floor, he dashes out of sight.

"Oh du meine Güte!" Fräulein Gretchen cries, hurrying over. She bustles me to the fire, fretting about my rosy cheeks, and helps me take off my coat and boots. "I was so worried! Look at the weather!"

I don't bother to explain that the snow is the least of our problems. Instead, I just ask, "Fräulein Gretchen, do you have something I can borrow to write with? My pencil's worn down to the nub."

Looking at me curiously, she hangs up my coat and produces the big iron ring of keys from her apron. Then she goes over to the door by the stairwell, opens it, and steps inside. Floor-length curtains block the windows. There's a big desk and heavy chair. Tall bookshelves line three of the four walls, tidy and organized. Clearly this is Dr. Blackcreek's office. Fräulein Gretchen comes back into the foyer, closing the door behind her.

"Here you are," she says, and hands me a pen case labeled WATERMAN'S IDEAL, along with a glass bottle of black ink. When I open the case, I discover that it's velvet-lined and holds a fancy black-and-silver-etched fountain pen. I've never written with anything so sophisticated.

"Now, where you have been? And what is this for?" she asks.

I answer quickly, "I had to walk around the whole island. I got lost." Technically, it isn't a lie. "And the pen is for a letter. I want to write my friend Beatrice."

Fräulein Gretchen tilts her head, as if she's recalled something. "Beatrice? Beatrice . . . Oh!" She perks up and walks to a table by the door, where there's a small stack of mail. "This came in the post before the storm. Is it the same girl you mailed a letter to just this morning? She must be a fast writer!"

My mouth falls open as I take the letter gingerly from Fräulein Gretchen's hands. The instant I'm alone in my bedroom upstairs, I open it.

Dear Essie, the letter starts out. Beatrice's handwriting is terrible. So is her spelling. Worse than usual, in fact, and that's saying something.

> *I have to right very quick becaus I want to put this in*
> *the leter carier's hand before he leaves. He's chatting up*
> *pretty Miss Becker. Essie, do you reemember the dime*
> *novel I red about the evil profeser? He kidnaped all the*
> *ladys who wore hatpins with blue jewls. Reemember?*

How could I ever forget? The ending she told me was awfully gruesome. A brash woman with a hatpin ten inches long had fought back unexpectedly and stuck the wicked professor right through. It was a shocking twist—the detective followed cries through an alley, thinking he was hearing the victim, only to stumble across the dying murderer. I had extra-horrible nightmares that week.

> *That villin was tuff because he was clever.*
> *If your stepfather really is up to truble, he's going to*

be clever too. If you think something is wrong, I need
hard facts—not suspisions. Where did he go to
univercity? What does he do every day on the island?
Is there a place in the house he mite hide personall
things? Right back soon. Tell me everything.

Yours truely,
Bea

At the bottom, there's a postscript in an even worse scrawl.

P.S. I just red what you wrote on the back page! The
woman on the beech was Mary Mallon!!! Man alive!
Oh no the leter carier is leav

The last word trails off into a scribble. After rereading Beatrice's letter one more time, I sit at my desk and start making a list—not of things that I fear, but of things that I know for a fact about my stepfather.

It starts off with, *From Germany.* And then I have to pause and think for a very long time. In the end, I come up with only a few more items, and none of them seem particularly useful:

Very straight posture while eating.
Collects drift glass on shore.
Doesn't sleep well.
Has cat.

Sighing, I put my forehead on my arm and close my eyes. This is going to be hard.

The snowstorm turns out to be one of the worst in several years. For almost a week, I'm trapped inside, penned up like an animal at the Central Park menagerie, unable to even mail a reply to Beatrice.

"You could see if the telephones at the hospital are working," Fräulein Gretchen suggested. "There is one in the administration building by the docks. It's easy to use. All you must do is pick up and tell the operator who to call."

For the briefest of moments, I imagined the comfort of hearing Beatrice's voice and almost agreed that would be a fine idea. But then my typical fears rushed in to take over. What if the telephone shocked me? What if it exploded?

"Oh, no," I said, walking backward. "I don't think I'm ready for that. Beatrice doesn't have a telephone anyway." Though that was true, I knew also that the shopkeeper down the street *did*, and he let people use it if they asked nicely.

To make my confinement during the bad weather worse, in the last mail delivery before the boats stopped running—the same delivery that brought Beatrice's letter—my new schoolbooks arrived. Fräulein Gretchen was insistent that we get right to work.

"I will do my best till we find you a governess," she said to me earnestly. "But you must do your best too. Education is everything, Angsthäschen."

So each day, my stepfather and Mam would trek back and forth to the hospital to tend to patients, and Fräulein Gretchen would tutor me in the small library upstairs. I liked the library. The chairs were plush and bouncy. The books had colorful bindings. I knew it would have been Da's favorite room—so many titles to choose from and no one to scold you that you're slow bringing them back. But I was constantly worried that one evening my mother would come home looking ill. That fear, along with a growing belief that Dr. Blackcreek might be a murderer, was enough to keep me always on the lookout for a way to get into my stepfather's office—surely the hidden "personal things" Beatrice had mentioned would be there. More than once, I tried hinting to Fräulein Gretchen that we have our lessons downstairs. Eventually, I even directly suggested it.

"It's just, there's so many more books to read in Dr. Blackcreek's office, you know? It feels more like a proper school," I explained as casually as possible.

She raised an eyebrow. "That is his place, not ours," she said simply. "And most of the books are in German. Do you want to study German now too? I can teach you that, I am confident."

I shook my head frantically and ducked back into the essay I was writing about Abraham Lincoln.

By the end of the week, snow has piled so high in some spots that it blocks out second-story windows. Freezing gales roar for hours on end. When I open the garden door and peek outside, New York City looks like an icy wasteland across the water, entirely coated in white. For all I know, it might be Antarctica on the other side of the river. It feels at least as far away.

Fräulein Gretchen calls that dinner's ready, so I walk to the dining room, only to discover that Mam and Dr. Blackcreek still aren't home. I know it must be that they're busy tending patients—the ill are suffering a great deal from the cold, my mother says—but I can't help feeling worried. Fräulein Gretchen can clearly tell something is wrong, because she asks if I'd like to eat with her in the kitchen. I perk up, surprised, and nod eagerly.

Inside the warm, bright room, the maid takes off her apron and hangs it on a peg by the stove. She serves us food straight from the pan to our plates—*schnitzel*, it's called. The dish is from Austria and is made of pork slices pounded thin and fried, served with a special berry jam. We sit down at the little wooden table together to eat, and everything is so good—the kitchen is so cozy and the food wonderful and the smells and sounds all familiar—it nearly feels like I'm home. This should make me happy, but instead, it just makes me think about Mam. I wish she were here. I hate that she's surrounded by people who might make her sick.

"I promise your mother is fine," Fräulein Gretchen says sympathetically.

I look up, amazed that she's read my thoughts, and then stare back down at my plate, forlorn. "It's just . . . every time I think of all the coughing and fevers and . . ." I swallow hard, unable to continue.

"When you are far apart, how can you protect her? Right? That is how you feel?"

I start to agree, but then see that she's smiling. "Essie, dear, you would worry if your mother worked in a pillow shop."

I frown. "Maybe. But do you know what pillows are stuffed with? Lice-infested animal hair. Diseased bird feathers. Once, I saw a cotton pillow sliced open and it was full of black mold."

Fräulein Gretchen blinks. "You are teasing me?"

My frown grows deeper.

"Angsthäschen," she says, sighing, then gets up to pour us some tea. "I know it is not easy to be isolated like this. I have been on North Brother several years, and it is still a challenge at times. I think, too, when the weather is bad, it is harder. It feels like the world grows smaller."

I know exactly what she means. But instead of telling her, I just shrug.

She takes her seat across from me again, warming her hands with her cup, then says softly, "When I moved here, I also left people behind."

I try to keep my eyes on what's left of my dinner, but it's impossible not to glance up. I remember the handsome man from Fräulein Gretchen's photo. I remember their smiles.

"Did someone force you to come here?" I ask. "Like how they forced Mary Mallon and me?"

Fräulein Gretchen shakes her head. "No. No one forced me." And then after a moment, she adds curiously, "If you have been ... thinking about Mary, you should talk to Dr. Blackcreek. She is a danger to other people, Essie—precisely because she believes she is not."

I open my mouth to defend Mary, but then see the look in the maid's eyes. She already suspects I've broken my promise to my stepfather. Besides this, I'm not entirely certain what I believe about Mary anyhow. Instead of replying, I shift uncomfortably and stay quiet.

Fräulein Gretchen leans back in her chair. "Before I came to North Brother Island, I lived with my brother and his family in Kleindeutschland. Little Germany. Do you know where that is?"

I shake my head, and because I'm feeling combative and stubborn, I shovel schnitzel into my mouth, pretending I don't want to hear more. But when Fräulein Gretchen starts speaking again, her voice is so sad that I swallow my bite and look up.

"I suppose many people have forgotten Little Germany. There is not much of it left." She purses her lips. "Well, that was our home. My brother. His wife and three children. Me. Six of us in one little apartment. Hard to imagine, isn't it, after living in a house of this size?"

"No. I can imagine," I say quickly. "We had a family of seven boarders once. With me and Mam, that meant nine people were in our apartment."

As soon as the words are out of my mouth, I flush. Instead of feeling proud of my home in Mott Haven, I'm suddenly embarrassed. I glance across the room at the Knickerbocker refrigerator. At the huge gas-burning stove. The fine dishes. The cutlery. The electric lights on over our heads. I mean to be frightened when I notice them, but instead my hands just curl into fists. I picture the frosted-glass light fixture in my bedroom—the silver-etched pen sitting on my desk upstairs. It wasn't till moving here that I realized how poor we had been. It wasn't till moving here that I cared.

"Nothing's wrong with sleeping six to a flat. Or nine, either," I say.

"Of course not," Fräulein Gretchen agrees. "In our tiny apartment, we had enough love to circle the world. This old house, for all its many rooms, has been absent of that for a long, long time."

She tightens her hands around the cup of tea, and the amber liquid ripples a little.

"Did something bad happen in Kleindeutschland?" I ask, cautious. I try my best to pronounce the word correctly.

Fräulein Gretchen nods. "A terrible tragedy."

I'm so filled with fear and anticipation that the deep breath she takes before continuing feels like an eternity.

"Afterward, many people in our community left. I think they needed to get away from the memories. But me . . . I wanted to be closer." She looks up. "Strange, isn't it? How differently we face our grief?"

I don't know what to say—I'm not even sure I understand—so I stay silent.

"When I saw Dr. Blackcreek's ad in the paper, the one for a maid-of-all-work, I knew I must apply. I knew he would take me on, too, even though I had little experience."

She stops speaking for so long this time I can't help it. Though it's rude and wrong of me, I pry. "Your brother died, didn't he? Because of the tragedy?" I'm so ashamed of myself that I'm cringing. "Was he . . . sick?"

The room is still enough that I can hear the snow falling outside.

Fräulein Gretchen shakes her head slowly. "Have you ever been so sad, Essie, that you cannot move? So sad that you cannot eat or speak—that you stay in your bed all the day, sleeping and waking to sadness and sleeping again?"

I feel suddenly dizzy.

Vials of medicine.

Wails in the night.

"Mam got that sad once," I say, though it's hard to keep breathing. My heart tightens up in my chest. "After . . . after Da died. She lay down and didn't get up, no matter how I pleaded. I brought her porridge in bed, but she'd only take the smallest bites. And after a while, she couldn't hold the spoon. I had to feed her like a baby."

I shut my eyes, wanting to push out the memory, but I can't.

The weeks Mam was sad were the worst of my life, worse even than the last days Da was ill. At least then, while he lived, I still had hope—foolish as it turned out to be. I lost that hope when he died. And then it seemed I'd lost Mam, as well. Each night I would cry myself to sleep, curled up under the window with the fire escape, feeling like I was stuck in a bad dream.

"I was certain she would die too," I say, and I'm crying just like in my memory. "I was certain I'd be left forever alone."

"There, there," says Fräulein Gretchen, reaching across the table and covering my hand with hers. She offers me a handkerchief and I wipe my tears. "I'm so sorry. I did not mean to upset you. Think now of the good things. Your mam did not die! There was nothing to fear after all."

I nod, sniffling as I calm down. "Yes. She got better."

"Tell me about that."

"A boy—a boy from the settlement house came with a letter.

It said Mam had lost her job. They called her 'unreliable.'" I look up quickly. "But she's not. She's the most reliable person I know. It was only that she'd been absent so long."

The letter offered condolences for Da's death in the same line it signed off on ours. Without money for rent, we'd be evicted. We'd starve. We'd lose all our fingers in the cold.

"I'm not sure why," I continue, shaking my head, "but when Mam read the letter, something changed. She sat up. She climbed out of bed. I remember her legs trembling because she'd grown so weak. But then she turned to me, and in a perfectly normal voice, she said, 'Come along, Essie, get dressed.' And we went to find work." I take a steadying breath. "It was like magic. All at once, she was better."

Fräulein Gretchen smiles kindly. "That's not magic, sweet Angsthäschen. It was your mam's love for you. That's what healed her."

I look up, but her expression changes suddenly, and I'm startled into silence.

Her eyes dance, unfocused. She glances from one place to another, like a tired bird desperate for somewhere to land.

"The tragedy in Little Germany took two of my nephews, and my brother got sad, like your mam." Fräulein Gretchen's voice breaks on the words. It crashes like waves on an icy shore, and all I can do is stand at a distance, watching as she sinks to the dark water below. "But my brother never got better."

Chapter Seventeen

Alone that night, in my bed, the mansion is as quiet as a grave-yard. But in my head, there is chaos. I hear Fräulein Gretchen's voice breaking. I picture the once-handsome man from her photo empty and gaunt.

Little Germany.

I was wrong. I had heard of it before. I just didn't make the connection till now.

I picture Da on the fire escape, and my eyes burn like they're stinging from smoke. I touch the scar on my hand.

I don't want to believe that Fräulein Gretchen's tragedy and the sinking of the *General Slocum* are one and the same, but there's no way to make my thoughts stop. They dash from terrible thing to terrible thing, dragging me along in their wake like a rag doll. With a frustrated cry, I sit up. And that's when the whistling starts.

First low and soft, then unmistakable.

The speaking tube.

I try not to panic. I try to stay calm. But I know exactly what's happening. Someone wants me to get out of bed—wants me to walk to the tube and press my thumb to the lever, put my ear up to that long, dark hole.

Someone wants me to listen.

"Leave me alone!" I shout suddenly, frightened by the pitch of my own voice.

The whistling stops. But it's followed by something much worse.

A metallic click and thunk. The movement of air. A cold draft.

I turn my head just as the lighthouse beam shines into my room, and watch as my door swings slowly open, all the way to the wall.

No one is there. The light vanishes.

In the shadows of the hall, something moves, and there's a soft rustling. It's like skirts being gathered and lifted. Though there's nothing to see, I can hear whatever it is step into the room. I scoot frantically to the side of my bed as the rustling sound passes me, heading toward the bookcase on the opposite wall.

I can't breathe. My heart is racing. Though everything is still pitch black, I'm wide-eyed and staring. Then the lighthouse beam spins back around. And I wish that I were brave enough to get up and run through the open door.

Because the middle shelf of the bookcase is empty.

The sick bell is gone.

"No," I whisper. "*No no no no no.*"

Darkness floods my bedroom just as I hear *ting-a-ling-a-ling-ling.*

When the beam returns—somehow brighter this time, like the lighthouse is closer—I know I am not dreaming. The bell is gone.

And out in the hall, down by the red door, I hear the ringing again.

I try to call for Mam, but all that escapes my throat is a whimper. When the darkness comes back, I start crying.

It can't be real. It must be like before, when Mam was sad and we were stuck, still sleeping in the bed where Da died, before we got our first boarders and moved permanently into the sitting room. We'd wake at the same moment, late at night, sure we had heard the bell ringing. My whole body would lock up in horror, but sometimes Mam tumbled from bed, crawling for her robe, weeping. I'd have to force myself to get up and help her—to insist that my father was dead, that there was no one for us to take care of. Again and again this happened. It didn't stop till Mam pulled the clapper right out.

The bell rings once more down the hall.

The lighthouse beam spears back through my window, bright and blinding as midday. And though the sound of the bell is still distant, still by the red door, at the foot of my bed I see the slver heirloom floating, ringing wildly and silently in the air.

I scream at the top of my lungs.

By the time Mam and Dr. Blackcreek burst into my bedroom, I'm on the floor, curled into a ball and sobbing uncontrollably.

"Essie? Essie!" My mother helps me sit up.

My stepfather, disheveled in his nightgown and cap, turns on the electric light.

"No!" I scream at him. "No! Shut it off!"

He does, then fumbles to light the oil lamp in the dark.

"Essie, what in God's name is the matter!" cries my mam. "Did you fall out of bed? Oh, Alwin, she's hurt herself. Her head's bleeding!"

I don't try to explain that I got tripped up in my sheets. I just point at the doorway and shout, "Someone's here! They took the bell!"

Dr. Blackcreek finally gets the lamp lit, and the disorienting contrast of the shadow and light from the spinning beam vanishes, replaced by an orange glow. Immediately, everything feels warmer and safer, but I know this is a lie.

"No one's here but us, love," says Mam, pressing her hand to my cut forehead, holding me to her and rocking us both. "Wake up. You're dreaming. No one else is here."

She's right. We're alone now. But I wasn't asleep. I know that what happened was real. I know someone else was in my room— someone I couldn't see.

Because the bell is back on the bookcase.

And it's sitting on the wrong shelf.

Chapter Eighteen

Dearest Beatrice, my reply letter starts. *Things have gotten so, so much worse.*

It's been two days since the night I saw the sick bell ringing by itself in my room. Though I've had some time to sit with the fact that, without a shred of doubt, I'm living in a haunted house, it hasn't made things any easier. Each night, I'm a bundle of nerves going to bed, and I beg Mam to stay with me till I fall asleep—which itself has become increasingly difficult. Fortunately, during my isolation in the snowstorm, I've had lots of time to write Bea, which helps ease my mind.

Included in this letter, at the very end, is a page stating all the things I know for certain about my stepfather.

The page in question is still nearly blank. To make up for this, I've reported as much as I can of my harrowing experience on North Brother Island, not just because I know my friend will find it entertaining—inappropriate as that is—but because I hope she might see some important, overlooked detail. I've recounted all the strange happenings at night, given careful descriptions of the girl in the wet dress, and drawn a complicated chart that updates Beatrice on the changes I've made to the List of Unspeakable Fears. In the face of such bone-chilling horrors, several more ordinary ones have been removed. *Moldy Pillows* and *Sea Monsters* and *Paper Cuts* just don't make me flinch like they used to—not by half a mile.

Writing to Beatrice helps me feel better. It lets me picture how she might react to a line or respond to a question. And that's a pleasant break from the rest of my time on the island, especially since Dr. Blackcreek has been asking about my dreams again. He thinks I need to start taking medicine, something that will help me sleep at night. He's also suggested to Mam that my door be locked after I'm settled in bed every evening. This is, quite possibly, the worst thing I could ever imagine—allowing a murderer to drug you and trap you in your room. Just the thought is enough to send me spiraling into fits of anxiety.

Mam insists that the medicine and precautions are for my safety—that both she and my stepfather are afraid I'll run from my room and fall down the stairs in my sleep. It's taken a great deal of pleading to convince her to go against Dr. Blackcreek's requests, and I suspect I'll lose the fight soon enough. This makes it all the more important to finish my letter and get it to Beatrice.

Fortunately, the snow has stopped and the skies are starting to clear. At breakfast, Fräulein Gretchen tells me she thinks that the boats will be running again by tomorrow, and I'll be able to post my now very, very long letter. Of course, this means I need a few more facts about my stepfather—and I need them immediately.

I glance across the table as he puts down his utensils, politely excuses himself, and leaves the room. Hopefully, I can get Mam to talk.

When we're alone, though, my mother clears her throat and says, "Alwin would like to take you for a drive."

I go stiff as a board.

"I can't," I say immediately. "I'm busy today. Lots of school-work."

"This isn't up for debate. Your schoolwork is postponed." My mother frowns. "You didn't tour the island with me, so you'll tour it with your father."

I cringe. I hate it when she calls him that, but the more important thing right now is to avoid arguing and get her on my side—especially with such a dangerous proposition at hand.

"I don't need to go for a drive," I say. "I could tour this place from a high window at the right angle. And I already walked the whole shore on my own, so there's nothing left to see."

"You need fresh air, Essie," says Mam. "Besides, Alwin wants to talk to you about something."

I'm fairly certain more frightening words have never been spoken.

"Please. *Please don't make me go!* Please, Mam! *Please!*"

She sighs. "Essie—"

"He's a murderer! He killed those nurses!" I say frantically. "He suspects I've learned something and means to interrogate me. My life could be in terrible danger!"

"Heaven help me, Essie O'Neill! This is ridiculous! Now he's a *murderer*?! Where do you get such ideas?"

I'll be in trouble if I answer that question, so I simply stay silent. Mam stands up, pressing both her palms flat to the table and staring me down with furious eyes. "Not another word of this fantasy! I mean it. Not a single word! And rest assured, if you don't go get ready right this instant for your drive with Alwin, your life most certainly *will* be in danger!"

Since my fear of Mam's wrath is even greater than my fear of my stepfather, I quickly find myself out on the front porch in my coat, blinking in the sunlight. The stairs and walkway are wet with melted snow. The sky is clear and bright. To my left, an engine cranks to life, and I turn to see Dr. Blackcreek walking around the front of his auto. He opens the passenger door and smiles tightly, gesturing awkwardly with his cane.

Resigning myself to my fate, I bow my head and climb in.

Thinking of the dime novels Beatrice has told me about that detail intense interrogations, I expect this drive will go one of two possible ways. Either my stepfather will start immediately into a hard line of questioning, intending to throw me off guard, or he'll ease me into a false sense of security by beginning with tedious small talk. No matter what, I'll be trapped in the auto with him, and if I say the wrong thing, my life might soon be in danger. Just at the thought, I feel my heart speed up.

"I'm glad to have nice weather again," Dr. Blackcreek says once he's seated beside me in the automobile. He has to yell to be heard over the engine. "How does your head feel this morning?"

The latter tactic it is then. I take a shaky breath.

I touch my bandage gingerly, freshly wrapped by Mam. "It's all right," I say, not wanting to show any weakness. The truth is, even though it's been a couple of days, the bump still hurts quite a lot.

"Mm," my stepfather says. "Good." And then he doesn't say anything more.

Several minutes later, both of us still silent as we bounce along down the road, noisy engine whirring and sputtering, I begin to wonder if there's a third tactic I didn't predict. I keep my guard up, just in case, and watch him out of the corner of my eye.

For the rest of the morning, my stepfather drives me around North Brother Island, pointing out buildings and people, occasionally shouting terse explanations. It all seems rather innocuous, and paired with the unseasonably warm sunshine and bright weather, I find it difficult to stay alert. It doesn't seem likely that Dr. Blackcreek would do anything evil, out in broad daylight like this. By the time we round the southern tip of the island, I'm relaxed—if not even a bit bored—leaning back in the bouncy seat and watching the East River churn past. When I see the lighthouse, though, I realize where I am and sit up straighter. Mary's cottage appears ahead.

Surely my stepfather will say something now. Surely he'll use this as an opportunity to try and trick me into admitting that I disobeyed his order—that I visited with Mary. Since he's clever, like Beatrice said, he'll likely root out every last thing I've learned. Then he might pull off somewhere out of sight and try to murder me, too, in an effort to cover his tracks.

My hands grip the edge of the seat cushion. I hold my breath, tense as we get closer. And then, in a blink, we're past the little house. I watch it go by in confusion, almost frustrated.

"The church is lovely," I say, pointing quickly to the old building next door to Mary's cottage. If we're going to have this fight, I want it now. My stepfather just nods, though, not slowing the auto.

"What's that there?" I ask, pointing to the next building. It's long and made of brick, with dark windows. There's a little shed out back with the door propped partially open. I glance over my shoulder at Mary's cottage one more time, absolutely bewildered. It's already growing small in the distance.

Dr. Blackcreek looks toward the red building we're passing and frowns. "That's the laboratory," he says.

My blood goes cold. I hadn't realized, when I was with Mary, that we were so close. Though I suppose, in reality, everything is close on North Brother Island.

"What's inside?" I ask, and immediately worry that my stepfather will hear the fright in my voice. I can't help but picture the most grisly things: bodies cut into pieces and sewn back together, cloudy jars full of still-beating hearts. But again, he doesn't act like anything is amiss.

"Heavy equipment," he answers me, still watching the road. "Dangerous chemicals. Do not go anywhere near it."

Not for a moment do I think this is the truth, so I study him closely.

His right eye twitches. His hands grip the wheel a bit tighter.

There's something significant in that building, all right! Something more harrowing than equipment and chemicals.

After we've made it back to the northern end of the island, my stepfather turns down a road that leads through the center. Frank is out in front of the staff house, clearing fallen branches and other debris left over from the blizzard. He waves as we pass. Soon we spot a small group of women taking an early lunch outside the nurses' home. They call to us, but we can't really hear what they're saying over the rumble of the engine. Dr. Blackcreek pulls the automobile to the side of the road and shuts it down. For a moment, the world hums in the quiet.

I'm not too worried about what he'll do next, with other people in sight. We've probably stopped so he can introduce me to the nurses. He's done the same, yelling to be heard, with a few people already. So it's unexpected when Dr. Blackcreek doesn't get out of the car, instead pointing to a large square patch of dirt on our right, outlined with construction materials.

"Tennis and handball courts," he says. "At least it will be."

I lean forward. The space isn't much of anything yet, but in the late morning sunlight, it's easy to picture what it could become. It's easy, too, to picture Mam and me laughing together as she teaches me, just like she taught Da. I remember the way he would dive for the ball with his racket, no matter how impossible the shot seemed. Da put his heart and soul into everything that he did, never caring if the odds were against him.

Despite my best intentions, I smile, but my stepfather glances at me, so I sit back and erase the expression.

"There's no one here I could play with," I say. "When it's built, Mam will still be working all the time."

He watches me for a moment before turning away. "That is part of why I took you out today. There's something we need to discuss."

I feel a thrill of fear at the tone of his voice, but then, when

I really hear his words, turn suddenly hopeful. "Are you going to make Mam stay home?"

Dr. Blackcreek's brow furrows. "I have told you already. That is not my choice. If she wants to volunteer at the hospital, who am I to tell her no?" He clears his throat when I frown and changes the topic, pointing to a spot a little farther off. "See that area over there? Near the young maple trees?"

I nod obediently, but I'm back in a bad mood.

"Come this spring, that will be the location of a brand-new schoolhouse," my stepfather says. "I wanted you to know first, before the official announcement."

I blink at him, confused, before asking slowly, "You're building a whole schoolhouse? Just for me?"

He snorts, glancing down, and then regains his composure when he realizes I'm serious. "No. No, not just for you," he says. "I have hired several new nurses. A few asked to bring their children to live with them, and I agreed—provided, of course, that we first build a schoolhouse. I will not have anyone's education interrupted." He looks at me down his long nose, and I realize the strange, pained expression edging up on his face is an attempt at a friendly smile. "It will be a small school. Just one room. But once it is complete, it will mean you will have someone to play with. And I expect a proper schoolteacher is preferable to Fräulein Gretchen's tutoring, yes?"

I'm surprised, so it takes me a moment to reply. "I couldn't prefer anyone to Fräulein Gretchen."

Dr. Blackcreek smiles so broadly for a moment that it doesn't even look like he's wearing the same face.

"I'm pleased to hear that," he says. "But I should still like you to be educated by a professional." He purses his lips, clearly having trouble with the next words. He swallows, glancing away. "I wouldn't have anything less for my daughter."

My whole body goes stiff.

Dr. Blackcreek takes a long breath. "I realize that I am not the easiest person to grow accustomed to. I've been alone for quite some time. And to be honest, even before that, strangers were sometimes put off by my customs. Unlike your parents, I did not move to this country until I was an adult. I know some of my habits may still seem unfamiliar to you." He takes another breath. "I also know that I can be rather . . . distant. This may be a coping behavior, due to traumatic events in my past."

I'm fairly certain that even if I fully understood what he was saying, I still wouldn't be able to react. As it is, all I can do is stare.

"If anyone can empathize with what you have been through, Essie—losing your father—I assure you I can. Five and a half years ago I lost my own family."

If there were a word for this feeling, it would go on my list. My stomach is so tight it hurts. My face is hot and I know that it's red. I want to cry and yell all at once. I want to hate him. I want to hate him *so much*—for talking about Da, for calling me his daughter, for marrying Mam—for all the other horrible, *unspeakable* things that I'm absolutely certain he's done.

Because I am certain, aren't I?

For the first time, I have doubts.

"Dr. Blackcreek! Dr. Blackcreek!" someone cries, and we find one of the nurses from the bench running toward the automobile. "There's trouble in the surgery!"

Behind her, in front of the nurses' home, a new woman has joined the group having lunch. I can't fully see her, since the others are crowding around, but I can tell she's wearing protective clothing and shoes, so she must have come straight from the hospital.

"What's happening?" I ask, panic rising.

Dr. Blackcreek glances back at me. "Stay here," he says, and then gets out of the auto and hurries toward the women.

I kneel on the seat and turn around, heart pounding as I try to get a better look out the back window. I see my stepfather shout something to Frank, who at once puts down his gardening tools and starts off in my direction. When he gets to the auto, he starts it up, moving from the inside to the front to crank the engine.

"What's going on?" I ask, frightened.

"Oh nothing, nothing," Frank says, too loud and too fast. "The doctor's just needed at work. Have you had lunch, Essie? Let's see if Fräulein Gretchen's made one of her meat pies."

We head back to the house. I crane my neck, looking out the window as we pass the nurses' home and everyone gathered outside it. The woman who came from the hospital is sitting on the bench now. Her face is in her hands, and the way her shoulders tremble, it looks like she's crying. Dr. Blackcreek is kneeling down in front of her, talking, so I can't get a good view.

Not till we're a ways away.

Not till my stepfather stands up and runs straight toward the hospital.

The woman's smock is covered in blood.

Chapter Nineteen

A red door.

A dark hallway.

A terrible feeling of dread.

I want to run. I want to leave. To get out. But I'm trapped. I spin around, but the door is still there, right in front of me. Even when I take a step backward, it gets closer. The light around the frame glows hot and bright, and every time I try to squeeze my eyes shut, they snap open.

That monstrous door! The wooden frame, etched with brambles and roses, is seeping, rotting, and the closer I get, the more the etchings distort. They turn into real things, living things, *faces*. The closer I get, the more those faces become people I know: Mam, Beatrice, Fräulein Gretchen.

They start to move. Their mouths open. Their eyes look my way.

Essie! Essie! Essie! they wail.

Using all my strength, I raise my hands up to cover my ears—and suddenly everything stops. There's no more door. No more wailing. There's nothing at all. It's entirely silent and dark.

Something has changed.

For the first time in as long as I can remember, I'm not in the same nightmare anymore. I'm no longer standing in the hall. Instead, I'm on my back, lying down, staring up at the ceiling. Beneath me is a ratty old blanket spread out on the floor. My chest tightens.

This is my apartment in Mott Haven. This is a memory, not just a dream.

Down the hall, the sick bell is ringing.

When I wake up, I nearly fall out of bed for the second time in one week, barely saving my forehead from another encounter with my little side table. I'm panting and sweating. Tears streak down my cheeks. I wait for the beam from the lighthouse to illuminate my room, but it doesn't come. For a moment, I panic, fearing that I'm still stuck in the nightmare, but then I remember my new curtains. Dr. Blackcreek suggested them. After my tumble and my insistent descriptions of strange shadows and floating bells, he determined that the spinning beam from the lighthouse was "triggering a state of disorientation." Fräulein Gretchen started sewing thicker, heavier curtains that same day. When we came back to the house for lunch this afternoon, Frank put them up.

I climb out of bed on shaky legs and pad across the chilly wooden floor with bare feet. When I reach the windows, I throw the curtains open and am relieved by the immediate burst of bright light. Disorienting or not, I've grown used to the spinning beam. Its absence is worse than the anticipation of what it will reveal.

For a while, I stand there at the window, basking in the light like I'm soaking up sun each time the beam comes back around. At first I don't notice the shadow on the beach, which elongates each time the beam runs across the shore. Finally, though, the oddity catches my eye, and I squint, realizing the shadow is being cast by a person—a person down by the waves, far, far away from the house.

A tall person, walking with a cane.

My stepfather. Out again in the middle of the night.

My first reaction is urgency. I want to wake up my mother and show her. Though I'm still confused by Dr. Blackcreek's kind behavior today on our drive, maybe it means nothing at all. I've known kind people before who did awful things. Sometimes the face someone shows you isn't his real one, especially if he has something to hide. Or sometimes a person can be good and generous one moment, and then cruel the next. A neighbor might mend your doll when it tears, but slam the door in your face when you knock at night, begging for help.

I cringe, pushing out the memory, and try to stay focused. What good will waking Mam do? My stepfather's walks are unusual, yes, but they're not proof of anything, and she knows about them already. I need hard evidence about what Dr. Blackcreek is up to. Photographs or murder weapons or documents. Now that the weather is better, if I can get to the laboratory—

The speaking tube starts to whistle.

I tense, turning halfway, then move only my eyes. The mouthpiece is visibly vibrating from the sound.

I'm so scared my heart throbs in my ears. But this isn't a coincidence. The speaking tube hasn't made a single noise since the night the bell rang. And here it is, calling me, when my step-father is once again out on the beach.

Someone has something to tell me. I just have to be brave enough to listen.

I make myself walk across the cold wooden floor. It's only a piece of metal sticking out of the wall. It's only tin and brass piping. It can't hurt me. There's nothing at all to be afraid of. Still, my fingers tremble when I reach the far side of the room and lift my hand up to the mouthpiece. I press the lever with my thumb, and a small cover with a tiny hole shifts out of the way, revealing a deep, round, dark space. The whistling stops.

For a moment, I'm sure I've been a fool. I imagine something foul and freakish wriggling suddenly out of the pipe, grabbing for me. But nothing happens. So I gather what courage I can and lean forward, standing up on the tips of my toes.

I whisper, "Hello?"

And then I force myself to do the hardest part yet. I turn my face and press my ear to the gaping hole. After a silent moment, there's a feathery sound, like soft breathing, and I hear a reply.

"Esssssie . . . ," a voice says, so thin and light my ear tingles. I want to jerk away, but I hold still. "Essie . . . the office . . . the attic . . ."

And then it's gone.

I step back, letting go of the lever, and the little cover slaps into place. For a long time, I stare at the speaking tube. And then it hits me. *My stepfather is out.* My mother's asleep. Fräulein Gretchen, too. There's no way I'm going into the attic—not ever—but the office . . . that doesn't frighten me half as much. And now's my opportunity to get in. I just have to find the keys.

I take a deep, shaky breath, slip on a robe, and light my candle. Then I tiptoe out into the hall and down the stairs, avoiding the creakiest steps. At my stepfather's office door, I try the golden handle. As I expected, it doesn't budge.

Look closer, Essie, I hear Beatrice say. *Don't give up now.*

I hurry through the downstairs hallways and into the kitchen. I pause often, listening, making sure no one has woken and that Dr. Blackcreek hasn't returned. Next to the stove, hanging on a high peg, I spot Fräulein Gretchen's apron. I walk over and find the key ring right away in a pocket. I press it close to my chest so it won't jingle as I rush back through the dark halls. At the office door again, I set my candle down on the nearby side table and search till I find the key Fräulein Gretchen used when retrieving the fountain pen. It's larger than the rest and heavy. My hands are shaking when I push the key into the lock, but on the very first try, the bolt thunks open loudly. I pause, listening once more to the house, and when I'm certain there's no sound of footsteps, I grasp the knob and turn. The door opens.

At first I can't see a thing. I swallow hard. Stepping into that pitch-black room will be like diving into a deep pond in the dead of night. There's no way to tell what's lurking in wait. But I grit my teeth, snatch my candle back up, and walk in anyway. I close the door behind me and wait for my sight to adjust. Slowly, it does.

When Gretchen retrieved the pen for me, I got a peek inside this room, but now, with floor-length curtains blocking the lighthouse beam, everything more than a few feet away is a murky shadow. My little flame details only what's nearby—as if I'm standing in a bubble of light. Objects in distant corners are hulking, ominous shapes. It takes courage to make myself move.

I stay close to the walls and their bookcases, all built right into the house. There must be hundreds of books, many that have shiny gold words and ornate designs on the spines. I try to sound out one of the titles: *Die Traumatischen Neurosen*. Unfortunately, Fräulein Gretchen was right. Most of these books are in German. I won't learn anything from them.

My candle casts gigantic dancing shadows as I move into the center of the room. There's a standing globe near a huge desk, but I don't spin it. Beatrice would surely advise me to touch as little as possible. In the dime novels, the criminals always make some foolish mistake that gives them away. They leave boot tracks on the floor or forget to put a piece of furniture back in its proper place. I blush, realizing that in this case, I'm the criminal—I'm the one trespassing.

Up above, I hear a noise coming from the second floor and go still. After a few moments, though, the sound doesn't return, so I walk around the desk and try the drawers. Of course they're all locked and need keys smaller than the ones on Fräulein Gretchen's key ring. On top of the desk is a stack of documents, however, so I set my candle down, take a seat in the big office chair, and start going through them.

Annual Expense Reports . . . Smallpox Study . . . I'm careful not to disturb anything else on the desk, setting everything aside in order. *Immunizations . . . Contamination Procedures . . .*

With language like this, the documents might as well be in German too. I sigh, going more slowly, scanning for anything that seems important. It's tedious work, and though my stepfather's handwriting is exquisite, in most cases, I simply don't understand the complicated medical words. I feel a twinge of sadness, thinking of how frustrated Da must have felt—even pretty easy books were complicated for him. I remember sitting and trying to help him with the novels he checked out from the library. Sometimes he'd pick ghost stories or other things I didn't like, but I never minded. He was so eager to learn—and with him beside me, I always felt safe.

There's another noise from upstairs. This time it sounds like someone's in the hall. I go still for much longer, but once again, nothing comes of it. I tell myself it's just the old house being noisy, like Fräulein Gretchen said. I try not to think of girls in wet dresses or eerie voices or the floating sick bell.

At the bottom of the stack of documents, I find an over-stuffed leather folder tied together with a string. The title reads: *Employment History*. The papers inside are mismatched. There are applications, notes from interviews, termination documents—information about everyone who works, or *worked*, on North Brother Island. There are even some photographs of important people, like previous directors of Riverside. It seems the last one left in 1903 and they didn't get an official replacement until September 1904. That replacement was my stepfather. There are a few scant details here about him, like the name of the city in Germany where he was born and went to school. I commit it all to memory.

After the pages about the hospital's directors, there are seemingly endless documents concerning the nurses and other staff. I frown. The rate that people leave Riverside appears to be quite high. And rarely does it seem they leave because they've lost their position.

Husband demands wife return home, explains one document.

Contracted illness, says another, and my heart skips a beat.

The word *Melancholia* is repeated frequently. I know this is a disease, but I'm not sure what kind.

Flipping faster now through the folder, I come to a divider. The first entry reads, *Absent without leave.*

I stare blankly, uncertain whether I've truly found what I think I have. Leaning in closer, I search for other information. The start date for this nurse was six months ago. The end date was right before Mam and I arrived. There's a more detailed explanation about the woman's last day farther down on the page. The handwriting is my stepfather's.

Quarters found empty in nurse's home. Some personal items remained. Will ship if she is located.

I gasp. This is one of the missing nurses! When I turn the page, I find a nearly identical document for a different woman, who vanished only a few weeks before the first.

Roommate says she left on the early morning ferry, Dr. Blackcreek's note reads.

The next page reveals similar information for the third missing nurse, who disappeared some months ago. I assume my work is done. I'm only concerned with these three women, after all. But I turn the page once more, out of habit.

Absent without leave, says the document, and I blink. A fourth nurse. A year ago.

I flip again. Another missing nurse. I flip again. Another one.

Flip. Flip. Flip. Flip. My fingers are flying, my eyes wide as can be. The records go on and on and on. The entire section is filled with people who've gone missing from North Brother Island!

But something's wrong. Something doesn't add up.

I pause. The documents in this section are in order by year. There are still dozens left, presumably all missing, and the date on the page where I've landed reads *1902*.

I'm distracted when the noise comes again. This time, there's no mistaking it. Footsteps. And now they're on the stairs.

I close the leather folder and tie it shut. I quickly place the rest of the documents back on top and scoot the whole stack to its original place, but at the last moment, a set of folded papers slips out and spills all over the floor. I dive to retrieve them. A familiar creak on the staircase tells me that whoever is coming down is halfway here.

I gather the fallen papers, my heart pounding, put them on top of the stack, and crawl under the desk. I go absolutely still. My breathing gets shallow. Seconds pass with excruciating slowness.

The footsteps stop outside the door. And then something runs its claws right down the frame, letting out a terrible cry.

"MRrroooOOOwww!"

My breath escapes in a whoosh, irritation rising up after it.

"Old Scratch, you wretched pest!" I crawl out from under the desk.

The front door of the house opens.

I slap both my hands over my mouth.

"Stop that! Stop it, Scratch! You'll ruin the woodwork!" Dr. Blackcreek whispers angrily. He shoos the cat away and says something in German that sounds like a curse. "Why do you want to go in that room?"

I hear his hand on the doorknob.

And I remember my candle, still sitting on top of the desk.

Chapter Twenty

My hand darts up, and I snatch the little silver handle on the candle plate, bringing the light down to my hiding spot. I lick my fingers and pinch out the flame just as the office door opens.

For a few harrowing moments, my stepfather stands there, half in and half out of the room. I can't see him, but I can sense his presence lingering. I can tell he's deciding whether to come farther inside. All the hairs on the back of my neck bristle. I pray to every saint I can name that he leaves.

"Katherine?" Dr. Blackcreek whispers.

My heart nearly stops beating. And then I frown, confused, because I realize it's not me that he's calling for. After a moment longer, my stepfather sighs, laughs lightly to himself, and goes back into the foyer. He locks the door behind him, and soon the staircase is protesting underneath each of his steps. The old floorboards are so noisy, I can tell exactly where he is in the house all the way to the master bedroom.

For a very long time, I'm too afraid to come out from under the desk, even after I'm certain Dr. Blackcreek is gone. I grip my flameless candle, staring at nothing, not understanding. *Katherine.* Who did Dr. Blackcreek think was in here?

Even if I dared to spend more time in the office, combing

through records, I don't have any light to read by. So, finally, I get up and feel my way across the room. I expect this to be terrifying, but I make it to the door without any trouble.

Just as Beatrice would surely do, I cover all my tracks from sleuthing. I lock the door behind me. I scurry back into the kitchen and put the key ring in the correct apron pocket. Then I creep up the squeaky staircase. Even though I'm careful not to step on the loudest boards, the sounds still echo through the whole mansion. When I pass by the master bedroom, I'm anxious that Dr. Blackcreek will open the door and step out, but he doesn't. And soon I'm back at my bedroom. Before I can go in, though, I pause. There's a familiar *scritch-scritch-scratch* at the attic door.

"Old Scratch?" I whisper, and he looks up from his handiwork—a worn spot of claw marks along the floor. "You naughty beast. You almost gave me away!"

He pads over, purring obnoxiously loud, and rubs his body along my legs. I stiffen at first, but then relax. When I go into my bedroom, I find I don't even care that he follows me. It might be nice, after all, not being alone.

"You can't sleep in my bed, though," I warn him once my door is closed. "I'm sure you have fleas." I tilt my head, curious. "When did you come upstairs, anyway? I didn't hear you."

And then a chill passes through me.

I heard Dr. Blackcreek go up the stairs. But before that, I'd heard someone come down. And it couldn't have been the cat. If I didn't hear him come upstairs before me just now, that means he's too light to make the floorboards creak.

Perhaps Katherine—whoever she is—was in the office with me after all.

In the morning, even though I'm very tired, I get up early to finish my letter before Frank picks up the mail. I want it to be on the first ferry out. On the last page, I add more things to the short list about Dr. Blackcreek. Items of note include:

From Ingolstadt, Bavaria. Much better than just *From Germany*—and I'm fairly certain I've remembered the correct spelling. In fact, it's almost like I've heard the name of the city before or seen it written some other place.

Went to school in Ingolstadt too.

Became Riverside's director in 1904. This seems like it's important. Something about it is already nagging at the back of my mind.

Near the end of the letter proper, which, after a week of writing, is the length of a short book, I wrap things up.

What to do now, Beatrice? I'll search the laboratory, yes, if I can gain access. But if I do find the bodies, God save me, how should I go about exposing the crime? Do I call the police? There's a telephone at the hospital, but I'm scared to use it. I could tell Mam, of course, but there's a chance she won't believe me. And even if she does, that might be worse. You know how Mam is. What if she tries to confront my stepfather? Whenever good citizens take that sort of risk in your

dime novels, their plans go off horribly. My mother
might become a victim of the doctor herself!

I pause because I think I hear something in the hall. My heart is already beating fast, after imagining Mam coming to a gruesome end at the hands of Dr. Blackcreek. I'm perfectly still for a long while. It's important no one reads these words but Beatrice herself. If my stepfather finds out what I've learned, who knows what he'll do? Trembling a bit, my eyes return to the letter. The tip of the fountain pen, resting lightly on the page, has left an unsightly blot of ink.

I need your guidance, Beatrice. Now more than ever, I wish so very much you were here.

At the bottom, below the ink mishap and final lines, I sign my name.

Later that morning, after the letter is safely away, I'm barely able to stay awake for my tutoring session with Fräulein Gretchen. I'm supposed to be practicing arithmetic, but mostly I'm just trying not to fall asleep.

"How much must be paid for the keeping of—" I read aloud from my textbook, pausing for a big yawn. "How much must be paid for the keeping of twelve horses at the rate of eighty cents . . . eighty cents for four horses?"

I tilt my head at the problem, as if that will help me better understand it.

Finally Fräulein Gretchen eyes me sideways and asks, "Long night, little Angsthäschen?"

I sit up straight. "No! I mean . . . well . . ." Her look isn't accusatory. I don't think she knows about my investigation. "It's just that I'm not sleeping a lot."

"Is the lighthouse still bothering you? Should the curtains be thicker?"

I shake my head. "The curtains are fine."

"Then is it the nightmares?" she asks gently.

I start to shake my head again, but hesitate. "Well, yes. I'm still having nightmares. But that's not why I'm tired."

Fräulein Gretchen looks at me expectantly, waiting for more. It takes a moment to choose my words. I need to be careful about how much I give away.

"You've been here, at Dr. Blackcreek's house, for a long time," I say.

She nods.

"Do you ever . . . do you ever hear strange things? Like people walking around who you can't see?"

She goes so pale my skin crawls. Only once before have I seen her look at me like this—on the night I told her about the footprints coming out of the water. No matter what she says next, Fräulein Gretchen knows there's something going on in this house.

She folds her hands in her lap, clearly trying to stay calm. "That sounds very much like the talk of an Angsthäschen. You jump at shadows and think they are ghosts."

I frown. "You call me that all the time, but you still haven't told me what it means. And I never said anything about *ghosts*."

"Angsthäschen means 'fear rabbit,'" says Fräulein Gretchen.

"You are small and cute. And you are afraid of everything." She takes a breath and levels her gaze at me. "You didn't say 'ghosts,' but ghosts are what you are talking about. You are asking me if this house is haunted."

I cross my arms, looking away. "Isn't it?"

"Things happen here that are unusual. That is true. But I don't believe in ghosts."

My mouth drops open and I turn back to her. "How can you say that? If you've seen—"

"I have never *seen* anything," Fräulein Gretchen insists, and I go quiet again, realizing that she's trying hard to find the right words. "I believe that when people die, they can leave a small piece of themselves behind. It is like—like how you might smell someone's perfume in a room after they left, or how you see their imprint on a sofa where they were sitting." She shakes her head. "I have never seen anything in this house, but . . . but sometimes I hear things. Sometimes I feel something. The impression of someone. Do you understand?"

I nod. "Do you think that only can happen in the place where someone died?"

I'm proud of myself for how directly I ask this—I don't flinch even a little.

"No one has died in this house, if that is what you want to know."

I sigh and look down at my hands. "Maybe I am just a fear rabbit."

"Maybe," Fräulein Gretchen agrees, and when I glance up at her, she smiles. After a moment, though, she sighs too. "Or maybe, that piece of someone—when it gets left behind—maybe it isn't left at a place. Maybe it is left with a person."

We lock eyes, and my pulse quickens.

"A person like Dr. Blackcreek?" I ask.

Fräulein Gretchen closes my arithmetic book. "Why don't you go take a walk?"

Chapter Twenty-One

I shouldn't be where I am. I shouldn't be doing what I'm about to do.

I'm frightened, making my way across the still, quiet island, and I wish, for the millionth time, that I were only stuck in a dream—that I'd wake up in our crumbling tenement to Beatrice knocking on my door. If that isn't possible, I wish, at least, that she were here with me. I'm not brave like she is. I'm not brave like Mam or Da, either. And I don't want to do this alone.

But no one else is here. If I want proof of what Dr. Blackcreek is up to—if I want to protect Mam—I have to find it myself.

In the distance, I see the laboratory and puff out my chest, pretending I'm strong and can face this fear, even if I don't feel like it inside. I walk faster.

The trees and shrubbery that have been planted on the island are mostly still young, so there aren't many good places to conceal myself. This becomes even more apparent when I'm nearly at the back door of the long redbrick building, and I hear voices approaching. I'm so close to the laboratory by now that there's no way to lie myself out of trouble. There's nowhere else I could be headed. And I was specifically forbidden from coming here, so surely, no matter who spots me, word will get back to my stepfather.

I spin in a panicked circle, looking for somewhere, anywhere, out of sight. This would be a much easier task if it were dark, so I understand why Beatrice prefers sleuthing at night. I feel a bit of confidence, thinking of how proud my friend will be when she reads about my dangerous explorations. This motivates me enough that I don't run away. Instead, I take a careful look at my surroundings. The next nearest building is the church, but the voices are too close for me to make it in time. This leaves only the small lopsided shed to my left. I dart toward it, and when I reach the door, already ajar, I try to open it. The bottom is caught on something in the dirt. I can't tug it free. The voices round the corner, so I desperately wriggle my way into the shed, sucking in my stomach and yanking at my dress. Just as two men appear, I disappear through the gap, tumbling into a tight space filled with wooden boxes.

Luckily, the men are laughing, so they don't hear me bumping around. I take a steadying breath and then creep back to the gap in the door and peek through. Both men have large mustaches and slicked-down hair, parted neatly on the side. They're also wearing identical long white coats. Clearly, they're staff of some sort.

One of the men opens the back door of the laboratory building, and I get a direct look inside. The horrors exceed my expectations: rows and rows of strangely shaped glass bottles; shelves full of sharp metal tools; a long examination table with straps.

My heart is already on the verge of pounding out of my chest when one man calls to the other, "They'll be here any minute. We'd best hurry," and then turns and heads straight toward the shed.

"Oh!" I whisper, and for the first time, I look at the contents of the rickety little structure, hoping to find some sort of cover.

How the man coming my way doesn't hear me cry out, I'll never know.

Because the shed is full of coffins.

I nearly stumble backward into the door. I nearly give myself up and start screaming.

The man already inside the laboratory shouts something to his partner, and the man near me pauses. "What was that?" he calls.

When he paces a few steps away to better hear his companion, I should be relieved that I've been given a moment more to plan my next move. But all the blood in my body has rushed to my head. I'm paralyzed with terror. Something rubs against my leg and I jump almost to the roof, clamping a hand over my mouth to keep from crying out a second time. However, I quickly realize that the *something* is only Old Scratch—a horror I've become quite used to—and the sight of him brings me back to my senses.

I have to hide. I have to hide *now*.

I force myself to open the nearest coffin, a thin wooden box almost twice my height, and step inside, pulling the lid closed behind me.

"They've arrived! I'll be right back," says the man near the shed, and I hear him resuming his trek toward my hiding place.

Old Scratch starts rubbing against my coffin, doing his awful, broken meow.

"Shh!" I say desperately. "Not again! Be quiet!"

I kick a little at the lid, hoping to make him scamper off. Instead, he meows even louder.

The man is right outside the shed door, trying to work it free from the dirt where it's jammed, and I'm without any other options. I reach out of the coffin, snatch up Old Scratch, and replace the lid just in time.

"Mm. Which one, then?" the man says to himself, stepping into the shed.

I'm as far back in the empty coffin as I can go, holding the cat to my chest and staying as still as possible. This is complicated by the fact that Old Scratch is rubbing his head aggressively against my chin, purring so loud that I'm sure we'll be caught.

Finally, though, I hear the man drag out a coffin from the opposite wall, so I lift the lid of my own coffin for a peek. He's left the shed door wide open behind him, giving me a clear view of the commotion beyond. The man from inside the laboratory pulls on long rubber gloves as he comes to meet the two new staff members who've arrived. They're pushing a gurney between them. Someone is lying on top. The body is covered with a white sheet.

I'm squeezing Old Scratch so hard that he's stopped purring and is starting to squirm. I'm trying to breathe, but I can't.

As the gurney is lifted into the laboratory, a hand slips out from under the sheet and dangles down off the side. It's covered with oozing red blisters.

Chapter Twenty-Two

When Mam gets home that evening, I'm pacing my room, the List of Unspeakable Fears tight in my still-shaking fists. After running all the way back from the laboratory, I've refused to come downstairs—or even open my door—much to Fräulein Gretchen's distress.

I can hear her now, walking with my mother toward my room.

"She said she needed to speak with you at once. She would not say anything more. You should have seen her face, Mrs. Blackcreek. White as milk."

My mother knocks, hard and fast. Even though I'm expecting it, I still jump. Quickly I roll up my list and stuff it under my mattress. Mam comes in. She's wearing a dark blue jacket and skirt. As always, she's changed out of her nurse's uniform before leaving the hospital, since it's one of Dr. Blackcreek's strict policies that staff members not wear "contaminated" clothing home. When Mam worked at the settlement house, no one cared about that. They didn't care about handwashing, either—one of the many odd policies my stepfather brought over from Germany.

Before moving from one patient to the next, Dr. Blackcreek

requires everyone at Riverside to wash their hands in a chlorine solution. Apparently, someone named Semmelweis had come up with the idea decades ago, as a way to "decrease the spread of infection." And while anything that keeps Mam and me from getting sick sounds like a good idea, I can't help but notice how raw and red her hands are these days. *Hand Disinfectant* and *Empty Coffins* are both recent entries on my list.

"What's going on, Essie?" Mam asks. "You've given Fräulein Gretchen an awful fright."

I trust Fräulein Gretchen, I do. But I'm not brave enough to say these things in front of her. What if she gets upset? I whisper to Mam, "It's a confidential matter."

My mother takes a breath, practicing patience, and then smiles at the maid apologetically. "It seems I need a moment alone with my daughter."

Fräulein Gretchen's eyes widen. "Oh! Yes, of course," she says, and backs out of the room, closing the door behind her.

Mam raises an eyebrow expectantly. "Let me guess, this is something to do with Alwin?"

I cringe. "Please, please, just listen!"

My mother shakes her head, appearing incredibly tired. "Essie, it's been a *long* day."

"But I found proof!"

"Proof? Proof of what?"

"The murdered—" I only realize I'm shouting when I hear the front door open downstairs. My stepfather has arrived home. I lower my voice to a frantic whisper. *"The murdered nurses!"*

"Oh, Essie," moans my mother. She drags herself to my bed

and sits down hard, then lies back and covers her eyes with her arm. *"Oh, Essie."*

"I'm not overreacting. I'm not!"

She sighs dramatically. "What is it you found?"

"First you have to promise you won't confront him," I say, deadly serious. "No matter how angry you are."

"What?" She peeks up at me, confused.

"Promise," I insist. "If you confront him, after learning what I've discovered, there's no telling what he'll do! I've imagined so many horrible things."

"For heaven's sake!"

"Just promise!"

"Fine," says Mam. "I promise. Now *tell me.*"

I sit beside her on the bed, then start talking fast. "I wasn't going to trust Mary's opinion outright. I swear it. She's an awfully unusual person, and her dog is ferocious, but when we came up with the idea about looking in the laboratory—"

"Wait. What? Mary Mallon? You spoke to her again?" Mam starts to sit up, but I ignore her and go on. There's no time to fight about me breaking a few minor rules. Not in the face of such danger.

"Dr. Blackcreek told me *specifically* not to go near the laboratory. You should have seen him! It was so obvious he was hiding something there, which meant I had to look for myself, and guess where I wound up—trapped in a shed full of coffins! *Coffins!* It was so awful, Mam! And then . . ." I swallow a huge lump in my throat, not wanting to remember the next part. "And then I saw the body."

Mam's cheeks lose some of their color. "You *what*?"

I feel a rush of relief at her reaction, and it gives me the confidence to barrel onward. "A real one. A dead body. They took it inside the building, where there were all these frightening tools and devices. Oh! I forgot the part about the records. I found records, too. Dozens of nurses have gone missing, Mam! For more than a decade, with no explanation!"

My mother takes my face in her hands. "Essie! Stop. Did you just say you saw the body of a dead person today?"

She looks horror-struck, and it's so startling—so unnatural for her—that I fumble for words, slowing as I nod. "Y-yes. With a hand covered in blisters."

For some reason, I start crying.

"Oh, my sweet baby," says Mam, and she pulls me to her. "I'm so, so sorry. Oh, Essie."

I try to disentangle myself from her, confused. "What— what are you . . . ?" I wipe my eyes with my sleeve. "Mam, this is proof! The laboratory is where—"

"Where they perform autopsies," says my mother, and I blink, feeling suddenly incredibly small. Mam purses her lips. "I told you, your father is at the forefront of his field. He's searching for ways to help make people better. That means, sometimes, he has to do things that . . ." She pauses. "Well, that seem a bit scary. But they aren't. Not really. After people have died, looking at their bodies helps us understand why. Alwin just didn't want to frighten you. He didn't want you to see what you saw. That's why he told you to stay away from the laboratory."

"No," I say, shaking my head. "No! The nurses—"

"Your father didn't murder anyone," pleads Mam. "You have to trust me!"

"*You* have to trust *me*," I plead back. "I'm trying to protect us!"

My mother stares for a moment, as if at a loss for words. Her expression softens, saddens. "I *do* trust you, love. More than anyone. You saved me when I was sick. You saved us both. I'll always trust you. *Always.* But Dr. Blackcreek isn't what you think. You *must* let this go."

I feel a flutter of desperation before my insides fill with hurt. I look away. "You trust me, but you don't believe me."

"I do!" Mam touches my cheek, bringing my eyes back to her. "I believe you saw something awful today—something no girl your age should see. And I know you, Essie O'Neill. I know how the thoughts spin round and round in your head. But your father—"

"He's not my father! Stop calling him that! You're always calling him that."

Mam goes quiet. For a while, we stare at each other. And when she finally speaks again, her voice sounds even sadder than before.

"You're right. Alwin isn't your father. And that's what this is really about, isn't it?" She takes a deep breath. "I'm not trying to replace Da. No one ever could. Not in a lifetime of loving us both."

Tears well up again instantly. "This isn't about Da. It's about you and me and staying safe. You won't see what's going on because Dr. Blackcreek moved you into this big house and bought you pretty hats. He's controlling you!"

Mam gapes at me, but only for a second before laughing.

"Have you *met* me? You can't seriously believe that." And then she looks at me more carefully. "Alwin is just a person, Essie. Like us and Beatrice and everyone else. He has a past. He's lost loved ones too. He's not perfect. But he tries to lead a good life— he tries to help others—and that's what matters." She shakes her head. "If you insist on seeing him as a monster, though, that's what you'll keep seeing. You're the only one who can change your perspective."

I look up suddenly—not because of all the nonsense about my "perspective," but because she's reminded me that Dr. Blackcreek lost his family. I get a horrible feeling. I think of something I hadn't thought of before.

"Mam, do you know who Dr. Blackcreek's wife was?" I ask, my voice trembling. "Do you know her name?"

My mother blinks at me, surprised by the change in topic. "Emma, I believe. Why?"

I'm almost relieved for a moment, but then I ask cautiously, "Did he—did he have any children?"

Mam nods. "A daughter. She was about your age when she passed away. It's a tragic story. And before you ask, no. I won't tell you. Not tonight. Not after a day like the one you've just had. If you want to know what happened, you need to talk to your fa—" She catches herself. "Ask Alwin yourself. But make sure you're ready to hear it. It's very upsetting."

I don't care about my stepfather's story, though. Only one question matters.

"What was his daughter's name?"

Mam's eyes fill up with pity. "Katherine," she replies.

Chapter Twenty-Three

It's the middle of the night and I'm not alone in my room. I know it the moment I wake.

There's a feeling in the air, like a weight or a presence. There's the sound of a rustling dress.

How could I have been so simple? How did it take me so long to see? From the day I arrived in this horrible house—before I'd even stepped through the door—Katherine has been warning me. She's been trying to frighten me off.

Because she, of all people, knows what her father is capable of.

She knows what might happen to me.

I sit up slowly, but the room is pitch-black, and I can't see.

"K-Katherine?" I ask, my voice quivering. "Katherine, are you there?"

And then, outside my bedroom door, there's a sound. It's so quiet I almost don't hear it at all.

Ting-a-ling-a-ling-ling.

I swing my legs off the bed and dash to my window, throwing open the curtains. The spinning beam hits my room and I turn to face the far bookcase.

Once more, the sick bell is gone.

Ting-a-ling-a-ling-ling! Ting-a-ling-a-ling-ling!

"Stop it!" I shout. "I'm coming. Just stop!"

But the noise only gets louder. Someone is standing outside my room, ringing the sick bell as hard as she can. I press my hands over my ears and still hear it.

In a rage, I run to my door and yank it open. The hallway is empty and silent.

For a long while I stand there, breathing heavily, torn between anger and terror. The lighthouse beam shines into my room, illuminating the hall. It reflects oddly off the floor. I kneel down, feeling along the smooth boards. My hand touches something wet just as the light vanishes, and I gasp and fall to my bottom.

I can't see a thing. All I can do is hold my hand away from me—as far away as I can get it. What horrors have I touched!

The beam returns and I brace for gore, so it's shocking to see nothing at all on my wet fingers. No blood. No bile. The liquid is clear. After a moment, I crawl forward, feeling again for the spot. I twitch back when I find it, but then gather my courage and bring my hand up to my face. I sniff.

Water. It's a puddle of water. And it smells like it's from the East River.

The light casts the hall momentarily in brightness. My breath stops short in my throat. Wet footprints. Small. Bare. A child's. Leading from my room to the left.

Leading straight to the attic.

Ting-a-ling-a-ling-ling, comes the sound of the bell. Now it's behind the red door.

I stumble to my feet, so frightened my thoughts are on fire. I won't go! I just *can't.* Not there, of all places. I won't go, no matter what proof I might find. I turn, intending to dart back into my room and dive under my covers.

But I don't get past the doorway.

Because there's a soaking-wet girl sitting on the edge of my bed.

Her skin is pale, almost blue. Her brown hair is streaming in messy locks over her shoulders, fallen from a once-pretty braid. There's a white ribbon at the end, muddy and torn. Her dress is nice enough for church, decorated with lace, but when my eyes travel down, I can see it's burned at the hem.

The girl looks up at me with empty eyes. She raises the sick bell and smiles.

TING-A-LING-A-LING-LING!

I scream so loud I can't hear anything else. I scream and scream and scream until the whole world disappears.

Chapter Twenty-Four

I'm to be confined to my bed all the next day on Dr. Blackcreek's strict orders. No matter how I protest—no matter how I insist that there was a girl in my room—no one will believe me. I ran halfway down the hall before fainting. I was found dangerously close to the stairwell. And not a single adult will concern themselves with anything else.

Night terrors. A particularly aggressive attack. Condition exacerbated by exposure to frightening sights at the laboratory.

Dr. Blackcreek's diagnosis was aided by the fact that Mam told my stepfather where I'd been and what I'd seen. I'm furious with her. I've never been so mad in my life. Soon Dr. Blackcreek will have just what he wants. My door will be locked in the evenings. He'll administer drugs to "encourage sound sleep." And then I won't be able to catch him in the act on his nightly expeditions. I won't be able to hunt for more clues.

In fact, I now believe that if I'm not careful, he'll soon make certain I'm out of the picture entirely.

Outside, down the hall, I hear footsteps coming up the stairs. It's late in the morning, but my mother and stepfather must think I'm asleep, because their voices are hushed.

"I just don't think it's a good idea right now," says Mam.

"She's waking up nearly every night, absolutely petrified, and I know my daughter. Locking the door will only exacerbate her fears, I assure you."

My mother and Dr. Blackcreek have been at it off and on since dawn. Between their ruckus and the awful things I saw last night, I've hardly slept at all. To my relief, Mam hasn't completely betrayed me. She's at least fought for my freedom, even though it seems a hopeless task. My stepfather keeps insisting that his treatment plans are the right move, and it's clearly only a matter of time till he gets his way.

"She could have been seriously injured last night," Dr. Blackcreek says. I can picture his limp, his long beard and cruel eyes. I can hear the tap of his cane on the floorboards. "To keep her safe, there is no other choice."

I grit my teeth. Like he cares about that.

"And what if there's something else going on?" asks my mother. "This is so different from the nightmares back in our apartment. She never saw such awful things. What if—good God, Alwin—what if someone truly *is* getting into her room at night?"

My skin goes cold and tingly at the suggestion, even though I already know that it's true.

"Who would do that?" asks my stepfather, flabbergasted. "Who could even try?"

"A patient, perhaps? She's been speaking with Mary Mallon."

My eyes widen in shock. She's broken my trust a second time! What else will she tell him? What has she told him already? Does Mam know about me sneaking into his office? Does he know now too?

"I could have guessed as much," says Dr. Blackcreek. "Mary has been particularly troublesome recently. She listens to nothing I say. She's prideful and furious—more determined than ever to leave quarantine. For better or worse, I suspect Mary will see her wish granted soon."

"How so?" asks Mam. They're closer to my room now, their voices lower. "I thought her stay was indefinite. Isn't she still contagious?"

"Yes, but it seems the new health commissioner, Ernst Lederle, sympathizes with her plight." Dr. Blackcreek sighs. "It was naive of me to think Mary would give up on leaving Riverside after last summer's lawsuit. But turning my stepdaughter against me? To what end? Just out of spite?"

"Could it be Mary getting into the house?" asks Mam, sounding anxious.

"Absolutely not. That's preposterous. *No one* is getting into the house. There is a medical explanation for what Essie is experiencing, I assure you. Her night terrors will ease if you just give me the chance to help her."

A chance to *experiment on me* would be a more accurate way to put it.

Unfortunately, if I thought my mother telling Dr. Blackcreek about the laboratory and Mary and everything else was a terrible betrayal, I was a fool. Because the next thing she says is, "All right."

I roll over and stuff my head under the pillow before I can hear anything else. When Mam creaks open my door, I pretend to be asleep.

The letter is sitting on my bedside table. I'm not sure how it got there. I'm not sure when I fell asleep in earnest—perhaps with Mam's hand stroking my head, perhaps when she left the room after. But now I'm alone and there it is, a reply from Beatrice, right next to a cold bowl of porridge. I get out of bed quickly and open it up.

Dearest Essie, the letter starts. *I fear this time you're right. You and your mam are in incredibble danger.*

Anxiety rushes up into my chest.

I wanted my friend's help. *Of course* I did. One day she's going to be a brilliant detective, and if anyone can crack this case, it is her.

But in my heart of hearts, I'm growing tired. Tired of searching for clues. Tired of being so scared all the time. There's a part of me that just needs desperately for this all to be over—no matter what secrets my stepfather has. There's a part of me that wishes Beatrice's reply were filled with nothing important. Stories about crooks stealing ugly toupees. Stories about missing pet birds. I want to hear about normal life in Mott Haven. I want to know if Bea's youngest brother has again gotten caught swiping sweets. I'd even have taken a letter gushing about Mary Mallon and how jealous Beatrice was that I got to meet her and she didn't.

But I sent my friend a cry for help, and she did what I asked—what she does best. She investigated.

Next week is my birthday, Essie. I hope you haven't forgotton. I'm reminding you because you must come.

You must convins your mam to bring you to visit—say
it's for that, nothing else—and together you and I will
go to the polis with all of our evidence. By then I'm
sure I'll have more. But you must make this happin.
Because truly, I'm afraid there isn't much time left.

I don't want to turn the page. To my surprise, when I do, though, there are only a few words.

Are you sitting down, Essie? If not, please do.
Right now.

I turn to the next page, too frantic to sit.

I've discoverd something more horrible than you could
ever imagin. And we both know that's impresive. You
told me your stepfather was from Ingolstadt. Does the
name the Univercity of Ingolstadt mean anything to
you? It should. I know you red the book with your da.
I reemember you coming crying to me, telling me how
upseting it was.

The name does sound familiar, but I can't think at all why. I don't know what book it's from. Many books are upsetting to me, and my brain is fuzzy with panic.

I wouldn't have reemembered it, but Thomas Eddison
is making a picture show of the book right now. My

brothers are always wasting their newspaper money
at the nickleodeon, and they keep talking about how
the theater is going to play it next month. So I went to
the library to duble check the book. And sure enough,
I was right. I wish I wasn't, truly, but I was right about
where I'd heard the name.

"Come on, Beatrice!" I say out loud. "Just tell me already! I can't bear this!"

Are you sitting down, Essie? You must. Don't turn the
page till you do.

I cry out in frustration and sit down hard on the edge of my bed, then turn to the next page. And it's a good thing that I did as she asked, because I nearly faint for the second time in less than a day.

Your stepfather attended the same univercity as Dr.
Frankenstine!

My head spins. I'm barely able to breathe. I can't even read the rest of Beatrice's words. It's too much. It's too overwhelming. It makes absolute, perfect sense.

Chapter Twenty-Five

That night Dr. Blackcreek sends Mam upstairs with medicine and a key for the lock on my door. I plead and shout and make the biggest scene I can muster.

"But what if there's a fire?" I cry.

"There won't be a fire," Mam says.

"What if the electric lights put out vapors and I suffocate?"

Mam rolls her eyes. "Then I suppose you would have suffocated anyway, whether or not the door was locked."

This, of course, results in me sobbing hysterically.

"It was a joke, Essie!" Mam says, failing to comfort me. "Goodness, you're sensitive tonight. Would you feel better to know Alwin's already ordered a fire escape to be installed at your window?"

I look up slowly, sniffling, and nod, thinking only of Da, and how nice that would be, to have a fire escape of my own. But then I realize it's an odd thing for my stepfather to do. A fire escape would give me easy access to follow him on his nefarious expeditions. Why would he allow it?

"How long till it's ready?" I ask, wiping my nose with a handkerchief.

"You know how slow things are in getting to the island," Mam says dismissively. "A week or two, I suppose."

This explains it, of course. The fire escape will never be installed. Or I'll be out of the picture before it's arrived.

"What if you need me in the night and I can't get to you?" I try again to persuade her. "Or what if something awful's locked in the room with me and I can't get out?"

"Something awful? Like what?" asks Mam, and for a moment she looks sincerely concerned. I want to repeat my story about the girl in the wet dress—I want to tell her about Dr. Frankenstein and his monster—but if I turn this into another big fight, she'll likely just leave me here, all alone. She already did worse than that this morning, giving in to my stepfather's vile plans.

"A rat or a tarantula or Old Scratch," I say. "Any one of them could do me dreadful harm."

"There are no rats or tarantulas on the island." Mam sighs. "And I thought you were growing fond of Old Scratch. Fräulein Gretchen says she sees you together all the time."

I frown. "I'm not fond of him. He just follows me around." After thinking about this a moment, though, I feel a touch guilty. "Well, I suppose I don't mind him so much. An ugly, old cat is better than no one at all. And he's never mean." I remember the times he's nearly given away my investigations and say under my breath, "But he's rude."

Mam smiles solemnly. "I'm happy to hear you're getting along. He was Alwin's daughter's pet, you know. When your stepfather moved to North Brother Island, he couldn't bear to leave the poor thing behind. Katherine loved him so. I'm glad you're giving him a chance." She pauses before adding, "You might give Alwin a chance too—perhaps apologize for your recent behavior?"

She means, of course, the fact that I've barely spoken to my stepfather since the day before yesterday, when we went on our drive. Even when he asks me questions now, I refuse to do more than respond with the most direct replies. All I can see is him talking to that sobbing nurse, covered in blood; that blistered, lifeless hand hanging down from the stretcher; or the frightening ghost girl, who must be his daughter. *Katherine.*

But I don't want to talk about Dr. Blackcreek tonight—or *to* him, ever again, for that matter—especially not when this new horror is all his fault.

I change the subject and ask with the utmost desperation, "But Mam, what if in the middle of the night *I have to pee?*"

My mother smirks at me, using her foot to reveal a chamber pot already tucked away under the bed. I make a sour face.

"And here I thought you'd be glad to see something familiar," she laughs. "Aren't you afraid of the fancy toilet in the bathroom?"

"I was," I say, and then quickly continue, "It's just that there are more important things to be afraid of now."

In the time that we've been here, a great number of items have been marked off my list—some old fears, some very new. For instance, the speaking tube doesn't frighten me at all anymore. I haven't heard it whistle since two nights ago, when I went down to the office. And even if it does whistle again, I don't think I'll be scared. I put my ear right up to it, after all, under the most harrowing circumstances, and came out perfectly fine.

Mam retrieves a small, dark bottle of medicine from the bedside table and pours some into a spoon.

"It's not poisoned," she says before I can speak. "I watched him mix it myself. And it's just a small dose. We only want to see if it helps you."

When I stare back warily, my mother purses her lips.

"What if we make a deal?" she asks.

I cock an eyebrow.

"What if you promise to take this without a fight and tough out the locked door—just for a few days, just to try it—and I promise to bring you for a visit to Mott Haven next week on Beatrice's birthday?"

It's a bribe, obviously, but a good one. I mentioned the birthday visit to my mother when she brought me dinner, earlier in the evening. She knows how much I want to go, even if she doesn't know the real reason.

"You mean it?" I whisper, and it's hard to hide my eagerness. "You'll really take me? Just you and me?"

Mam nods, smiling. "If that's what you want."

I sit up straight, searching her eyes, and force down the lump in my throat. There's no choice in the matter. It's the only way out. I take the spoon from her hand and swallow the foul-tasting dark syrup in one go.

Mam leans forward and kisses me on the cheek. "Good girl," she says. "I just want you to feel better. That's all. You'll be asleep before you know it. You won't wake tonight with bad dreams. Not even once."

At first I don't feel anything, and for some time I lie alone in the dark. I tell myself I won't fall asleep, no matter what the medicine does. I'll stay on guard and watch the door. I'll check out the window to see if Dr. Blackcreek has gone for another walk.

But then my eyelids start to feel heavy. And no matter how I fight it, I can't help closing them. It feels as if I'm being pulled slowly down, sinking into my bed. Soon enough, all my hopeful thoughts of a reunion with Beatrice—a shot at escaping this dreary house and my stepfather for good—disappear. Soon enough, I'm standing before the red door.

Someone whispers my name. The sick bell rings. Dread and despair fill me up.

Mam was right. I don't wake tonight from the dream. I don't sit up crying in the dark. I don't call for her or fumble to unfold the pages of the List of Unspeakable Fears.

I thought I knew before what it felt like to be stuck in a nightmare. But after taking Dr. Blackcreek's medicine, I'm dragged down so deep that I'm left repeating the very worst part: my hand on the doorknob, the bell ringing loud as a fire brigade, tears clouding my eyes, sweat beading my forehead, water dripping somewhere in the wall. Heat. Misery. A sick smell.

I'm dragged down so deep that for the first time in three years, I realize the horrible truth.

The red door will never open. Forever, I'll be standing right here, just in front of it, imagining what's out of sight. Forever, I will be afraid.

Because in this nightmare—in this memory—I do something unspeakable.

The combination of nightly medicine and my locked bedroom door leaves me few options for collecting more evidence before my visit to Mott Haven. I'm incapable of following my step-father on his midnight excursions, and I can't search the house during the day because Fräulein Gretchen or Frank is always bustling about. Ads have been put in the paper more than once, seeking help at the mansion, but unsurprisingly, not a single person has applied.

The best I can do—the only thing, really—is take walks around the island during my breaks from school lessons. And even those have new restrictions. Because of the events at the laboratory, I have to check in with someone every half hour. Technically, I'm not supposed to leave sight of the house, either, though I've already gotten away with it several times. I use the tide table in the parlor to try and schedule my study breaks, attempting to get as close to low tide as possible. This makes it faster to get around, if I decide to go to the shore. It's also given me the chance to collect some drift glass, which I plan to give Beatrice when I see her.

Though the goal of my visit is much more serious, it would be a shame not to have anything for her birthday. And it's only three days away.

After a particularly miserable afternoon of penmanship prac-tice, Fräulein Gretchen finally lets me go free. I've been working on sentences with the fancy pen for what seems an eternity.

A friend is known in times of need.

Small gains are better than none.

My hand is weak from all the writing, and Fräulein Gretchen

agrees I've done enough for the day. On my way to the door, Old Scratch at my heel, I get my leather satchel and check the tide table book. I already have a pretty pile of drift glass for my friend, polished and sitting in a small basket on my desk, but I'd like to collect a few more pieces, and if I hurry, I might still have time.

I walk for quite a while, without any luck. The cat follows along, never more than an arm's length out of reach. The ground dips and rises underfoot. Before I know it, we've wandered farther from the house than we should. My thirty minutes must be spent. The tide was at its lowest around half past four, and it's already come some ways back in. The sun is starting to set. I stop and Old Scratch sits down beside me.

Across the water, the city twinkles to life. I hear the high-pitched honks of horns. I see the skyscrapers light up from the streets to the stars. The Fuller. The Singer. The Metropolitan Life Tower—the tallest building in all the world. Seeing New York City from this side of the water, in a way, feels like seeing it for the first time. I still miss Mott Haven. I still try to imagine where my tenement building might be—where St. Jerome's Church is and our little brick-and-limestone public library.

But I can't deny that the view is beautiful from this side of the East River too.

It reminds me of Da, climbing so high, insisting that from up in the sky, it was like looking down on a whole different world.

"It's as magical as a scene from a book," he would say to me, smiling. "The Great White Way lights up as if it's midday, like heaven itself has come down to the earth."

The wind gusts against me, and I wrap myself tight with my

arms, picturing the view from the top of the world. If I'm brave enough to stand here, would I be brave enough to stand there? Without Da holding my hand, I think not.

"I wish I was like you," I whisper.

After all this time, I still don't believe that I am. I still don't understand how you can climb up when you're terrified that you'll fall.

"It's the worst kind of torture," says a familiar voice, and I turn to find Mary Mallon a few paces away. "So close and yet still out of reach. I'll be glad to be rid of the sight."

I haven't seen her since the snowstorm at the cottage, so it's a surprise to find her here now. I thought maybe she'd already left, and strangely, the idea brought me both relief and dread.

"You're really going, then?" I ask. Old Scratch is warily looking around for her dog, but fortunately for us both, he's nowhere to be seen.

"Any day now," Mary says, full of pride. She glances at me inquisitively. "Have you thought more about my offer?"

"To run away with you?" I ask, and she blinks. I must sound more assertive than before.

To be honest, I've thought of it a great deal. But I know that in the end, I could never abandon my mother.

I shake my head. "I have my own plan. If things work out, Mam and I won't be here long either."

"You sound confident," says Mary. "That's good. You'll need confidence, dealing with an opponent like Blackcreek. He's put up a tough fight to keep me prisoner. I doubt there's a crueler man in all the world."

I flinch and don't even know why. I agree with her. I hate my stepfather. I still believe he's a murderer. I still believe he means us harm. Don't I? I must, after being forced to take his awful medicine. To make sure Mam doesn't cancel our trip to Mott Haven, I haven't complained even once, but the syrup makes me dazed and tired for hours during the day, even if I've slept a great deal. On top of that, Beatrice found a connection between my stepfather and the most famous evil scientist of all time. For all I know, Dr. Blackcreek might be following in Dr. Franken-stein's footsteps, creating horrible creatures late at night in his laboratory. I know he has secrets. Dark secrets. I'm certain.

But the trouble is, a part of me no longer is sure what those secrets are.

Even though Mam broke my trust, her logic is getting into my head. Worse than that, the very facts Beatrice encouraged me to gather aren't adding up right. There seem to be explanations for everything. I hate to put aside my friend's findings, but Victor Frankenstein, for instance, is only a character in a book. So what if my stepfather attended the same school? Even the warnings from the girl in the wet dress—who I'm sure is the ghost of Dr. Blackcreek's daughter—have only created more questions than answers.

As for my stepfather's general demeanor, there's been noth-ing cruel about him at all. Not openly. Not from what I've seen. In fact, if anything, he just seems . . . sad, and nearly as reluctant to speak to me as I am to him.

"Mary," I start quietly, "what if we're wrong? What if my step-father didn't experiment on any nurses?"

She looks at me curiously. "So you're thinking he killed them because they knew too much? About something even worse?"

"What? No. I mean, what if they aren't even dead? Or what if my stepfather had nothing to do with their disappearances?" When Mary just stares, I continue, "I found some documents with dates, and it doesn't make sense. Dr. Blackcreek came here in 1904, but there's proof that staff at Riverside were going missing long before then."

Mary just shrugs. "So other doctors were up to the same foul deeds. It's hardly surprising." And then she looks at me sternly, light from the water reflecting wildly in her eyes. "Listen well, Essie. Doctors are liars. Your stepfather is a *liar*. He warps the truth to take advantage of people and calls it science. *Science!*" she scoffs, and I take a step back because she looks a little unhinged. "Just because someone read a few books at school, I'm supposed to believe what he says? By God, I think not!"

I'm so startled, my stomach drops. Suddenly all the things I've learned about Mary sing in my head: that she's angry, that she's lonely, that she's scared and confused.

"Are you all right?" Mary asks after a moment, noticing the change in my expression.

"Yes," I say, but I take another step back. "I'm sorry, I—I have to get home. I'll be missed."

And I turn around and start walking. Then I start running.

What an incredible fool I've been! I feel sick with guilt. What have I been doing?

If Old Scratch is still with me, I don't see him. I can't really see anything, I'm so upset. Thoughts whirl in my head. My heart races. I'm questioning everything all at once. It's hardly a surprise when I trip over something and fall flat on my face.

I spit out sand. My big toe throbs like the devil, and when I twist around, I see the rock I tripped over, still half-buried. It's large and white and round.

I can't say why it is that I reach out and touch it. But I do. I stand up and tug it out of the sand.

A piece of it falls off and drops back to the shore. The rock isn't heavy like I expected. It's perhaps only a couple of pounds. In fact, it feels rather hollow. The top is smooth, but there are ridges along part of the bottom. My fingers find two large holes, oddly the same size. I turn the rock over. Dirt and debris fall away.

My hands shake. Sludgy, dark water pours out of deep sockets, soaking the front of my dress.

This isn't a rock.

It's a skull.

Chapter Twenty-Six

I'm running so fast and so hard that it feels like my heart will burst. The world around me is a white blur. The noise in my head is white too, repeating the same desperate thought: *I must get to Mam.* My legs burn as I lean into the wind, running faster.

I must get to Mam. I must get to Mam. I must get to Mam NOW.

When I first picked up the skull, it was light, but stuffed in my satchel and hugged to my chest, it's as heavy as one of the big boulders on the shore. I hate the weight of it in my arms. I hate the feel of it pressed against me through the soft leather, and the sound of it too. The loose jaw, which fell to the ground when I picked the skull up, clinks in rhythm with each of my steps as I race across the island.

To think that just a few minutes earlier, I was having doubts about the whole case, about Dr. Blackcreek and the murders and everything else.

And now, right here, in my arms, is real proof!

Once I deliver it to the right person—once it's in the hands of the police—Mam and I can leave this place. We won't ever have to look back. The nightmare will finally end.

When I reach the docks, I head up to the administration building. Though I've been on North Brother Island for almost three weeks, I've not once stepped into Riverside Hospital. Mam has offered to show me around the parts where the patients don't go, but I've refused.

"You'd be in full protective gear, just like a nurse," she always insisted. "I wouldn't let you see anything frightening. Some of the architecture is quite lovely. And there are lots of nice staff to meet, who I promise won't get you sick."

No matter what she said, though, my fear was too great. It was bad enough, Mam being exposed to illness—her and my stepfather possibly bringing it home. It was bad enough just imagining.

Yet now, somehow, in my determination to see Dr. Blackcreek exposed, all that fear falls away. Without hesitation, I march up the stone steps of the large administration building and burst through the front doors. The unfamiliar woman sitting at a desk in the reception area looks up in surprise.

"I need to see Aileen O'Neill at once!" I say, barely able to catch my breath. "I mean Blackcreek. Aileen Blackcreek. Where is she volunteering today? Which building?"

The woman blinks, slowly leaning to look around me at the doorway. I step back into her direct view.

"I'm alone. Aileen is my mother and the director's wife. Please tell me where she is!"

I expect this to receive an impressive reaction, but the receptionist just continues to stare, as if she's not sure what I am. Her eyes drift to the bulky satchel hugged to my chest.

"I don't know where she is," the woman finally says. "It's a very big hospital. I'll have to make some calls to the other buildings." She nods at the wooden cabinet hanging on the wall nearby, and I realize it's a telephone. Then she gestures to some files on her desk. "I can help you after I finish this up. There are chairs over there by the—"

"This is an emergency!" I shout frantically.

"And this is a hospital," the receptionist says in the same even voice, though now with a touch of irritation. "Emergencies are rather common here, so I'd appreciate it if—"

I'm fully out of patience, so I open the satchel and dump the skull on her desk. The jawbone bounces, clattering to the floor. The front teeth snap off and go skittering into the woman's lap.

The scream that follows is the loudest I've ever heard. It beats anything I could do by a mile.

When the first orderly rushes up to see what's the matter, the woman is completely inconsolable. Chaos ensues. Nurses and more orderlies flood the reception area. One is tasked with calming the hysterical receptionist down. Another covers the skull with a bedsheet. There's confusion about where it came from. My mother isn't among the onlookers, so finally I stomp over to the telephone on the wall, bracing myself. I pick up the piece dangling off the left side of the box and stand up on my tiptoes to reach the mouthpiece. It feels very much like using the speaking tube.

When I hear someone answer on the other end of the line, I plug my right ear with my finger to drown out the background noise of the Riverside staff.

"Hello. Is this an operator? I'm on North Brother Island and I need to speak to the police. There's been a murder!"

It was full dark out when the police arrive on the island. They employed the boatman at 138th Street to ferry them across the river at once, even though he usually only brings visitors to North Brother twice a week during the day in his little yawl. When the officers docked on the island and came up to the administration building, it started a second eruption of chaos. None of the staff at Riverside knew the police were even on their way.

Eventually, I pushed my way through the crowd and spoke up, explaining that I'd found the skull and made the call. The receptionist backed up my story by recounting the horrific scene of me upending the bones all over her desk. I thought she was overreacting, but it was enough to convince the four men from the city—each with a stiff hat and two long rows of silver buttons on his dark coat—that a young girl had called the station. Apparently, because of all the screaming in the background, they hadn't heard my voice clearly and realized my age.

I'm settled into a chair near the far wall, watching the police stand around in the brightly lit room. They take measurements of the skull on the desk. They write notes. One man has brought a folding pocket camera and is getting pictures from various angles. Another has just finished interviewing a young orderly who had nearly nothing of importance to say. This isn't a surprise to me, because I'm the one the police should talk to—but they won't, not till my parents are here. Everyone is frowning and quiet. The general look about the men's faces is clearly annoyance.

Finally Mam comes through the building's front doors, and I jump up, running to meet her.

"Essie!" she cries, catching me in a hug as she glances at the police. She's changed out of her hospital clothes but looks disheveled. "I heard something happened, but no one knew what! Are you all right?"

I start to answer, but before I can, an officer comes over to us. Mam makes me turn around to face him, staying behind me with a hand on my shoulder. The man has a mustache and squinty eyes and a large nose, all of which I can't help but think looks familiar.

"Mrs. Blackcreek, I presume?" he asks.

Mam sticks out her hand. "Yes. And you are . . . ?"

"Officer Grady," he says, puffing himself up.

I know little more about policemen than what Beatrice's brothers taught me, which was mostly how to identify which of the men who patrolled our street could be bribed and which would beat you senseless without even checking to make sure they'd snatched the right person. Beatrice always insisted that there were more than two types of police officers, and I hope, very much, that this Officer Grady is one of them. In any case, I can tell from his posture alone that he's in charge.

"I'm sorry for all this trouble, Officer Grady," says Mam in her most polite voice. "But I'm not even sure what's happened."

"I'm happy to explain, ma'am," the officer says, his small, stern eyes still on me. "I have a few questions for your daughter myself, as it is. But I'd prefer to wait till her father is present."

"He's in surgery," says Mam, no longer using her most polite voice. "I suppose her mother will have to do. Please go ahead."

Officer Grady blinks before clearing his throat and taking out a pad of paper and pencil. I realize I'm completely unprepared for an interrogation. I step backward till my mother grips both my shoulders and holds me in place. I tilt my head up, and her expression has gone from being relieved that I'm safe to being furious with me, so there's no use in pleading for help. But what if I don't tell my story straight? What if my words get twisted so it sounds like I'm the murderer? This should be happening to Dr. Blackcreek, not me! I'm on the edge of full panic when the officer starts to speak.

"It seems Essie here—is that right? Essie Blackcreek?"

"Essie O'Neill," corrects Mam. "Dr. Blackcreek is her stepfather."

Officer Grady looks up at this and clears his throat again, uncomfortable. "Well, it seems Miss Essie found a skull on the beach." He points to it over his shoulder. "She gave the poor receptionist a fright and got the smart idea, in all the commotion, to call up the station."

Mam doesn't say anything, but her grip on my shoulders tightens.

"It's wasted a good deal of police time," Officer Grady continues, frowning at me. "If we hadn't thought this was a murder case, we'd just as soon have sent someone along in the morning to make a report."

"But it *is* a murder case!" I shout suddenly. "That must be the skull of one of the missing nurses! There's been a serious crime here! Aren't you meant to uphold the law? Justice must be delivered!"

"Holy Mary, hold your tongue!" Mam cries. The rest of the room goes entirely silent.

I do my best to refrain from smiling. No one needs to know that I stole my lines from a dime novel.

Officer Grady's bushy eyebrows lift up high on his forehead. "Missing nurses?"

"Really, I'm so sorry," says Mam. "She's been at this since we got here."

"The nurses," I say. "The missing nurses. The ones who . . . who went missing." My voice falls to a whisper. The officer's expression is making me worried. "It's one of their skulls. It has to be."

Officer Grady points again at the desk and the man taking pictures. "That skull? There?"

I nod.

"That's the skull of a girl child," says the officer.

My mouth falls open. "But . . ."

"And there are no missing nurses," he continues, enunciating each word. Suddenly I realize why he looks so familiar. He was one of the men I spotted arguing with my stepfather on the first night I arrived. "That's done with."

My heart drops.

"The women have all been found?" asks Mam. "Thank goodness. I hadn't heard."

"That's right," says the officer. "It's not public yet, but our final report should be available next week."

Mam turns to me with a knowing look. "See? What did I tell you?"

My jaw might as well be detached like the skull's for how long it's been hanging open. The rest of the world blurs till there's nothing but voices and shapes.

"Seems all but one of the women are still in the city. The last went off to live with some family in New Hampshire, if I recall."

"I'm just glad they're safe. And again, I'm so sorry about this. Essie has an overactive imagination, and the isolation has only made it worse. She's been having terrible nightmares."

"Well, if any place will do that to you, it's here. I've a daughter myself, and if she wound up on this island, God forbid—"

The doors to the administration building bang open. Dr. Blackcreek is standing there, out of breath. I gape, horrified, and the officers do too.

"Is Essie all right?" he asks immediately. "I heard police were here. I came right away."

Officer Grady steps forward. "Dr. Blackcreek," he says. "So nice to see you again. It seems there's been a misunderstanding. Your daughter found a skull and—"

When my stepfather turns and spots it, all the color drains from his face. His eyes go wide. He limps forward, suddenly ignoring everything else.

This is it! I'm certain. The moment he'll give himself away!

"We were in the process of determining exactly where—" Officer Grady tries to continue, looking startled.

"It was on the northwestern shore," I say loudly. "It washed up during low tide, like the drift glass."

But Dr. Blackcreek doesn't hear me or anyone else. He's entirely fixated on the skull, and when he reaches it, he pushes aside the photographer. He hesitates, his hands trembling, then picks the skull up. Tenderly.

"A child," he says, overcome with emotion, and the certainty I'd recovered only hours before disappears. There are tears in his eyes when he holds the skull to the light. "A young girl."

"Yes, that's what we thought too," says the officer who'd taken measurements. "Because of where it was found, do you think perhaps—"

My stepfather's eyes suddenly lose focus. He sets the skull back down on the desk with a *thunk*, all the tenderness gone. And then he turns, stumbling through the room toward the doors, looking so lost and so distant, it's like he's stuck in a dream. Without a word, he walks out into the cold night.

Chapter Twenty-Seven

I'm curled up on the sofa in the parlor, hugging my knees to my stomach and burrowed into the blanket Fräulein Gretchen has brought from the linen closet. It's particularly chilly this evening, so I'm thankful for woven warmth, but unfortunately, blankets can't block out lecturing.

"I'm at my wit's end, Essie! I don't even know what to say!" shouts Mam, pacing in front of me. Clearly, she knows enough to keep going, though. "Alwin has done nothing but show you patience and kindness, and you repay him by embarrassing all of us? Do you realize that if the papers get hold of this, they'll have a field day? Do you understand what that would be like for us?"

I clench my fists under the blanket, but don't speak.

"Have you nothing to say for yourself!" cries my mother.

I keep silent.

By the fireplace, Dr. Blackcreek removes his round glasses and rubs his temples. "Aileen, might I bother you for an aspirin?"

My mother glances at him sympathetically, then steps out to get the medicine. For a moment, things are finally quiet. My stepfather stares down at me. I stare into the fire, watching it jump and pop.

"You hate me, and I would know why," says Dr. Blackcreek.

I look up, surprised.

"You're an evil scientist. You're a murderer," I say, but even as the words are coming out of my mouth, they feel wrong.

"And who is it that I have murdered?" my stepfather asks, his voice unnervingly calm. "The missing Riverside nurses? The ones who are all accounted for? Or is it my own patients I've been killing—the same ones your mother and I work so hard each day to save?"

My breathing is shallow, but I'm able to whisper, "I—I can't speak for your patients. But only the nurses who've gone missing recently have been found. Others—others are from years and years ago, and who knows where they are? You can't deny it. I know it's true because—"

"You snuck into my office. Yes. I'm aware." My stepfather takes a deep breath and sits down on the end of the sofa.

I think my heart will leap out of my chest. I scoot as far away as I can.

"Mam told you," I manage to say.

"She did not." Dr. Blackcreek smiles a little. "You spilled wax on my desk. And my organization system is quite precise. The stack of documents was not as I'd left it."

Beatrice was right. Even with all my precautions, I wasn't careful enough. He's too clever. I wait for his demeanor to change—for him to grow angry and vicious. But he doesn't.

"How exactly is it again that I managed to murder women who worked here before I arrived?" he asks, feigning contemplation. "I am just trying to get it all straight."

"Mary said—" I start, but then close my mouth. And it's

not even because of my stepfather's frown. It's because I don't trust her anymore. She's afraid of doctors and tests and being trapped on this island forever, and it's clouded everything that she thinks.

"I don't have all the answers," I admit, gathering courage. I thought that I would by now—that the pieces of the puzzle would make sense, not be more mixed up than ever. Things like this always work themselves out in the detective stories, don't they? "But I know you're hiding something. And I know if I ask you right out, you'll just lie."

"Goodness. You do think me quite the villain," Dr. Blackcreek says. Then he tilts his head. "I hope you will give me the chance to prove my innocence, though. I assure you, I can provide evidence in my favor, concerning the nurses. Is there anyone else you believe I have killed?"

I narrow my eyes but don't answer. If the nurses are no longer possible victims, that leaves only one choice. And even as bad as things have got, I'm not ready to say it out loud. Mam returns at this point anyway, holding a bottle of aspirin and a glass of water.

"I couldn't find the medicine box at first," my mother sighs.

Dr. Blackcreek takes his tablet, but I wonder if perhaps he never had a headache at all. Maybe he simply wanted to get me alone—to weasel out information while my mother was gone.

I'm outmatched. He's too smart, a professional, and I'm just a silly girl. If there's any chance of turning the tables, even a touch, I have make him reveal his true nature.

"Did you work out an appropriate punishment?" my mother asks, looking between us.

Dr. Blackcreek waves this away. "Let us leave it for the night. In the morning, we will all have clearer heads."

"No," says my mother, stern. "She's gone too far this time." When Mam turns to me, her voice is frigid. "I'm canceling your trip to the city."

I gasp. "You can't!" I'm up on my feet now, and tears are already forming in the corners of my eyes. "Mam, no! It's all I care about in the whole world! It's Beatrice's birthday, and I must be there. I must! *We both must!*"

"And that's exactly why we're not going," says my mother, unmoved. "I need you to understand the seriousness of all this. It's time you faced a real consequence."

"Mam, please! Please! No!"

"It's really all right—" starts my stepfather, but my mother puts a hand up and he stops speaking.

"I'm not changing my mind," she says simply.

I'm sobbing in earnest now, begging with all that I have. And I realize it's not even about proving anything anymore— not about gathering evidence with Beatrice, not about my stepfather at all. I just want to see my friend and my home. I *need* it.

"You're both horrible!" I finally give up and shout.

My mother's brows dart as high as her hairline. "Oh, do go on. This will surely get you what you want."

"He's horrible because even if he didn't murder those nurses, he murdered his last wife and daughter! And you're horrible for marrying him!"

I expect the cold silence that follows. I don't expect the incredible clatter from by the parlor doors. Mam and I turn to find Fräulein Gretchen just inside the room, where she's dropped a whole tray of tea. Pretty china is shattered all over the expensive rug, but the maid just stands there frozen. Dr. Blackcreek does not turn at the commotion. He is still. His face is aghast.

"Up to your room. Now," says Mam, seething.

"It's true!" I insist, and everything spills from inside me at once. "Katherine's been trying to contact me. It was her footsteps coming out of the river. Her ringing the bell in my room. She's been trying to warn me. About him!" I point at my stepfather. "About what he did to her and her mother!"

"How dare you!" says Mam, her voice trembling. "You have no idea what you're saying!"

"I do!" I shout back. "And if we stay here, we'll get sick and die or be chopped up into pieces for vile experiments!"

"Good God, child!" cries my stepfather.

And the truth is, it's still strange—his reaction. It's not what I expected. It's making me vastly uncomfortable. All my confidence is slipping away. His eyes look more hurt than angry. They certainly don't look like he's been caught in a crime. I glance at Mam, who's crying silently on the couch. Her cheeks have gone flushed and shiny. Dr. Blackcreek looks down at her, concerned, and feels her forehead. His expression immediately changes.

"You're hot as a kettle," he says, surprised.

"I'm fine," says Mam. "I'm just upset. Get up to your room, Essie, and *don't even dream* about coming out. Fräulein Gretchen, will you help me? I'm not sure I can manage the stairs."

"Of course, ma'am," says the maid, still shaken.

I step aside as my mother passes me, and the two women

disappear. For a moment longer, I linger across the room from my stepfather, who's watching me with an incredulous expression.

"I expected from the moment I met you that this would not be a battle easily won. I thought myself prepared for the challenge, though, even after so long without a daughter of my own." His accent is thicker. His eyes glassy. He stammers when he goes on, "But—but *this*? This I cannot believe."

For a heartbeat, I'm almost convinced by his performance, but the pieces must fall into place soon, mustn't they? *Mustn't they?* Otherwise, I've made a grave mistake.

Chapter Twenty-Eight

I wasn't always an Angsthäschen.

I used to be brave.

At least a little bit braver than now.

When I'd sit on the fire escape with my da, I'd hang my legs right off the edge. I didn't think about how far down it was to the street. I never pictured myself falling. I wasn't tough as iron, like Mam, or undaunted by danger, like Beatrice. I wasn't confident, like my da. But I could hide in a dark closet while playing with friends. I could use the sharp knives when cooking supper. I could introduce myself to a new classmate at school, even if she didn't introduce herself first.

I might never be the bravest person in New York City, but before my father died, at least I wasn't the biggest coward. At least I didn't always go straight to the worst possible outcome in every situation, imagining immediately the most horrible way things could go wrong.

I'll be hurt. I'll be killed. I'll get sick.

Or Mam will.

I'll be left all alone.

Before Da died, perhaps I was a rabbit. I suppose I've always been one. I might always be. I've never liked sudden, loud noises.

I hate being surprised. I've forever made a healthy effort to keep away from dangerous things. If the candle goes out, why risk stumbling around in a dark room? It's better to go back the way that you came and relight it.

On my sixth birthday, I wouldn't swim in the ocean on our trip to Coney Island and refused outright the scary rides at Luna Park. But I was still able to watch my parents enjoy themselves. I was able to laugh and relax, once I saw they were safe. Now, if I went on that trip—a trip that's become one of my fondest memories—I'd spend the whole time in distress, wishing desperately that I were simply back home.

Before Da died, perhaps I was a rabbit, but I wasn't an Angsthäschen. I wasn't hopeless.

As I lie in my dark bedroom now, the door locked, my breathing comes short and quick. My nightly ritual has been abandoned in all the commotion. No one turned down the covers. No one closed the curtains to keep out the lighthouse beam. My mother is usually the one to lock my door in the evenings. She always waits till I'm nearly asleep. She turns the key quietly so as not to give me a fright. Tonight, however, my stepfather came thudding down the hall, caring little if I heard. He jabbed the key into the lock. He yanked loudly at the doorknob to test it, and I jumped with every pull.

So now here I am, alone and fretting, unable to sleep. They've forgotten to give me my medicine. And while at first this seemed a relief, it's fast becoming a curse. My head is spinning. One question leads to another and another and more after that. I'm swept off on a current of my most painful memories, my most upsetting thoughts.

And it's left me questioning everything.

What if Dr. Blackcreek isn't a villain? What if he dearly loved his wife and daughter and I've accused him of the most heinous things? What if he really did mean to be friends with me? What if I've broken his heart? What if now, he'll kick us out of his house, off the island?

Do I want that anymore? Do I still want to go back to Mott Haven?

Since I arrived on North Brother Island, all I've done is remember the good things about home—my friends, our apartment, the comfort of familiar sounds and smells and routines. But now that I'm far enough away, I can see all the things that were bad. I've grown accustomed to electricity, even if I still don't touch the switches. Indoor plumbing is convenient, not frightening. The kitchen here is always stocked with fresh food. The rooms are always warm. In Mott Haven, I wore torn, dirty dresses. I mended my socks so many times they had hardly an original stitch. We shared our walls with rats, our bed with lice, and our apartment with unpredictable boarders who constantly moved in and out of our lives.

If I left, I think of how much I'd miss Fräulein Gretchen. I think of how much I'd miss my walks on the shore. I think of how happy Mam's been—tired, yes, but always smiling. Once again, she has a sense of purpose. Once again, she has someone who loves her, someone other than me. Whatever else might be said of my stepfather, I can no longer pretend that's not true. He does love her. Very much.

Have I ruined our chance at a good life?

If I'd been just a bit braver—if I'd not seen shadows around every last turn—might this have all been avoided?

The lighthouse beam spins into my room, and I shut my eyes, but it's so bright the backs of my eyelids turn red. At the door, I hear the lock clunk open.

I sit up at once, just as the light fades away. Mam. It must be. She can't sleep either. She was so terribly upset. Perhaps she's feeling better now—well enough to scold me. Perhaps I can apologize, and if I'm persistent and honest, I might still make things right.

In the dark, I hear the doorknob turn and the door creak open as my mother peeks inside.

"Mam?" I whisper, clinging desperately to the thought that we might still find a way to be happy—that I haven't ruined everything after all.

Light floods the room as the beam comes back around.

My door is wide open. No one is there. And then, down the hall . . .

Ting-a-ling-a-ling-ling!

It's coming from near the red door.

My eyes dart to the bookcase on the other side of the room. Again, the little silver heirloom is gone. I hold my breath, listening. The beam moves across my bed twice before I finally slide my covers away and lower myself to the floor.

My bare feet land in a puddle of freezing water.

Instead of screaming or jerking away or falling dramatically—all things my brain contemplates in the space of a stabbing heartbeat—I simply go still. Gooseflesh prickles over my skin.

It starts at my toes and races like so many centipedes straight up my legs. My back swarms and tickles. My chest. My neck. I wouldn't be surprised if the hair on my head was frizzy and standing on end—the hair on my arms certainly is.

After what seems an eternity, I finally regain control of my limbs. Moving ever so slowly, I bend forward and open the little drawer of my bedside table. I take out the matches and strike one. The room glows orange. I think I see something dart away into the shadows. Shaking, I light a candle, and a reassuring bubble of light surrounds me.

Stepping out of the puddle one foot at a time, I look down at the floor. It takes every last ounce of my willpower not to go frozen again.

I'm now standing directly in a pair of wet footprints, almost exactly my size.

They lead out of the puddle, across the room, out the door. I hold my light up and can see where they turn left down the hall.

Ting-a-ling-a-ling-ling! rings the sick bell.

I'm trembling all over, but I make myself move. I cross the room. I venture slowly out into the hallway. The candle flickers as my eyes trace the line of wet footprints, glimmering and dancing in time with the long shadows. The trail stops just in front of the attic door. Old Scratch is there, perched like an ancient, decaying gargoyle guarding castle gates. His black fur shimmers in the glow. His yellow eyes glint. Two flicks of his ratty tail and then, still staring straight at me, he wedges a paw under the ornate red door and pulls.

It creaks open.

Through the dark crack, I see half the face of a girl.

Katherine.

Her one visible eye blinks right at me. She tilts her small head. She's so pale it's as if she has no blood at all. Wet hair clings to her cheek. Water drips from a strand to the floor. Her face vanishes, but within the same breath, a finger appears—just one. I'm not even sure it's attached to a hand.

She gestures for me to follow, then is gone.

Ting-a-ling-a-ling-ling! rings the sick bell, higher now, up the attic stairs.

My heart is thumping so hard that I'm shaking. Wax has dripped all over my hand, all over the faint scar from Da's spilled coffee. Hot as it is, I barely notice.

"Mewroooow!" Old Scratch croaks at me. Then he slips through the crack.

I haven't always been an Angsthäschen.

I'm afraid, yes. I'm so scared that shivers come in waves up my spine. But I can choose to keep walking forward. I can choose to finish opening the red door. And I do. I do choose it. Because North Brother Island has taught me something important.

As I stand there in the dark, in the middle of the night, all alone, a dead girl gesturing for me to follow, I realize that she hasn't been trying to frighten me. She's only been trying to lead me. Horrible as it might be to face whatever comes next, I must continue. If I don't go up these stairs, I'll spend the rest of my life fearing something I never even saw. I'll spend the rest of my life making choices based on what I imagine the worst outcome to be, instead of what's actually real.

I open the red door and step into the shadows.

Because I finally understand what my da meant, all those years ago on the fire escape, watching the skyscrapers he'd helped build light up the night sky.

"You're so brave," I said, thinking of nothing but how high he'd climbed.

"Little love, don't you know?" he replied. "Every single time I climb up, I'm terrified that I'll fall."

Only now does it finally make sense.

Only now do I understand that you can't be brave unless you're afraid.

I take the stairs slowly. It's clear no one besides the cat has been in the attic for a very long time. Cobwebs are thick on the wooden railings. They hang low from the slanted ceiling, tangling in my hair. I try my best to duck out of reach, but I feel them stick to my skin anyway, and I shiver, imagining spiders nesting behind my ears and skittering into my nightgown. When I step on something that crunches—and shudder in horror at a gooey brown slime on the sole of my bare foot—I almost bolt right back to my room.

But then there's movement out of the corner of my eye, and I look up just in time to see the pale flutter of a girl's dress disappear around a precarious tower of old hatboxes.

Gathering all the courage I can, I scrape the bottom of my heel off on the edge of a step and continue upward, watching my feet much more carefully. Finally I reach the attic proper, peeking first with my candle just over the rim of the uneven floor, then climbing the rest of the way cautiously up. The ancient, musty storage space is wall-to-rafters stacked with crates and trunks and outdated laboratory equipment. Everything's covered with a thick layer of dust, so it's easy to spot the trails of paw prints all over the broken furniture and piles of yellowed books. How has Old Scratch been getting up here? Has Katherine been letting him in? I suppose it's not too hard to believe—if she unlocked the door for me tonight, she could do it for a cat as well.

"Merrow!" the beast screeches, brushing up against my exposed leg. I kneel down, set aside my candle, and pet his head. He starts purring, so I pick him up, looking at him closely for the first time. He's dirty, yes, but I realize that's probably because he's so old he can't properly clean himself anymore. I realize also, from the fogginess in his eyes, that he's mostly blind. This must be why he follows me all over the place. Suddenly whatever lingering bad feelings I had for him vanish. All I feel is pity and sadness.

"I'm so sorry," I say, stroking his head. "I've been a brat, haven't I?"

Old Scratch responds by snuggling roughly under my chin. When he starts to wiggle, I put him carefully down.

Ting-a-ling-a-ling-ling, rings the sick bell, coming from behind mountains of forgotten old things. The sound is closer, but quieter, too. Old Scratch meows meaningfully, then walks a few steps forward. When I don't follow at once, he stops and looks back, meowing again.

"You two are in this together, aren't you?" I say.

In response, the cat slinks away into the darkness. I pick up my candle and continue. A big moldy box tinkles with the sound of broken glass when I walk past. The faded writing on its side reads *Blood Vials*, but I don't let myself panic. I just keep moving, following fresh paw prints past a gigantic cracked mirror, which elongates and warps my reflection eerily. I squeeze by a headless canvas mannequin. Beside her is another, child-sized. Its shoulders have burst at the seams and horsehair stuffing is all over the floor.

Floorboards creak. Shadows stretch. Shapes in the dark bend and sway. But I don't let any of that stop me. It's not because I'm not afraid. I am. I just keep moving forward despite it.

The sick bell rings again, very close now. The sound is even softer than before, though, as if the person ringing it has grown tired.

Ahead, Old Scratch jumps on top of a dented examination table, then hops down. I search for a way around. When I turn back, Katherine is right there, right in front of me, on the other side of the table.

Her wet hair is still stuck to her face. Her white ribbon, once tied prettily to the end of her braid, is dirty. Her skin is pale blue in the candlelight, her eyes lifeless.

But she smiles, and I know it's sincere. She doesn't mean to be scary. She can't help the way she looks. It's my own fault if I can't see past that.

She turns slowly, as if moving through water, and points at something off to her left. I take a deep breath, then drop down and crawl under the examination table. Broken leather straps hang over the edges, scraping along my back like rough fingers.

When I get to the other side, I stand up, brush off my knees, and exhale. I lift my candle, peering around.

I don't notice the girl at first, sitting on top of a huge steamer trunk, her feet crossed at the ankles. She's grown incredibly faint. Anyone who didn't know to look for her might mistake the outline of her body for a trick of the light. She's so faded I can see right through. Brass bed frames and dusty vases seem to make up her organs and bones.

Old Scratch appears from nowhere and jumps up, right into the same space as Katherine's half-invisible lap. She smiles and strokes his head. He leans in, purring again, as though he can feel her touch. And as the last of her vanishes, she starts sinking, straight down into the trunk.

Chapter Twenty-Nine

Old Scratch, suddenly alone, looks surprised that the girl is gone. He cranes his neck, trying to figure out where she went, then meows pitifully when he can't find her. I sit down and put the cat in my lap, petting him just the way Katherine did. I feel silly that I was so scared of him before. He only missed his friend.

At the front of the old, peeling trunk, right in the center, there's a big latch with a keyhole. It's broken, so I don't need a key, but the lid seems to be stuck. When I finally wedge it open, it falls back into a brass bed frame. Old Scratch ricochets off my lap, and I cringe at the clatter. Dust whooshes up everywhere, sparking the little flame on my candle. My first fear is that someone heard the clamor—that I'll be discovered and dragged away before I can finish my investigation—but that thought is immediately overshadowed when I start gagging.

A horrible, rancid smell is coming up from the trunk.

Covering my mouth and nose with my arm, I rise onto my knees, lean forward, and hold up my light. The first thing I spot is entirely unexpected.

The sick bell is sitting upright in the midst of the trunk's disheveled contents.

Clearly, this luggage has been shut up for a long time. I

daresay it hasn't been disturbed since Dr. Blackcreek moved to the island. But there the bell is anyhow—the very same one. I reach in, hesitate, then pinch the silver handle, picking it up. There's no doubt that it's mine. I spot familiar nicks and scuffs. I turn it up and see it's still missing the clapper. I take a breath and set it down on the floor.

I'm not sure what I think I'll find as I lean back into the mess of forgotten clothing and papers and dishes. Before tonight, I believed Katherine was leading me to some sort of terrible proof about my stepfather's misdeeds. Perhaps I thought she needed my help putting her spirit to rest. But now none of that is quite right. My feelings about her father are changing. And Katherine isn't vengeful or angry. I know this from her smile—from her gentleness with Old Scratch. When I was scared of her, it's like I wasn't looking at the same person. All I could see was what I feared.

I brace myself, steeling my heart, and promise that whatever I find—whatever Katherine has worked so hard to show me—I'll see it through to the end.

The foul smell in the trunk is due to mold. A corner of the lid has a crack, and from that place, dark stains stretch down, contaminating the whole left side of the luggage. Everything in that area is unrecognizable. The remains of what might have been a bonnet or sash sit in a pile of muck. There's an embroidered handkerchief, but I can only tell what it is because of a tiny *E. B.* still faintly visible on one edge. There's a little lace dress, for either an infant or a doll, but who knows what color its bows once were.

I stick in my arm, trying not to touch the most vile items, and shift around the first layer. There are envelopes tied together with twine—letters, I think, but so damaged they're likely illegible. There are broken teacups wrapped in soggy newspaper. There are framed photos and documents, but most are obscured by shattered glass. I find one photo still intact—a family studio portrait, I believe—but all the faces are distorted and blurry. I swallow hard. It's upsetting to look at, all these precious memories ruined. The thought makes me sad, and feeling sad makes me afraid.

What if there's something alive, down beneath all the rot? What if I can't see the faces of the people in the photos, but they can see me? What if I cut my finger and mold gets under my skin and disease seeps into my blood?

I almost abandon my task. I nearly stand up and hurry back to the stairs. But then I stop and try to calm down. I remember all the frightening things I've already faced. I start breathing more steadily. And soon the outrageous thoughts seem just that—*outrageous*. I get back to work.

Digging again into the trunk, I feel something silky and smooth. When I pull the edge out, I see that it's a pink ribbon. The end is frayed, but otherwise it still looks pristine. The pretty piece of cotton belongs to Katherine, I'm certain, even though it wasn't the one I saw in her hair. Without pausing, I reach deeper, giving the ribbon a tug. It's caught on something. A book. In fact, the length of it is pressed between pages, marking a spot. Careful now, I excavate my find and pull it out, then wipe the book with my nightgown.

The volume is autumn red, and amazingly, it looks almost completely intact. I bring my candle closer. The cover has a worn drawing pasted in the center. At first it's difficult to make out, but when I tilt the book in the light, my heart catches in my throat.

A ship ablaze, people leaping over railings into churning water.

New York's Awful Steamboat Horror, reads the title.

I flip to a random page and read the first line my eyes catch.

Clouds of smoke engulfed the sky, through which the ascending jets of fire shot with the fierceness of lightning.

I continue flipping pages and skimming text, faster and faster.

. . . even more terrifying than the Chicago Theater Fire . . . writhing figures in the burning wreck . . . a thick clustering of women screaming . . . separated from their little ones, never to look again into their loving faces . . . went down to a watery grave . . . ill-fated passengers on the General Slocum . . .

I slam the book closed. My heart is pounding so hard I fear I'll be sick.

It's a memorial book.

I remember the fire escape with my da. I remember watching the ship smoke in the distance, barreling past Hell Gate, headed straight for North Brother Island.

I don't want to read any more. I'm upset enough by what I've already seen. And with the pieces of Dr. Blackcreek's story I know—with the little girl's ribbon marking a page—I can guess the rest of what I will find. It's horrid and grim.

But I promised myself that I'd see this through.

With trembling hands, I open the book again.

And then, almost against my will, I start really reading.

It was a bright and beautiful June day. Children were running and playing. Women were chatting gaily and herding their young ones away from the rails, lest they tumble accidentally into the water. Everyone on board the *General Slocum* was abuzz with excitement. They'd been looking forward to this excursion all year. It was the seventeenth annual picnic of St. Mark's Lutheran Church in Little Germany. Of the nearly 1,400 passengers traveling to Locust Grove on Long Island, almost all were women and children.

The *General Slocum* was a popular steamboat and fine-looking, too. A three-decker, newly painted, the mahogany interior filled with red velvet and wicker furniture. A band had been hired by the church, and the musicians on board played the excursionists off with a favorite hymn: "Ein Feste Burg Ist Unser Gott"—"A Mighty Fortress Is Our God." The sun was shining, the passengers singing. American flags whipped in the blue sky.

In less than an hour, more than a thousand people would be dead.

Most died in the first fifteen minutes of the fire, such was the panic and chaos. A fourteen-year-old boy who survived said he warned the captain about the flames as early as Eighty-Third Street, while passing Blackwell's Island. He said he was told to shut up and mind his own business. The captain later vehemently denied such a story.

What cannot be debated is that instead of making straight

for shallow waters, the captain steered the *Slocum* toward North Brother Island, traveling quickly, fanning the flames higher and higher. He defended his choice after the fact. He was one of the few to survive. He said he tried more than once to dock, but his ship was turned away from nearby piers because of fear that the fire would spread.

Pleasure and business boats alike sailed past the burning steamer in cold disregard, leaving little hope for the terrified women and children. Even a strong swimmer would struggle to stay afloat in the swift Hell Gate waters, and most of the passengers could not swim at all. Putting out the fire was impossible. The fire hoses had holes, and the crew, untrained in fire drills, for the most part simply saved themselves. Only one steward died, drowned because he was weighted down with a bag of coins he'd hoped to protect.

The only choice for most of the passengers was to leap into the water. But many of the racks of Never-Sink life preservers were empty, and the ones that were full contained only torn, rotten rubbish. Some of the life preservers were even filled with bits of scrap iron mixed in with the cork—a cheap trick for passing safety inspections based on weight. The few lifeboats were wired to the deck, and the panicking crowd prevented their launching. Even the *Slocum*'s lovely new coat of paint proved fatal. It was highly flammable and helped spread fire to the whole craft.

Survivors of the disaster described children in flames. They described mothers throwing their infants into the water and watching them sink. A happy pleasure cruise turned into a nightmare. There were some stories of heroism, of course. Eleven men from the Bronx Yacht Club saved 110 people from drowning. The staff and patients of North Brother Island swam out into the river again and again, rescuing those that they could. They kept the kitchens at Riverside Hospital open all night, preparing soup for the survivors.

But for every good deed or happy ending, there were a dozen stories of sorrow. There were countless children left orphaned. Countless mothers whose babies burned. There were fathers back in Little Germany, too many to name, who lost their whole family in under an hour, never to even know whether they'd suffered.

I close the book slowly, in tears.

I collected clues diligently these past weeks on the island. I spread them out and examined their edges, wondering how they might fit. But the problem was that the picture I wanted to make wasn't real. It never existed. Maybe, all along, I knew the truth, but I was just too scared to see.

Wiping my cheeks dry with the back of my hand, I finally turn to the page with the ribbon. A newspaper clipping falls out in my lap and I move to retrieve it, but first a photograph in the book catches my eye.

A shoreline strewn with bodies. Sheets cover their top halves, leaving only boots and skirts exposed. A tree is off to the right.

I squint, following the tree to the house in the background. This shore. This house. This attic window.

And the tall, dark figure bending to inspect one of the victims? My stepfather.

My heart clenches with sadness, and I have to wipe my eyes

clear again. The text explains how, on the day of the disaster, after a few hours the recovery of bodies slowed. But then at five o'clock, the tide went out, and the dead began to wash up on the shores. It was suspected that low tide would carry grim offerings to North Brother for a long time to come.

I think about the house full of drift glass and my step-father's walks on the beach. I remember the records I found in his office. Dr. Blackcreek took the job on North Brother Island only months after this book was printed—after this photo of him looking for his family was taken.

I try to steady myself. It's too much too fast. But I'm so close to the end—and I must finish what I started, for Katherine's sake, if not mine.

The newspaper clipping that fell in my lap is in German, dated weeks after the tragedy.

After seeing the ship burn on the river, Da talked about it all the time. He followed the stories in the English language news-papers as long as he could, but they grew bored of the *Slocum* within a few days. It was tragic, yes, but after all, the victims were foreigners. And there was war on the horizon—always one or another—and political scandals and articles about why women couldn't handle the responsibility of the vote.

How could the German papers of New York City write about anything else, though? Weeks wouldn't wash away the enormity of the grief. Months wouldn't either. Not years. Not decades. It would take a generation or more. Because in a single day they'd lost an entire community.

I stare down with wet eyes, scanning the column of unfamiliar words. In the center are two oval pictures ringed with drawings of flowers. The woman's hair is high on her head and styled curly up front. She's wearing a round brooch on her collar. The girl's dark eyes look right into mine.

I expected this. I'd already guessed what I would find. Yet still, I feel my heart break.

Because I know those eyes, those thin eyebrows. I know the braided hair and small smirk.

Directly below the pictures is text:

Frau Emma Blackcreek und Tochter Katherine.

I don't need to be able to read German to understand what this says. I don't need any help translating the rest, either. These are Dr. Blackcreek's wife and daughter. They died on the *General Slocum*.

Chapter Thirty

I was sitting by Da in bed. I was seven years old. It was early fall and there was a chill in the apartment, so we were cuddled up, reading out loud from a book. *The Hound of the Baskervilles* by Arthur Conan Doyle. In truth, the words were too difficult for us both, but I was doing my best to help where I could.

"Foot . . . footprints?" said my father uncertainly.

I leaned over, looking. "Yes. That's right."

He pulled the book toward himself with a smug expression, coughing.

I bit my lip anxiously. "Maybe we could stop now? Mam said you should rest. And . . . this story's getting scary."

Da grinned. "You mean, it's getting good! We have to finish the chapter." He cleared his throat. "Where was . . . aha. '"Footprints." "A man's or a woman's?" Dr. Mort—'" He paused, glancing at me. "'Dr. Mortimer'"—another smug expression—"'looked strange—strangely at us for an . . . instant, and his voice sank to almost a whisper as he answered. "Mr. Holmes, they were the footprints of a—a . . ."'" Da frowned and squinted. Then he gave in, showing me the page.

I considered the word for a moment. It took a couple of tries to sound out. "Gigantic," I finally said, confident.

Da winked at me. "Such a bright one you are." He coughed again, looking back at the page. "'They were the footprints of a gigantic hound!'"

I gasped, but all it took was Da's smile before I was smiling, too. The story was frightening, for certain, but I was too proud of him to be afraid. I beamed until his coughing fit got worse. Then I took the book away and held up a glass of water.

"You have to rest," I repeated. He ignored me.

"If Beatrice wants to be a detective," my father said between drinks, "she needs to forget those Nick Carter stories her brothers like. Sherlock Holmes is far more clever."

"She likes those stories because they're short. She wants to finish the mysteries fast, so she can see how they end."

"A good story takes time, though," Da said. "You want it to boil up slow."

On the table next to us was a newspaper with an article about the Giants' prospects for the upcoming World Series, which they'd won last year. The story had all sorts of statistics about Da's favorite players. I thought he might enjoy it if I read that to him next—and it would keep him from talking and hurting his throat for a while—but before I could start, Mam pushed open the red door and stepped into the bedroom. She was carrying tea and a thin glass fever thermometer.

"I'm about to be off," she said.

Da had been sick for a long time. Sometimes he'd get better for a while, but then he'd lose his appetite and start looking tired. Recently, he'd gotten much worse. He often ran a fever. He never seemed to stop coughing. Mam had brought my father the best doctor we could afford, but her suspicions about something serious were dismissed.

"He's smoking too much. Drinking too much alcohol, too, I'd expect," the doctor had said, looking around our tiny tenement.

Mam had expressed concerns about tuberculosis, but that had just made the man puff up, annoyed that a woman would question him.

"I've given you my diagnosis," he'd said.

Now, though, Da had a headache and fever almost all the time. We couldn't afford another visit from a doctor—not with my father still out of work—so Mam and I tried our best to take care of him. We slept in the small sitting room on the floor and let him have the whole bed. When my mother was home, she'd change the cool cloth on his forehead. She'd help him eat. She went to him quickly when he rang the sick bell, even in the middle of the night. She fetched him blankets and brought him water. When she was out visiting patients, it was my responsibility to do all these things. And I was happy to help. I loved Da more than I worried about getting sick. I wasn't yet scared of that—at least not so badly. There were no night terrors then. There was no List of Unspeakable Fears.

"It's just a bad cold," my father said as Mam came over and I put down the paper. He'd lost so much weight so quickly that his cheeks were hollow. "Word on the street is colds are very fashionable right now. Everyone's getting them."

I giggled a little, mostly because I was nervous, but Mam had fully transformed into a nurse. She gave us both a stern look, then shook out the thermometer with a few practiced flicks of her wrist before sticking it in Da's mouth. He flinched dramatically, like she'd hurt him, and she shushed him.

"Be quiet or you'll make it take longer. And I haven't time. Mrs. Dragos says her eldest son's quite unwell and the others in the family are starting to show symptoms. She couldn't explain what they were. Her English is still very basic, poor dear. I know she's frightened. Anyway, I'm going right now to check on them." Mam looked at me, but I was busy trying to see if the silver liquid in the thermometer was rising. "Essie, are you listening?"

I perked up, nodding.

"You're sure you'll be all right on your own?"

I slid off the bed and stood up straight. "I can take care of him."

"What if he vomits?" asked Mam, gauging my reaction.

I tried not to look squeamish. "That's okay," I said. "Really."

And it was. I was seven years old. I could lift the chamber pot in time. I could clean up if needed. I could take care of my father. He always took care of me when I wasn't well.

Mam removed the thermometer from Da's mouth. Her brow furrowed as she tilted the glass stick in the light from the window. "This is certainly not just a cold. Are you still having chest pains?"

Da made a *not really* face, but I couldn't decide if he was telling the truth.

"So what's wrong with him?" I asked, frowning.

Mam just shook her head and sighed. His face was flushed like a cooked lobster. It was clear he was in pain, even if he wouldn't admit it.

"Maybe I should stay in after all," said my mother, taking his hand. "If you get worse suddenly, I want to be here."

For a breath, my heart grew a bit tighter. If Mam was worried, I should be too. But then Da gestured to me, smiling, and the tension immediately went away. He'd always had that sort of effect. You couldn't stay worried around him. You couldn't be frightened or angry. With one look, he could charm it all better.

"I've got the best nurse in the city right here. What do I need you for?" he teased my mother. "They couldn't care for me better at a fancy hospital." Suddenly, though, his expression turned serious. "And we need the money from your visits. If I'm not back to work by—"

Mam shushed him again. "Rest. No worrying. Nurse's orders."

She fluffed the pillow under his head, kissed her fingers, pressed them to his cheek, and then reached into her pocket. She handed my father the sick bell.

"I'll be back soon," she said.

When we were out in our little kitchen, the red bedroom door closed behind us, Mam started talking, hushed and fast.

"Don't let him smoke, even if he makes all sorts of promises. And don't give him too many blankets. We want his fever down, not up."

I made mental notes, following her to the door. My mother's black nurse's bag was waiting. She already had on her uniform with the big puffy sleeves. At the mirror, she pinned a little cap on her head and adjusted her long white apron. The deep pockets were empty now, but soon they'd be full of medical tools.

I silently prayed the family she was going to see wasn't very ill. I hoped they didn't have influenza. They'd only recently arrived from Romania—fleeing persecution because of their religion, Mam said—and most of them couldn't speak English. The food here was different. The clothing. The houses. They surely felt lost and alone. And of course, they couldn't afford a real doctor. If it wasn't for Mam, their only option would have been one of the awful quarantine islands. And everyone knew if you went to one of those, you'd never come back.

Ting-a-ling-a-ling-ling! Da rang the sick bell.

"Stories!" he called, breaking off in a cough. "I need stories right away! Another pillow fluff too!"

Mam glanced over my shoulder, rolling her eyes. "You'll have a long night ahead of you." She smiled. "Go on, then. I won't be too late."

If that had been true, perhaps things would have ended differently. But as it was, what my mother found waiting for her at Mrs. Dragos's was more serious than she'd guessed—and the illness had already spread. Mam was overwhelmed. She lost track of time. So when things took a turn for the worse, I was alone.

My father had been quiet for hours. I made him gruel, thinking a meal might give him strength, but he would not eat. Instead, he grew less and less like himself. The sun set. His fever went higher. His bedsheets became soaked with sweat. He started saying odd things.

"If we're not careful, soon all the oysters will be gone," my da whispered, running a hand along the exposed mortar, speckled with shells, where the wallpaper had torn.

"You must eat something," I begged, holding a special cup to his lips. It had a little spigot, and I'd watered down the gruel till it was nearly liquid, thinking I might get him to drink it.

"You should only buy oysters in months with an *R*," said my father. His eyes drifted up to the ceiling and filled with tears before he lifted a hand, shielding his face from the light of the oil lamp beside the bed. "There were whales in these rivers. But now they're just full of sewage and it's making us sick, sick, *sick, sick, sick . . .*"

When he started sobbing, I started too.

And then he started coughing again. It went on and on, harsher and harsher, his body shaking violently with each wave. He pressed his handkerchief to his mouth. I reached out to touch his shoulder, to help brace him, but flinched away in surprise at the feel of his skin. His temperature was dangerously high. Heat radiated off him like a gas stove.

"Da!" I cried, and he closed his eyes, the coughing finally past. He leaned back in bed, wheezing now.

"What's Colonel Ruppert hiding in that summer home? What treasures?" he whispered.

I knew then that my father was no longer with me. He was no longer in the same room. I turned and hurried to the door.

"I'm going to get help!" I said. "Just stay here. Don't worry. Someone will come!"

I ran straight out of the apartment and banged on the door of our closest neighbor. She'd always been kind to me before. Sometimes she gave me baked treats. Once, when my parents were away, she'd even mended my doll because it had torn at the neck.

But that night, she barely gave me the chance to explain.

"Get back! Get away!" she'd cried. "And don't you dare call the authorities or they'll round us all up. Do you hear? They'll inject us with poison and take away your father and my little ones too!"

"But I need help!" I sobbed. "Da needs help! I don't know what to do!"

The woman must not have cared, because she didn't reply.

The other neighbors I tried were the same. It was a miracle if they even cracked open their doors. Beatrice's family, who I knew would have done something, was away visiting relatives.

There was no choice but to tend Da alone.

Back in my apartment, I slumped against the kitchen wall, crying. Finally I forced myself to get up, to walk to Da's room. I wet rags from the sink again and again, trying to bring down his fever. The whole time, he kept ringing the bell. More than once, I grabbed at it, wanting to stop him, but he still had strength enough to keep it tight in his fist. My head spun. I was so tired I could hardly stand straight. Da drifted farther away. His coughing grew weaker. There was blood on his handkerchief. The moon sank in the sky.

My father stopped ringing the bell. He stopped saying strange things. I no longer could get him to open his eyes.

Eventually I stumbled from the bedroom and sat back down in the kitchen, against the far wall. I stared at the red door. Not moving. Not crying. I was stuck, neither awake nor asleep. And for the rest of the night, till Mam finally came home, I did the most unspeakable thing in the world.

I did nothing.

A pipe was leaking behind the wall next to my head, making me dizzy with its repetitive drip. A spider crawled around on my leg and I didn't even swat it away.

Sometimes I thought I heard Da say my name.

Sometimes I thought I heard the bell ring.

Ting-a-ling-a-ling-ling. Ting-a-ling-a-ling-ling.

I pressed my hands to my ears. Was it an echo inside my head? A twitch of his fingers out of habit? Or, if I went back to him, would he be better? Would he know me again? I wanted to open the door. I desperately did. But the fear of what I might see—of what I might never unsee—left me paralyzed.

By the time Mam got home, it was so late it was early. The sun was rising over the river, glinting off the metal railing of our fire escape. When she'd reached the Dragos family's apartment, one of their children was already dead. Another was dying. Smallpox. The whole tenement was likely infected, and maybe the ones next door, too. Maybe the whole block. Authorities had to be called, despite the protests of Mam's patients. She had to wait for them to arrive so no one would flee. Everyone knew that when the Board of Health officials showed up, they'd take anyone with a fever and quarantine them on North Brother Island or Ellis Island or somewhere else just as awful. There was no other way to contain the disease, and if it wasn't contained, the whole city would soon be at risk. A dozen deaths would turn into a hundred. A thousand. Two thousand. More.

Mam and Da and I had had the smallpox vaccine, so there was little fear of us catching the illness. My father was sick with something else. Later, a doctor would tell us that he had had tuberculosis, like Mam had first feared, and that it had spread to his brain, causing swelling. For a long time, Mam would worry that she and I would also get sick. There was no vaccine and no cure for tuberculosis.

I would worry too about illness and death. I would worry worse than I ever had in my life, so much that I began to have trouble sleeping. And then Mam would get sad, and I would start worrying about new things, no matter how big or small. I would start worrying about *everything*. Before long, it would feel normal, being scared all the time.

But that early morning, when Mam came home and found me curled up in the kitchen, hugging my knees to my chest, I didn't feel anxious or fearful. I felt empty.

The red door was tightly closed. My voice was ruined from crying. My hands were still pressed over my ears. Mam pulled at them, but my arms stayed locked to my head, as if they'd never come free, so she went into the bedroom. It was then that she started crying too.

We didn't know what had gone wrong. We didn't know how much things were about to change, either—not just in our lives, but inside us.

All we knew in the world was that Da was dead.

Chapter Thirty-One

"Essie . . ." Five seconds of chilling darkness.

"Essie . . ." Five seconds of burning light.

"Essie, where are you?" It's my father down the hall, but I don't understand why the beam from the lighthouse is here. There was no lighthouse outside the window in Mott Haven.

"Essie, please." *Ting-a-ling-a-ling-ling. Ting-a-ling-a-ling-ling!*

Darkness. Then light. I can smell the East River. I can feel a cold breeze. I can hear the creak of the old house's bones. But that's wrong. The red door—the first one, the real one—wasn't in a house at all. It was in a tenement building made of tan-colored brick and oyster-shell mortar.

"Essie!"

My father needs me. He needs me to stand up. He needs me to open my eyes and take my hands from over my ears. Before, I was too filled with grief—too heavy with fear. But the dream is different this time. North Brother Island has changed it.

I've seen things and read things and heard things that have frightened me, but they've made me stronger, too. I know now that when I face what I'm afraid of—when I look it in the eye—it often isn't as bad as it seems. I know that being scared is the first step to being brave. I can't save my father. I can't go back and stop him from dying. But I can live in a way that he would be proud of.

In three years of dreaming the same dream, I've never moved forward. Not a foot. But tonight I reach out and touch the red door. I put my hand on the knob.

I open it.

"Essie, you must wake up."

I blink and look around, surprised to find I'm in the attic in the mansion on North Brother Island. Muted gray light is shining through the nearby window. I must have fallen asleep going through the rest of the trunk. Still groggy, I turn and am surprised a second time, because Dr. Blackcreek is kneeling beside me, gently shaking my shoulder. His cane is on the floor next to him. He's wearing the same clothes from last night. And all around us are the remnants of my investigation—photos, books, newspaper clippings. Fractions of a shattered family history are smoothed flat on the dusty floor, organized in a timeline. Pieced together. At the end of it all is the pink ribbon.

My stepfather picks it up. He looks at it for a long time before tucking it into his pocket.

I wait for him to speak. I'm ashamed for so many reasons. I'm sorrowful and sorry and mad at myself all at once. I can't imagine anything worse than Dr. Blackcreek finding me here, asleep among his grief—especially after the wrongs that I've done him. I'm sure this will be the last straw, that he'll start shouting and kick me and Mam out. If I hadn't ruined everything last night in the parlor, I've ruined it now with my snooping. Who could be anything but furious about someone discovering your darkest secret, especially when your darkest secret is that your heart is so broken it can never be put right again?

"I thought you would never wake up," Dr. Blackcreek says, his expression unreadable. He lets go of my shoulder, but I can't tell if he's angry. "You must come with me. We've had a message from the hospital."

For a few moments, I don't react, and when I do it's only out of confusion.

"What?" I ask, tilting my head. I go to rub my face with my hand, but then stop because I've realized I'm holding something. The sick bell.

"Your mother wants to see you at the hospital," says Dr. Blackcreek. He helps me stand up and starts leading me back through the attic. "It's urgent."

I just blink, wobbly on my feet as I follow. The labyrinth of boxes and furniture and hat stands is all much less menacing in the morning light. This only adds to the sensation that I might still be dreaming, that I'm not even in my real body. It's not till we're back down the stairs and in the hallway that I realize my stepfather is still talking.

"—was given a bed right away. Her fever is very high. It seems the illness has progressed a great deal already. I tried to convince your mother to stay here, but she insisted on going to Riverside. I'll bring you there once you're dressed. You won't be allowed to enter the infectious ward, but—" He looks back at me, where I'm frozen by the red door. "Are you all right? Your mother said you would be very worried."

I can't move. My heart is paralyzed in my chest. Though

only minutes before, I was sure I'd grown braver, I crumple inside the moment I understand.

"Mam—" Her name catches in my throat. "Mam is sick?"

"No!" says Dr. Blackcreek, surprised, but I'm already panicking. My whole body is already trembling. "No! Not your mother. I said *Beatrice*. Is that not your friend's name? She arrived on the first boat this morning. Smallpox, they think."

My head swirls. I don't even know when I started to cry.

"Mam is all right?" I ask between sobs.

"She is perfectly fine. The hospital sent a message to the house because Beatrice is asking for you. She seems to think you are in danger." If my stepfather shows any emotion at this, I don't notice it. "Your mother went straight ahead to the hospital. She hoped you'd meet her there, so you can talk. But when Fräulein Gretchen came to wake you, she said that you weren't in your bed."

I stare at him, still swirling. "Mam is all right?"

"She is all right."

"But Beatrice . . ." When I see his pitying look, I lose all control. I start crying so hard that I'm gasping. He puts a hand on my back. He tries to get me to breathe. But I glance down at my fist, white from clenching, and through my tears I realize I'm still holding the sick bell.

I bolt past my stepfather so fast, he cries out. "Essie! Wait!" he calls after me.

But I don't. I don't slow for anything. Not as I race dangerously down the stairs. Not to pick up a coat. Not in the grand foyer, when Fräulein Gretchen comes in looking distressed, and shouts, "Essie! Where have you been? Where are you going?"

I make it to the back door, then keep running. Through the garden, past the tree, down to the shore. I run straight into the freezing East River, all the way up to my knees. The shock of the cold water makes me come to a swaying halt, and I almost fall forward into the waves. Gripping the sick bell in my right hand, I pull back my arm. I grit my teeth. In my mind, I see it spinning out over the current. I see it soaring past the Bronx, past the tenement buildings, past my school and church, past the library, past all I ever knew. The people at the tops of the skyscrapers will see it go by. I'll throw the sick bell so far it will land in the Harlem River or even the Hudson. It will sink *down down down* into the polluted oyster beds and rest with the whale bones and glittering mountains of drift glass.

For a long time I stand there, braced to throw. But finally my arm grows tired. Finally it falls to my side. I turn around and wade to the shore, still sobbing, and collapse on the rocks.

Dr. Blackcreek is waiting for me. "It is all right now," he says. "Everything is all right."

He wraps me in a blanket and helps me dry off. He walks with me back toward the house. In the bare garden, I sit down on the bench and he sits beside me, not saying a word.

"I thought I wasn't an Angsthäschen anymore, but I am," I say. Though I've calmed down, my voice is still small. "Beatrice is dying and I'm not even brave enough to meet Mam at the hospital."

"I never said she was dying," my stepfather reassures me. "She's well enough to ask for you. Her condition might not be too serious."

"That's how it started with Da," I say, my voice getting higher and tighter. "We thought he wasn't very sick. Even the doctor said so. And then, in one night, he was gone."

My stepfather watches me for a moment, and I expect, when he speaks, that he'll tell me I'm being ridiculous. I expect him to say the same things everyone says. *It's fine. Don't worry. You're overreacting.*

Instead, though, he replies solemnly, "I understand why you are afraid. Things can go bad so quickly. You're right. Diseases spread. Tsunamis topple great cities. Fires start that cannot be put out. Even on a beautiful day, people die."

I look up, confused. His reaction is wrong. He should be annoyed at me. Exasperated.

"That's not what you're supposed to say," I whisper, and for some reason I almost start crying all over. "You're supposed to tell me I'm being childish!"

My stepfather's eyes widen. "There is nothing childish about what you have gone through, nor what you are going through now. Your friend has taken ill. You lost your father to sickness before. You are frightened and anxious."

This only confuses me more. "But . . . but Mam always just tells me not to be afraid."

"Your mother tells you that because she does not want to see you hurt. And maybe, sometimes, such reassurance is exactly what you need. But I think that right now you need something different," says my stepfather. "I think you need to hear that these bad feelings you have, adults have them too. It's only that some hide it better. We have more practice, is all." He looks at me meaningfully. "And why should I lie to you when the truth is more comforting?"

"There's nothing 'comforting' about Beatrice being in the hospital."

"But isn't there?" asks Dr. Blackcreek patiently. "She has people to care for her now. People who know about medicine."

"That doesn't matter." When I continue, my words crack like I'm breaking apart. "Her family wouldn't get the smallpox vaccine. They thought it was dangerous."

I understood this. I was afraid of it too, at first. But Mam explained how important vaccines were—that they kept everyone safe. Unfortunately, the Murphys didn't believe her.

"*Beatrice could still die,*" I say.

My stepfather purses his lips. "Maybe," he says. "But maybe not, too. I believe in science and facts, Essie. I trust experts. I do my best not to worry until I know that there's cause. Before a tsunami, there must first be an earthquake. If there is a fire, we will smell smoke. Once the doctors learn what type of smallpox your friend has, and how far it has progressed, we can decide whether to worry or not. But till then, what good will it do?" He smiles kindly. "Trust me on this. Please."

When I don't smile back, though, he sighs.

"I suppose that is our problem. We have no trust between us, you and I." He shakes his head, looking away. "Since you arrived, we have both kept our distance. And we have not been honest about how we feel. We have not been honest about our pasts, either."

I bristle, hunching up my shoulders. "There's nothing I need to be honest about."

"Not even your nightmares? If you told me what haunts you so—"

"I can't," I say quickly, my heart again starting to race. I squeeze the sick bell in my palm till it hurts. "I can't say it out loud." After a few breaths, though, the tension eases. He looks so sincere. He sounds sincere too.

"Maybe . . . maybe I can be honest about other things. If you think it will help." I look at him, hard. "But you have to be honest too. About everything."

Dr. Blackcreek nods seriously. "Very good, then. We have a deal. You are welcome to start."

This surprises me. "Start what?"

"Asking questions. I know you have many. I will tell you the truth. Even if I'd rather you didn't hear it."

For a long time, I don't know how to respond. I've put so much effort into figuring him out—into searching for clues about who he was and what he's done—and now everything is an open book laid in front of me. All I need to do is ask. Was it really this easy all along? I'm so overwhelmed I think I won't be able to speak, but then, suddenly, everything comes in a rush.

"What sort of experiments are you doing in that horrible laboratory? And why do nurses and staff so often leave Riverside?" I frown. "Whose skull was it that I found? Why would you move here in the first place? Why do you go for walks late at night? The *real* reason. And why, why, *why* did you marry my mam? Don't you realize she still loves my da? She won't ever stop, you know." My voice is trembling now. "I won't ever stop either." I look back down at my hands clutching the bell and ask softly, "Do you hate me? Because of the cruel things I said?"

My stepfather's mouth is open when I glance up, but he closes it fast, then removes his glasses and cleans them off with a handkerchief from his pocket.

"That is a lot of questions," he says.

I squeeze the sick bell harder and stare at my toes.

"Difficult ones too." He's quiet for a moment longer before continuing. "First, let us clear up your confusion about my profession." When I glance over, he's trying to hold in a smile. "Though it would be much more interesting to claim I was a night prowler or mad scientist, I am only a doctor."

"A doctor who studied at the same school as Victor Frankenstein," I mutter.

"What?" says Dr. Blackcreek, blinking. Now he cannot hold back the smile. "What is this?"

"You're from Ingolstadt. You went to school there too. So did the evil doctor in Mary Shelley's book." I cross my arms. "Beatrice figured it out. She's going to be a detective."

"I see," says my stepfather. "I applaud her for her ambition. But we both can agree that Shelley's story is fiction, yes? It is a compelling perversion of scientific fact, I will admit, but it is not real."

I don't look him in the eye. "Yes. But . . . I thought maybe the University of Ingolstadt was."

"It was," he agrees. "But it goes by another name now and is no longer in Ingolstadt. In any case, I only went to primary school in my hometown. I left to study medicine elsewhere. Dr. Frankenstein and I did not attend the same university. And again, well—"

"He's not real. I know." I sigh. "Beatrice was just so proud of the discovery. And it did seem to make sense."

"Anything will make sense if you want it to badly enough." He gestures to the island around us. "This place, for instance. If you want to believe it's a prison, that is what it will be. But the truth is, the purpose of North Brother Island is to heal the sick and keep them from spreading their illnesses to others."

"And the laboratory?" I ask, still suspicious.

"It helps us conduct research. We analyze samples and examine patients who have died." My stepfather grimaces. "I realize it all sounds quite morbid. And I realize, when you saw the equipment and the body, it was upsetting. That is why I tried to keep you away. But the information we find in that laboratory, using those tools, helps us make vaccines and medicines. It helps us develop new treatments for those who get sick, like your father. Like Beatrice." His expression turns apologetic. "Hiding things from you only made you more confused and curious, though. I see that now. If you would like a tour of the laboratory, I will take you myself. I can show you in person that our goal at Riverside is truly to help people, not harm them."

I look down. "All right," I say softly. "Maybe."

"As for the missing nurses, I wish I had a more satisfying answer about why so many go. If I did, perhaps I might help prevent it. But I think the reality is simply that this is a hard place to stay for a long time. Lots of people leave without notice. Matrons. Orderlies. Even doctors."

"You're not making your case any better," I say as kindly as possible. He laughs a bit.

"I know. But just take a moment and think about it. We are isolated. The patients we treat here are poor. Many have no family or friends. And their diseases are often untreatable. The nurses at Riverside see all of that. Every day. There is suffering on this island all the time, and for many it will never ease." Dr. Blackcreek shakes his head. "Not everyone is like your mother, Essie. Most people cannot experience so much sadness and still find a reason to smile. And we all handle stress differently. Perhaps the ones who leave suddenly, without saying why, are ashamed. Perhaps they feel they have failed or that they are abandoning those in their care."

He sighs. "People get spooked here too. Quite often. I will admit, I have had my fair share of starts late at night—thinking I hear something down the hall or feel a hand on my shoulder. I have sworn more times than I can recall that I've seen a door open by itself or an object move, without explanation, from its proper place. On an island of this sort, it is to be expected, though."

"Because of all the people who've died here?" I ask timidly.

"Well, yes and no," my stepfather says. "I do not think it is because of their ghosts, if that's what you mean. But I do think the hardship of living here—with the memory of so many deaths—makes you see shadows where there is nothing at all."

I make a face, because what I've seen is no shadow.

After a moment, Dr. Blackcreek goes on. "As for the skull, and my move to North Brother, and my walks late at night and the rest, well, you have already figured that out, have you not?"

I look up, surprised, but then reluctantly nod. "Yes. I guess so. Your wife and daughter . . . they died on the *General Slocum*."

"They did."

"Do you think the skull was your daughter's? Is that why you walk the shores at low tide? You've been looking for them?"

Dr. Blackcreek is quiet for a long time. "I am a man of science, Essie. But I am still human. I still have a heart. And sometimes the heart is more powerful than the mind. Even when you know something is impossible—outrageous, ridiculous, illogical—you still can hope for it." He glances down at me. "Or fear it."

I look at the sick bell again. I cup it close in my hands.

"Perhaps, once, part of me hoped I would find them. Perhaps that is why I interviewed at Riverside and took the job when it was offered. And perhaps, at first, that is why I walked the shores." My stepfather turns to look out over the gray water. "But there were hundreds of young girls on that boat. There were hundreds of women. There is no way to tell whose skull it was that you found. And what good would that do, anyway? Putting the bones of my wife and daughter in the earth will not bring them back."

He takes the pink ribbon out of his pocket. He cups it in his hands.

"It will not stop me from missing them."

"If it were my da's bones that were lost, I'd search for them too," I say, and I mean it. "I'd walk the shores every night no matter how dark it was or how cold." I hesitate before adding, "But I think you're right. Even if you found their bones, I don't think you would stop hurting."

He looks back down at me. "I know you and your mother will always love your father, Essie. I know because I'll always love my wife and daughter. But that is why your mam and I married. We thought that together, we might be happy again." This time his smile isn't sad. "And no. I do not hate you. I am not sure that I could, even if you had succeeded in turning me in to the police. You remind me too much of my Katherine."

"She was scared of everything, like me?"

"Everyone is scared sometimes," Dr. Blackcreek says. "But what reminds me of her is not that. It is . . . little things. The sound of your footsteps in the hall. Your school papers left on the table. You make me feel like a father again—even if not a good one."

I press my lips together, and the desire to tell him how I feel now, the truth of it—how I've been feeling for quite some time—is so strong I nearly give in.

But then he asks, "Why did you try to throw your pretty bell in the water?"

My chest tightens up. I cringe miserably.

"It was your father's, yes? Brought from Ireland?" he asks, and I nod.

I'm certain I won't be able to speak. I'm certain that I'm not ready. And yet . . . I open my hands one more time. The sun peeks through the clouds above. Light reflects off the silver.

"It reminded Da of his mam," I say. "When he rang it—when he was ill or had a nightmare—she always came. He loved the bell very much."

"We had one just like it," says my stepfather. "Katherine was always stealing it to play with." He tilts his head. "But these are happy memories. Why would you want to forget them?"

"Because . . ." I hesitate, and when I speak again, my voice comes out small. "Because there are bad memories too. On the day that Da died, he kept ringing it. Sometimes I still hear it. Even in this house." I look up slowly. "Katherine . . . Katherine has been ringing it. Late at night."

My stepfather goes still.

"I was telling the truth about her. She's the one who opened the attic for me. She showed me the trunk. She's been visiting me since I arrived. At first I thought she meant to scare me, or maybe to warn me about, well . . . you."

"Oh?" says my stepfather, and this time, it's his voice that's small.

"Now I know, though, that she never meant to be frightening. She just wanted me to follow her. She wanted me to understand why you were so sad."

"I see."

If he's angry or irritated, I can't tell.

"Maybe . . . ," I continue, trying my best to sound confident. "Maybe it's also like you said. That Katherine wanted to play with the bell." I'm not sure if I should go on. I fear I've gone too far already. But I can't help asking, "Would you like to try it?" I hold out the bell. "Do you want to keep it for a while and see if she visits you?"

Dr. Blackcreek doesn't smile, but he doesn't frown either.

"I think I would like that very much," he says softly.

And I'm so caught up in the moment—I feel so safe beside

him—that I whisper, "My nightmares are also bad memories. About the day that Da died. Mam was away and I was alone. I tried to help him but . . . but then I just stopped. I don't know why. I just sat down in the kitchen and stared at the door and I couldn't do anything else. I couldn't move. And then Mam came home and . . ." I start to cry. "Because I was so afraid, I couldn't help him. And I'm still scared because—because if it was my fault that—"

My stepfather reaches over and puts a hand on top of mine.

"It wasn't," he says. "Traumatic neurosis. That's the name of what happened to you. It's as real as smallpox or tuberculosis or a broken leg. You knew your father was dying and you suffered an emotional shock. I am not surprised at all that you still dream of it."

I look down at his hand on mine. I look up at his face. "I—I was sick?"

"In a way," he says. "How you feel still—being scared all the time—that could be a sort of sickness too. But now that I understand, I can help you."

I take a breath, and I do feel a bit lighter already. "I hope so," I say.

"I know it is hard to talk about things like this," says my stepfather. "It is hard for me, too. But in time, I promise it will get easier. And the people who love you will always listen." He smiles, and it's warm and it's real. "I am right here. You are not alone."

Chapter Thirty-Two

Mam stays late at the hospital, taking care of Beatrice. My step-father joins her for a long while. Fräulein Gretchen spends the day fretting over me. She doesn't make me do any schoolwork. Instead, I take a warm bath and she bakes me German chocolate cake. I help her with chores and we read together from a book in the parlor. I feel a little bit better that night.

It's no surprise I turn in early, though. After sleeping so little—on the attic floor no less—and after so much heartache, I'm worn out. I still won't go see Mam at the hospital. It's not like I'd be allowed to visit Beatrice in her room anyway, even if I were brave enough. When I'm getting ready for bed, though, my stepfather comes home and checks on me.

"Your friend is doing much better," he tells me. "But her fever still hasn't dropped."

"Do you know what kind of smallpox it is?" I ask quietly. "Do you know if we should worry?"

"Not yet," he says. "But I will know more tomorrow. In fact—" He hesitates. "I do not want to give you false hope. If what I suspect is correct, though, there is no need to worry at all. If you want—if you are ready—you might even be able to go visit her in the morning."

For a brief moment, I'm relieved, but then my fears rush back in.

"I can't," I say quietly, feeling awful. "I can't go."

"All right," says my stepfather. "That's all right."

He's about to leave, when I remember something. "Wait!" I say. "My medicine. I need to take it."

Dr. Blackcreek turns around in the doorway. "Oh, Essie! I am so sorry. We forgot last night too, didn't we?" He sighs. "I am not doing so well at this, am I? At being a father again."

"You're not doing *that* badly," I say. When I look up, I smile, and so does he. Then I shrug. "Besides, I was glad for you forgetting the medicine, actually."

"Oh? I thought it was helping you sleep."

"Yes, but . . ." I pause before continuing. "It's just that it makes me feel funny. Sometimes, in the day, everything's fuzzy. And sometimes I sleep so deeply that my nightmares are worse."

"Oh dear," says Dr. Blackcreek, looking concerned. "I wish you had told one of us sooner."

I'm suddenly frightened. "Is the medicine hurting me?"

"What?" He waves the idea away. "No. No. Nothing like that. It is just that there are lots of different types of medications. And different ones are better for different people. It is important that we find one that is right for you. We need to try something else."

I relax. "At first I worried Mam might not take me to see Beatrice in Mott Haven if I complained. Not that that matters now." I frown and then shrug again. "I suppose I also just thought that was what the medicine was supposed to do."

"I see," says my stepfather. "In the future, though, you should tell someone if something makes you feel bad." He smiles kindly. "After some time, we'll try stopping the medicine too. If your night terrors have gone away, you won't need to take it."

This makes me happy to hear, but before I can say anything, my stepfather gets an odd look on his face. "I just realized, if you did not take your medicine last night, perhaps it is possible you had trouble sleeping soundly for that reason? Maybe you were stuck again, dreaming or only half-awake, when you walked up to the attic? That would account for . . . what you saw."

"Yes," I say slowly. "But I saw Katherine lots of times before. Even during the day. And weren't you the one who locked my door last night? If she didn't unlock it, who did? How did I get out of the room?"

"Mm," says my stepfather, stroking his beard. He looks away, thinking.

I can tell how badly he wants to find an explanation. It's strange, though, him not really believing, since he agreed to borrow the sick bell. And I remember him calling his daughter's name in his dark office on the night I snuck in. Clearly, some part of him hopes I'm right—that Katherine's still with him. For a moment, it doesn't make sense. Why won't he accept that it's possible?

Then I recall what he told me about adults and fear—about how grown-ups are just better at hiding it. And I realize that the things people are most afraid of can't always easily be put down on a list. Fires and illness and red doors—all that's awful, yes, but a fear of feelings can scare you worse than anything else. We don't want to hope for something too hard and risk heartbreak later.

It's not really the red door I'm scared of, after all.

It's the memory of how I felt when Da died. It's the dread that I'll feel pain like that again. It's the fear that I did something wrong, or didn't do enough.

It's the fear of always being afraid.

Only now, I'm not afraid of that last one anymore.

Dr. Blackcreek is looking at the little basket on my desk when I reach under my mattress and pull out my list.

"Is this your birthday present for Beatrice?" he asks, pointing to the drift glass, and I nod. "It is a very good present."

I hand the list to my stepfather.

"A letter for her too?" he asks, curious, then unfolds the papers and scans them.

I start to regret what I've done almost instantly. What if he tells Mam? What if he thinks it's a problem? What if he gets angry at something I wrote? I remember the word *Germans* was once on the list—and even though I've crossed it off, I'm still ashamed.

"I just . . . I wanted to show you," I say. "It's a list of things I'm afraid of. I'm not supposed to have it anymore. Mam told me to get rid of it a long time ago. But I think it's helped me. I wanted you to see that I'm not as scared as I used to be. It's half as long as it was when I got here. And I don't look at it as much anymore."

My stepfather leans against the doorframe, still reading.

"You're afraid of alligators?" he asks. "You do know it is unlikely you'll meet one?"

"They found one in the city sewers. Beatrice told me."

Dr. Blackcreek raises an eyebrow before reading on. "'Talkative Strangers,' understandable. Looks like you scribbled out 'Cats.'" He flips through a couple more pages. "You have crossed off so much, Essie. I think that is a good sign."

"I still add things once in a while. But not often," I say quickly, as if confessing a sin. "For instance, I really, really don't like those new Hoover Electric Suction Sweepers everyone's advertising. They look dangerous. So I put it down there. See?" I point to the entry, then grin. "But look at this." I walk over and push the electric switch on the wall. The lights overhead go off. After taking a deep breath, I push the opposite button, and they come back on. "I crossed off 'Electric Lights.' Just this afternoon," I say proudly.

"Impressive," says my stepfather. "I expect that will help you in the coming years. Everything will be electric soon, I am quite certain." He purses his lips, serious. "And for the time being, I will tell Fräulein Gretchen to hide the new Suction Sweeper."

I gasp and Dr. Blackcreek smirks.

"I am joking," he says, and I let out my breath. "But do not be surprised if she orders one eventually, especially if we cannot get any new maids. At least, we have finally had some applicants."

He hands the list back, and I look at it a little warily.

"You don't think it's a morbid obsession?" I ask.

"You said it helps?" When I nod, he answers, "Then no. What was that name at the top, though? 'Unspeakable' something?"

"The List of Unspeakable Fears," I say. "But it doesn't really fit anymore."

"Why not? Sounds rather clever to me."

"Yes, but things are different." I smile. "Now I can say them out loud."

Dr. Blackcreek mixes me a new medication. I don't feel as strange when I start to fall asleep. And I don't dream at all about the red door. I know I will again. It's not that I believe it's gone forever. But I think now that I'm not so afraid of it, the dream will happen less often. And when it does, I'll be fine.

I also think Dr. Blackcreek is right. Now that I've told someone about how I feel, it might be easier next time. Especially since I have someone to talk to.

In the morning, I wake up and find Old Scratch at the foot of my bed. He must have been hiding in my room when my stepfather tucked me in. I yawn and stretch and he mimics me. I get dressed and head for the door with him right at my heel. Hopefully Fräulein Gretchen has already unlocked it and I won't have to call for her. As I'm about to touch the handle, though, my eyes catch something out of place on my desk and I pause.

The sick bell.

A chill starts but then stops almost immediately. There's a folded piece of paper underneath. I walk over and pick up the bell.

Ting-a-ling-a-ling-ling!

I nearly jump out of my skin. For a heartbeat, I'm certain something supernatural has happened again—in broad daylight, no less—but then I realize that the sound is different than before. Brighter. Quieter. I turn the bell upside down and peek inside. Someone has installed a new clapper, made out of a tiny piece of drift glass. I unfold the paper.

> Dear Essie,
>
> I meant to share breakfast with you this morning, but someone needs me at Riverside and, well, you know how it is.
>
> I am sorry to say that though I kept the bell close last night, I did not see Katherine's ghost. It is not that I don't believe you. I want to believe. So very much. Perhaps I need to be patient. Or perhaps I am not ready to see her. Maybe I can borrow the bell again sometime, when I am ready. If you say you have seen my daughter, then that is enough. It is a good thing, I think. Katherine must want us to be friends. And now, I believe you do, too.
>
> I know you will be happy to hear that I have learned more about Beatrice's condition. She does not have smallpox at all. Just a bad case of chicken pox, it turns out. It can be easy to confuse them, especially if you do not see how they start. Your friend has been moved to a part of Riverside for children who are not seriously ill. I think she would like very much if you visited her. Your mother has already left for the hospital, if you feel up to meeting her there. Know, though, that it is all right if you don't.
>
> I must be off now, but I will see you later today.
> Alwin

P.S. I hope you do not mind that I gave your bell a new clapper. I thought it was a shame, such a treasured thing and no voice.

I put down the note and hold the sick bell up to the light. It's been polished. It glints in the sun. I think of the good memories I have with my father. I think of how much I love him.

I hesitate. I take a slow breath. I ring it.

Ting-a-ling-a-ling-ling.

It's funny, because it doesn't scare me at all.

Chapter Thirty-Three

Beatrice is in room 304. It's late afternoon. Mam holds my hand as we walk down the hall. We're both wearing masks, rubber shoes, and protective smocks over our clothing. My friend is still contagious, but since I had chicken pox when I was little, Mam isn't worried. I still shouldn't hug Beatrice or kiss her, though, just to be safe. I'm sad, but I understand. And the moment I walk into the small room, I'm so happy to see her, I don't care anyhow.

"Essie!" Beatrice shouts, her eyes wide in shock. "You came! I can't believe it! You came!"

I start running forward, but then hesitate, glancing back at Mam. She nods, and I go a few feet closer, but no more. My friend's face and neck, arms and hands—basically all the parts of her I can see—are covered in red blisters, a few of which have started to scab over. She keeps reaching to scratch them, then looking apprehensively at my mother.

"Horrible, isn't it?" Beatrice asks me, gesturing to her whole body. "Aren't you scared?"

"A little," I admit, and then smile. "I'm glad it's you and not me, though. It's terribly itchy."

"It is!" Beatrice cries dramatically. "And your mam threatened to wrap up my hands if I don't stop scratching. She also made me take a bath in oatmeal. *Oatmeal!* And said I couldn't eat any of it. What a joke."

Beside me, my mother rolls her eyes. "I'll leave you two alone for a bit. But no scratching, Bea. Otherwise you'll get scars."

"I really don't care about that," insists Beatrice.

I glance at my mother. "She's telling the truth. She doesn't care."

"No scratching," Mam repeats, then sighs and walks out of the room.

Immediately, Beatrice starts scratching frantically all over. "Heaven help me, Essie! This is the worst."

"Better than smallpox," I say sternly. "I thought you were going to die."

Beatrice stops and grins. "Of course you did." And then her expression turns serious. "Quick now. Update me on the situation. Before your mam comes back. What more have you learned about your stepfather? He came in to see me yesterday. Took all these notes. I understand why you're so scared of him. He looks villainous. And that accent!"

"Yes," I say awkwardly. "I've actually learned a great deal more."

"Go on, then," Beatrice says eagerly, sitting up. "Details! Details!"

"I found a skull on the beach."

My friend's mouth drops right open. "That's incredible! What did it look like? How heavy was it? Could you tell if it was a man or a woman? There are ways to tell that, you know."

"It looked like a skull. It wasn't that heavy. And it belonged to a girl our age."

"By Jove," says my friend, enchanted.

"I found something else, too," I say, before she can recover. "I found out we've been wrong the whole time."

At this, Beatrice sits back, suspicious. "What on earth do you mean? All the clues—the skull—*Dr. Frankenstein!*"

"Dr. Blackcreek is not who I thought," I say simply. "He's a good person. He's kind. He came and helped you, didn't he?"

She makes a face. "So what? That's exactly something—"

"A criminal would do, to throw us off the trail," I finish for her, and Beatrice looks up. "But I'm telling you. We were wrong. He lost his family in the *Slocum* disaster. That's why he's so distant— why he came here in the first place. And a lot of the things about him I thought were strange, well . . . I think some of them are just because he's from Germany. And being afraid of someone because of where they're from—how they look or sound or the habits they have—it's not really fair, I think."

Beatrice considers this. "I suppose you're right." After a moment, though, she looks at me curiously. "So you're giving it up? The whole case?"

"Yes," I say. "But if I need help with another one, you know I'll call on you first." I smile. "I might even use the telephone. I've done that once already."

She gapes. "You? A telephone? I can't even picture it. Seriously?"

"You should see my list now," I say proudly. "I even pet cats."

Mam knocks lightly at the door, and we both turn to look.

"Sorry, girls," my mother says. "You can visit more later. But Beatrice needs to rest."

Beatrice raises her hands in the air. "I didn't scratch even once."

Mam makes a face. "I'm sure." Then she looks at me. "Essie, didn't you have something . . . ?"

I perk up and step outside, where I put the little basket. I get close enough to set it on Beatrice's bedside table.

"Happy birthday," I say, smiling. "I hate that you're itchy, but I'm so glad I got to see you." After a second, I add, "And I'm glad you're not dying."

We both laugh and then say our goodbyes. My friend picks up her present and admires the pretty pieces of drift glass as Mam and I leave the room.

"That was very brave of you," my mother says.

"Now that I've come here once, I know it's not so scary. Do you think tomorrow I can come by again? I could bring a book and read to her, like Da and I used to do." Mam glances at me, and I know it's because of how easily I said his name. "I think Dr. Blackcreek has some Arthur Conan Doyle in his office—hopefully in English. Beatrice really needs to start studying better mysteries."

"That's a wonderful idea," says my mother.

My stepfather is waiting for me outside the building with the automobile. Mam still has a few patients she wants to check on before she goes home, so she helps me get out of my protective clothing and wash my hands in the chlorine solution—it doesn't hurt like I thought—then walks me to the front entrance. I hesitate at the door, though.

"Mam," I say slowly, "I want to . . . I want to apologize."

"It's all right," she says. "We both said things we didn't mean in that fight."

"No. I don't want to apologize about that." Flustered, I add quickly, "Well, I mean, I *do* want to apologize about that, but—" I stop myself, trying to collect my thoughts. Mam watches with raised eyebrows. "Let me start over. I want to apologize for the way I've been acting. About you getting married. About Dr. Blackcreek. About the island and the missing nurses."

I'm not sure I can say the next part out loud. It hurts to even hear the words in my head. But I know I'll feel better when I do. And I know Mam needs these words too.

"Since Da died, I've been sad. And it's not just that I miss him. I do. Terribly. I miss him all the time. But I also miss . . ." My voice breaks and I have to catch my breath. "I also miss *me*. What I was like before I got so, so scared."

I go to wipe my eyes with my hands, but then remember I shouldn't touch my face, since that spreads disease. I wipe my eyes on my shoulder instead. Mam doesn't bother. Tears run freely down both her cheeks.

"When Da got sick, I did too," I continue. "Dr. Blackcreek told me that. It's not like tuberculosis or smallpox. It's a sickness in my heart and my mind." I look up, and my voice fills with hope. "But now that I understand what happened, I already feel a bit better." I smile as best as I can. "And I wanted to let you to know I was wrong. Dr. Blackcreek is good. He loved his first wife and daughter, and I think he loves us. I'm happy that you got remarried."

Mam laughs a little, even though she's still crying. "You can't imagine how glad that makes me. I care for Alwin very much. But if you'd never come around . . ." She shakes her head. "You're my little love. No one matters more."

We don't hug, since she's still in her hospital clothes, but it's enough that we want to.

"It won't be forever, you know," she says earnestly. "Staying on North Brother Island. Alwin and I have already talked about other hospitals where we both might find work. I know this is a hard place to live. But for now, I'm happy you're all right. I always knew you were brave enough. You always have been. Whether you realized it or not. You're much braver than me."

I look at her like she's delusional. "That's *not* true."

"It is," my mother says seriously. "After everything you've faced and overcome? You're by far the bravest person I know."

There's a honk outside from the automobile, and I can see Dr. Blackcreek waving through the windows. I'm about to go to him, but then I remember something and turn back to Mam. I reach into my dress pocket and pull out the sick bell. I ring it once before offering it to her.

She stares for a moment, surprised.

"I don't need it anymore. Truly," I say.

Mam's eyes fill with tears again as she takes the little bell in her hand, and I walk out the front doors.

Chapter Thirty-Four

"Would you fancy a ride?" calls my stepfather as I come down the stairs.

I smile, hurrying to cross the walkway and climb into the front seat beside him. When I'm settled, he taps the gas and we putter off. We take the long way home, driving down to the south side of the island and then up the western shoreline. The sun is setting over the horizon, glowing red on the river and glinting off barges. Near the docks, my stepfather pulls over and turns off the auto. We sit quietly together, enjoying the view.

"Strange, isn't it?" he asks. "How something can be so beautiful but still make you sad."

I nod, feeling much the same way.

"I have something to tell you," says my stepfather. "I'm supposed to keep it a surprise, but I thought about it and realized you might not like surprises."

I appreciate this. "That's very true."

"I know how much you were looking forward to celebrating Beatrice's birthday. But now, of course, everything's changed. When she's well, though, would you like to go visit her in the city? We might make a day out of it and see the zoo?"

I light up. "That would be wonderful!"

"And then . . . I realize it is still quite far away, but your own birthday is in July, is that right?"

I'm impressed that he knows. "Yes, it is."

"Often, looking forward to things in the future can help us get through hard times. So I thought we could make a plan now. I was trying to decide what to do, and then your mother told me that once, for a birthday, you went to Luna Park on Coney Island and loved it. Maybe we could all go together—Beatrice, too, if you want. We can buy lots of sweets and ride all the fun rides." He gives me a quick look. "Only the *safe* ones, of course."

I'm so thrilled that for a moment I don't know how to respond, but then suddenly, unable to contain myself, I dive across the leather seat and wrap my arms around his neck.

"Oh, thank you!" I say. "Thank you! Thank you!"

Dr. Blackcreek laughs nervously. He pats my back. And though it's all a bit awkward, when I sit down again, he's smiling too.

By the docks, someone shouts something profane, disturbing our happy moment. It seems luggage is being loaded onto a ferry and there's a complaint about how it's being handled. My stepfather leans forward, looking out the front window, and sighs.

"That will be Mary," he says. "The boat is very late setting off."

"Mary Mallon?" I repeat in disbelief. "She's really leaving the island? Right now?"

Dr. Blackcreek nods. "The health commissioner finally agreed to her pleading, though only on the condition that she not take up work again as a cook."

I make an uncertain face. "Do you think she'll do as they ask?"

"I hope so," he says. "But she has built her whole life around her profession. And she is quite talented. I do not imagine she will happily accept a position doing something less respectable—and for less money, too." He sighs again. "If she can even *find* work, that is. You know how hard it is for us immigrants. And she is a single woman on top of it all. It must feel to her as if the whole world is stacked against her."

"If the health commissioner is the one letting her leave, then he should help her find a job," I say.

"He should," agrees my stepfather. "And maybe he will. I just . . . worry. Mary still does not believe she was the reason for the spread of typhoid before. And if she does not believe in the science, how can we expect her to act responsibly?"

I purse my lips and then open the door.

"I'm going to say farewell to her," I say.

"Essie, I am not sure—" starts my stepfather.

"I won't be long," I assure him. "It's all right."

He reluctantly agrees, and I walk around the car, then down to the docks. I cross the swaying ramp all on my own, doing my best not to look at the river below, and meet Mary on the top deck of the ferry boat. She's scolding a crewman who looks rather irritated. Something's familiar about him. Maybe his shoes. In any case, when he's through taking the scolding, he just shakes his head and leaves to get more cargo. I'm left alone with Mary and her fox terrier, who's sniffing everything in his leash's range with intensity. When I come near, he almost strangles himself trying to jump on me.

"Stop that at once!" shouts Mary, pulling him back. "Why is it, when you're around, he loses all memory of his training?"

"Are you certain he's *been* trained?" I ask, keeping out of the dog's reach.

"Ha!" Mary flashes a grin. She looks down at the mustached animal and makes a gesture with her hand. "Hop!" she commands. "Hop! Hop!"

The dog snaps out of his interest in me and starts bouncing up and down on his back legs with his nose pointed up, as though he's a seal at the circus. When Mary stops commanding him, he stops bouncing and returns to sniffing everything, including me.

"See?" says Mary. "It's your fault."

"I guess so," I say, smiling. "Then I'm sorry for being a nuisance. But I wanted to tell you goodbye."

Mary crosses her arms and takes a slow breath, looking me over. "You do know I can see your stepfather in the auto, yes? He obviously sent you here to deliver some thinly veiled threat." She shrugs. "It's pointless, though. I'm no longer his prisoner. And I never will be again."

"He didn't send me," I insist. "It's not like that. I really just wanted to wish you well."

"Hmph," says Mary, but her guard seems to drop. "I assume, if you're riding around like two old chums, you've decided he's not a murderer? Or is this part of some new elaborate plan?"

"He's not a murderer," I say. "I was wrong about him. I was wrong about a lot of things here." I hesitate, then add uncertainly, "Hopefully, I'm not wrong about you, though."

"What do you mean?" Mary frowns.

"You act tough because you've been treated unjustly. You're angry. And you have a right to be. But beneath it all, you're a good person. I know it. You're a hard worker. You care about the people around you, even if you pretend that you don't. Beatrice— my friend, I mean—she's quite inspired by you. I wish you could meet her, but she's got the chicken pox."

Mary's eyes are wide, and for once, she doesn't come back with anything spicy.

"Beatrice was always reading me your stories in the paper," I go on. "I know you don't like those stories, but I think she saw them in a different way. She was always standing up for you. She said you took care of the children who caught typhoid in the houses where you worked. She said you stayed all night by their beds, not even caring that you might get sick too." I look at her sternly. "So I know it. You're a good person."

"And a good person would stay here. Is that what you're saying?" Mary asks, and there's fury in her voice. "A good person would give up all her liberties and her freedoms and quarantine herself on this nasty island for the rest of her life?"

"No," I say calmly. "I don't think you should have to stay. At least, not if you're careful. But you need to trust what the doctors have told you. There's something dangerous inside you, Mary. It's not your fault. It's not fair. But it's true."

Her mouth opens as though to retort, but then she closes it and looks away.

The sun dips down past the city skyline. The lighthouse beam spins.

Five seconds of darkness between us.

Five seconds of light.

In those few heartbeats, Mary's face looks so deeply conflicted I pity her. But then I remember that that's not what she would want.

"I know you love cooking," I say. "But if you really do care about others, you can't be a cook anymore. You could hurt people you don't mean to hurt."

In the growing dark, she says solemnly, "I suppose it's not a sacrifice if it's easy."

"Just like it's not bravery if you were never scared."

"True enough."

Mary looks out over the river, the city mirrored and moving in its current.

"No matter what, I'm never coming back here," she says. "I swear it on my life." When the lighthouse beam spins around, illuminating her face, the mischievous smile I've come to know her by returns with it. "You know, it's not too late for you, Essie. I could stall the captain a bit longer, divert your stepfather's attention. It wouldn't be a challenge, smuggling you on board."

I blink at her and then laugh, disbelieving.

"I'm serious," Mary continues. "I'd help you find work in the city and a nice place to live. It wouldn't be cushy, of course—not like you've gotten used to. But you'd be free of this cursed, horrible place."

The last of the skyscrapers light up on the other side of the river. New York City shimmers. And for a moment, I think I know what it looked like to Da, standing on top of the world.

From up there, the horizon stretched forever, filled with endless possibilities and joy and people who made him smile. I close my eyes and picture it. A shiver runs through me. At first I think it's fear, but then I realize it's more complicated than that. Fear, yes. But also courage. And love. So much love.

"No, thank you," I say. "I think I'll stay where I am."

Author's Note

When I started writing this book, we lived in a very different world. I remember having coffee with my editor on the plaza outside Rockefeller Center, talking about Essie and North Brother Island and the research I'd been doing in New York City. It was a busy, crowded day. As we chatted, people passed by all around us, strangers brushing shoulders. Of course, no one was wearing a mask. Looking back, it almost doesn't seem real.

To say that the COVID-19 pandemic changed *The List of Unspeakable Fears* is an understatement. Though the book was always a ghost story, and though it was always set in the same time and place, the pandemic turned Essie's fearful personality into something much more meaningful. It also transformed my feelings about Typhoid Mary.

With Essie, what changed was that I realized we had something in common—we both had anxiety disorders.

There are many different types of anxiety disorders, all with different symptoms and causes. Some people, like Essie, experience a traumatic event, which can either trigger the disorder or make it worse. My disorder is mostly hereditary, meaning that other people in my family have a history of mental health issues too.

I'm not afraid of everything, like Essie—in fact, I love scary stories, and if I were a character in a horror movie, I'd be the first person to investigate the spooky noise in the basement, even if the power was out. But I worry a lot about small things, like driving my car or waking up on time to teach a class. In fact, I worry so much, and so often, that I can make myself sick. I take medicine for this, which helps me, but when big, stressful things happen, sometimes even the medicine isn't enough.

Needless to say, living through the pandemic has made my anxiety disorder worse. At times, I've felt so filled up with worry for my family, myself, my friends, my students, my neighbors— for strangers all over the world—that I feel like there's no room inside me for anything else. I think that's how Essie feels sometimes too, and I think that's why I connected with her so much while writing her story.

In New York City in 1910, there was a lot to be anxious about. The study of modern medicine was still fairly new. Doctors had a long way to go before they would understand the causes of, and find cures or vaccinations for, many very common, very deadly illnesses. There was also a great deal of poverty and many people lived in dark, overcrowded tenement buildings, where it was always too hot or too cold, and where disease spread as fast as fires.

Things were particularly difficult for immigrants. Almost five million people lived in New York City by 1910—and 40 percent of them were born outside America. Though Essie's family came from Ireland, and Dr. Blackcreek's family came from Germany, immigrants in NYC at the time came from many other places as well, including Italy, Eastern Europe, and China. They all had different reasons for leaving their homelands, of course, but most were in search of a better life, trying to escape starvation or persecution. Unfortunately, after docking in the United States, many found something very different from the American dream waiting for them.

Even in the best of circumstances, moving to a new country is incredibly difficult. I know this because I've done it. For five years I was a teacher in Japan. I loved my job and my friends and the food. I loved living in such a beautiful, interesting place. But at times, it was hard, too. Integrating into a new culture, especially when you're not fluent in the language, can feel impossible. And living so far away from your own culture and family can become very lonely.

Essie and Dr. Blackcreek also dealt with another difficulty: prejudice. Many people weren't happy about the number of immigrants coming to America. They didn't care about the hardships the immigrants were fleeing, perhaps, in part, because they didn't always see the immigrants as humans. There were different, harmful stereotypes for people from different places. Some had it much worse than others. For most immigrants, though, getting a good job or a good education wasn't easy. Laws often worked against them. Their contributions, as well as their tragedies, were frequently overlooked.

For instance, excluding pandemics and natural disasters, only a handful of events in the United States have had a higher death toll than the sinking of the *General Slocum*, where more than a thousand German immigrants died. Yet I'd never heard of the *Slocum* before beginning research for this book. To put this in perspective, less than a decade later, about 1,500 people died on the *Titanic*—and it's safe to assume that everyone reading this note knows that story.

Between the challenges of her life as an immigrant and the dangers of illness in 1910, it's no surprise that Essie developed an anxiety disorder—even if doctors wouldn't have called it that back then. The pandemic helped me see the truth about her fears by helping me recognize how much Essie and I had in common. But that wasn't the only change COVID-19 brought to my novel.

Before starting research for this book—before the pandemic—I had fairly simple opinions about Mary Mallon. I saw her only as a victim of prejudice and misogyny, and I believed her forced stay on North Brother Island was unfair. I didn't doubt she was a carrier of typhoid fever, but I felt that, if she had been given the opportunity, she could have lived her life among other people without posing a threat. And then I started my research, and I learned that she *had* been given the opportunity. Though at the end of *The List of Unspeakable Fears*, my fictional Mary is certain she'll never return to North Brother Island, the real Mary Mallon did return, in 1915.

Five years after being released from quarantine, she was found working again as a cook—this time, in a maternity hospital. Twenty-five people there were already sick with typhoid fever. Two would die.

I still do believe that prejudice and misogyny played a part in Mary's story. It's also clear that she wasn't given the support she needed when she left North Brother Island. Since the newspapers had ruined her reputation and she wasn't allowed to use her skills as a cook, it would have been hard for Mary to find a good job. We don't know a lot about her life during those years, but we know her initial attempt to work as a laundress didn't last, in large part because it paid very little money.

But all that said, learning that Mary had broken her promise not to work as a cook again made things complicated for me. By all accounts, she wasn't a bad person. Why would she knowingly put others in such danger?

When the pandemic reached the United States in early 2020, I found my answer.

Like typhoid fever, COVID-19 can infect people without giving them symptoms. Suddenly, I was hearing Mary's words everywhere. People were testing positive for the virus but felt totally healthy. Some of them were upset that they had to quarantine or wear masks, because they didn't believe they were actually sick, no matter what doctors said.

I suppose, even 110 years later, a few things haven't changed.

It wasn't Mary Mallon's fault that she had typhoid fever. I also don't think she ever meant to hurt anyone. But she didn't believe in science. She didn't trust doctors. And because of this, people died.

Education might have solved this problem, but many obstacles stood in the way. The study of germs was fairly new. Mary may not have had access to good schools. And, perhaps most importantly, there wasn't really an Essie or Dr. Blackcreek, who might have sat her down and explained everything with patience and kindness.

Maybe my Mary Mallon doesn't make the same mistakes. I like to think she doesn't—that in a world with Essie, Mary keeps her promise.

In any case, we have the chance to make different, better choices today than the ones made in the past. The world can be a scary place. Now, more than ever before in my life, this is true. But if Essie learned to be brave in the face of her fears, we can too.

And I'm certain, if we trust in science and do our best to take care of one another, one day soon we'll be brushing shoulders with strangers again.

Acknowledgments

From the very first image in my head of a young, frightened girl on a dreary New York City island to the final draft of this novel, I've been fortunate to have the support of many wonderful people.

Thank you to my incredible editor, Reka Simonsen, for your belief in this book from the start and for your guidance as it found its shape during such a challenging year. Thank you to my awesome agent, Yishai Seidman, who has helped me turn my childhood dream into a career. And thank you to the rest of my amazing team at Atheneum, including Justin Chanda, Michael McCartney, and Kristie Choi. I must also mention the talented Deena So'Oteh, whose marvelously creepy (and equally beautiful) cover illustration perfectly captures Essie, North Brother Island, and Old Scratch.

Like any work of historical fiction, this novel required a great deal of research. Thank you to the knowledgeable tour guides at the Tenement Museum in NYC for your patience in fielding my many, very specific questions. Thank you to the staff at the NYC Public Library, especially those working in Archives and the Map Division. And thank you to the librarians at the University of Tennessee at Chattanooga, who never judge me for how many books I order at once or how strange the titles sound.

To my dear friend Dominik Heinrici, I cannot thank you enough for all the research assistance with German culture and language. The same goes to Jess Redman and Rajani LaRocca—thank you times a million for your insightful feedback concerning mental health and medical practices. As always, any remaining inaccuracies are my own.

To all my friends and family who've supported me during this journey, you know I couldn't have made it without you. Special thanks goes to Dr. Sarah Einstein and Dr. Kayla Wiggins, who both helped me hone my writing as a student, and who continue to do so with their friendship and feedback. Special thanks also goes to my brother, Connor Miller, and his better half, Lara Muir, who shipped me an emergency package of fancy coffee and bath bombs when the writing got tough. Extra triple special thanks goes to Jessica Graves, who provided quality memes and text check-ins every day for several weeks straight so that I would meet my deadlines, which I didn't meet anyway, but please don't say anything—there's no need to disappoint her.

Thank you to John Kramer for the family heirloom that helped inspire this book.

Thank you to Kim Swanson for the sick bell.

Thank you, Mom and Dad, for my love of stories and ghosts.

And thank you, forever and always, to my partner in everything, Dustin Kramer. Not only are you the best first reader in the world, you're my best friend, and you have been for more than half my life now. Absolutely none of this would be possible without your love and support.